Praise for Maia Strong's *The Ballad of Jimothy Redwing*

"Maia Strong is a fresh and vibrant new voice in fantasy fiction. She's my new go-to author for m/m fantasy romance."

~ *Kate Davies*

"...The magic-fueled intrigue of the plot is deftly balanced with its more down-to-earth elements of love, friendship, politics, duty and desire. Jimothy himself is a delight, worldly but not jaded, while Ricky maintains a charming humility even as he determinedly pursues the man he wants."

~ *Kirsten Saell*

"It's a joy to read every single aspect..."

~ *Elisa Rolle*

"If you like your romance full of rich detail, likable characters, and a touch of mystery, Maia Strong's "Ballad of Jimothy Redwing" is just your cup of ale."

~ *EroticRomanceWriters.com*

"The romance displays intimate spice, along with a bond between two strong, loving men. I enjoyed this impressive tale."

~ *Literary Nymphs*

"I love well written fantasy stories that transport me to another world and THE BALLAD OF JIMOTHY REDWING by Maia Strong is an excellent example. I found myself immediately drawn to Jimothy and the world in which he lives. Ms. Strong does a wonderful job of bring[ing] Couvin and its residents to life."

~ *Romance Junkies*

The Ballad of Jimothy Redwing

Maia Strong

A Samhain Publishing, Ltd. publication.

Samhain Publishing, Ltd.
577 Mulberry Street, Suite 1520
Macon, GA 31201
www.samhainpublishing.com

The Ballad of Jimothy Redwing

Print ISBN: 978-1-60504-176-6
Digital ISBN: 1-60504-036-3

Editing by Sarah Palmero
Cover by Anne Cain

First Samhain Publishing, Ltd. electronic publication: June 2008
First Samhain Publishing, Ltd. print publication: April 2009

Dedication

To:

Susan, who invited me into another world;

Jenny, who first encouraged me to write the "naughty bits";

and

Kati, who never expressed a shadow of a doubt.

Foreword

I've never been a fan of politics. Give me a bit of romance, a sword fight or two, and a little comedy, and I am content. Unfortunately Wand'ring Minstrels have never had the luxury of ignoring politics. At this point, though, I think one particular Wand'ring Minstrel would be content with the simple luxury of a roof and a fire.

Chapter One

It was the kind of day that poets never write about. Jimothy could think of half a dozen ballads, at least four epic poems, two sonnets and a limerick, all of which related to the weather, but none of them recounted the sort of relentless drizzle that had assailed him since before dawn. He knew the tale of a blasted, desert country, cursed by its own gods. He could tell the story of mountains eternally blanketed in snow to hide the Druids that lived within. He was positive that he could sing at least a song apiece about hail, sunshine, snow and even ordinary overcast skies. This, though…this frankly sucked.

He raised his head enough to look around through the grey mist. The landscape that had so captivated him since he'd put the city of Tesna behind him was still there, only now a blanket of wet covered it. Jimothy put his head back down and slogged on. There was no point in stopping yet, even if he could have found a place that wasn't just as sodden and soggy as he was. The sun—what he could see of it through the overcast—was still high; there were several more hours before it began to set. The days were getting shorter as the equinox approached, but they still outlasted the nights. He was glad of it. He had a lot of walking to do to reach Couvin and the longer he had daylight, the farther he could get each day.

He continued to plod along under the leaden sky. He knew

from his map that the route from Tesna to Couvin was relatively straightforward; he simply headed north and east and he would arrive as quickly as his feet could carry him. The information he had also said there were waycabins scattered throughout the country—if only he could find one. Unfortunately his map gave no indication where they might be located, and the only other information he had on them was entirely historical.

He paused to shake out his cloak from inside. It had little effect. The rain was just heavy enough to wet everything, but not heavy enough to cause it to collect and roll off. The boiled wool kept him dry for a long time, but inevitably the damp seeped through. He wished he could have afforded an oilskin cloak to keep him as dry as the case he'd commissioned kept his demiguitar. *Not likely on a Minstrel's "salary".* Fortunately he'd been able to save up for the case thanks to that winter job he'd found with the Benoits. A lascivious smile turned up the corner of his mouth as he thought about the journeyman textilist who'd made the case for him. The relationship they'd developed before Jimothy left had been a welcome side benefit of the commission—and it had won him the gift of the oilskin satchel he wore under his cloak.

He willfully pulled himself from the fond memory and continued his trek towards Kanbec's capital city, determined to reach it as quickly as possible. The letters he carried were mostly private correspondence, but there was one missive that was more time-sensitive than the rest. He was the second carrier of it and had no desire to hold onto it any longer than necessary. He looked forward to handing over the letter and its responsibility to its addressee.

The lush green of the land tinged with murky brown where his footsteps turned up the underlying mud. He kept walking until the sun began to drop below the cloud layer. Despite being wet and weary, he paused to gaze at the rainbow it caused as sunlight poured through the falling water, appreciating that even in this depressing weather there was beauty. Then he picked up his feet and trudged on.

At last, with the sun beginning to set behind him, he reached a fall of stones that he'd spotted earlier. The natural overhang had kept the ground beneath safe from the worst of the rainfall. Jimothy slung his pack off one shoulder and his demiguitar off the other, leaning them against the dry stone. "As if they needed it," he muttered, speaking for the first time that day. He cleared his throat. It wasn't smart for a Wand'ring Minstrel to spend entire days in silence. He knew better. He'd just never quite gotten used to the habit of talking out loud to himself.

Before settling in for the night, he stepped from his tiny refuge, found a spot well downhill, and relieved himself as quickly as he could. It wasn't difficult with the encouragement of the rain egging him on. He returned to the minimal sanctuary of the stones. His stomach growled, reminding him that he'd skipped lunch in his haste to get through the day and on his way. He fished in his pack and found the slightly misshapen clay mug he'd bought at a discount due to its malformity. It had been a good purchase, one he still took pride in since the mug had yet to scratch or chip in all the years he'd had it. "Funky but sturdy," he said fondly. Pulling up his hood, he ducked back out into the rain. He'd seen a small rivulet of clear water running not far away and he hurried to it. He pressed his mug against the spongy ground, catching the water. It was a challenge keeping grass and mud from dirtying it, but it was a skill he'd honed over more than a decade of traveling in all sorts of terrain and weather. He let the mug fill, ignored the rain that fell on his upturned face as he drank it down, and filled it again. Then he once more headed to cover.

Jimothy made himself as comfortable as he could under

the stone canopy, sitting cross-legged with his back to the rock. Pulling his satchel onto his lap, he dug out the apples and cheese and the last of the mutton pasties he'd gotten at the market in Tesna. He took a bite of one of the small, blush-red fruits, followed it with a bite of hard yellow cheese. They tasted good and he smiled around the sweet and savory mouthful. He leaned his head back against the cold, hard rock and closed his eyes, chewing thoroughly to get every scrap of flavor from the food. He ate his meal slowly. Finishing the apple, he took another but stalled with it halfway to his mouth. He stared at it for a moment, contemplating its shape, its size, its color and its current scarcity. "You've at least two more nights on the road. You haven't seen so much as a single rabbit to snare and your knife won't shoot down a quail," he reminded himself. He put it back in his pack, wrapped up the rest of the cheese, and tucked it away as well. Then he nibbled at the little mutton pie until all that was left were crumbs and grease. He licked his fingers clean and sighed. It had been a long, tedious day and he was tired.

He looked out at the lengthy shadows cast by the stones and the few scattered trees. The sun would be down soon. It would be dark with the new moon approaching, and it would be just cold enough to be uncomfortable, if the past night was anything to go by. Jimothy figured it was. He pulled his hood over his head, wrapped his cloak around him, and settled himself to sleep as best he could.

His thoughts wandered back to the textilist who'd made his satchel and case. A smile curved his lips as he conjured the young man's image in his mind's eye: straw-blond hair perpetually tousled as if he'd just risen from bed; hazel eyes that caught the light and sparkled with flecks of green and gold; full lips that were earnest and shy to smile. Jimothy's inner eye moved down the memory picture: wide shoulders and arms toned and strong from his work stirring dye vats full of fabrics and lifting and sorting the wet, heavy stuff; hands wiry and nimble from his work cutting, piecing, and stitching. Jimothy remembered his surprised delight when he'd discovered the soft covering of pale hair on Thaniel's chest. Just enough to play with, Thaniel had joked once, almost embarrassed. Jimothy had been quick to reassure him that it was indeed just the right amount as he'd run his fingers through it, tugging lightly and tracing teasing circles around the younger man's nipples.

Jimothy shivered and smiled at the memory. He yawned and relaxed. Long hours of walking were conducive to sleeping, even in his less than ideal situation, and he drifted off. Sleeping mind followed the path laid out by the waking and he dreamed of Thaniel.

The two broke the kiss almost as passionately as they'd begun it. Thaniel caught his stolen breath and Jimothy grinned at him. "Did you learn that in your apprenticeship?"

Thaniel shook his head. "No more than you learned it from your masters at the Sect, I expect."

"Not from the masters, no," agreed Jimothy, pulling him closer and bumping his groin into the other man's, toying, testing and finding his own desire amply mirrored. "That's strictly forbidden. Now the other students..." He pressed his erection hard against Thaniel's, heard him moan a little. "...that's another matter."

"Bless the other students, in that case," declared Thaniel. He tugged at the lacing to his breeches, had them down in a second, and turned his attention on his lover's. Pants at their ankles, they rubbed against each other's hardness. It was a matter of moments before their movements caused them to trip and tumble onto Jimothy's bed. It wasn't the most comfortable bed, but the small room above the inn's kitchen was at least private—more than could be said for Thaniel's shared room in the guildhouse.

Jimothy kicked off his pants and sat up to yank Thaniel's from him. He massaged, licked and bit his way back up the other man's legs. Reaching Thaniel's cock, he took it in one hand and his own in the other. Thaniel leered up at him, eyes hungry for more. "Door's open whenever you're ready to come inside."

"Heya. That must be some good dream."

The voice shocked Jimothy into wakefulness. He blinked several times, squinting into the early morning sunshine. His startled eyes met the square-pupiled gaze of a chestnut mare and for a brief moment he thought it was the horse who'd spoken. Then good sense asserted itself and he looked upward. He couldn't make out the face of the mounted man, but the amusement in his voice was obvious. Jimothy quickly assessed his state and was certain the fellow couldn't have seen the rapidly-fading erection hidden under cloak and trousers. *So what is it he finds so funny?*

"I beg your pardon?" Jimothy said aloud.

"Smile like that on your face first thing in the morning can mean one of two things. In this case, I'm guessing it was a mighty fine dream you were having."

"In that case, aren't you going to apologize for interrupting it?"

The fellow laughed. "I suppose that was pretty rude of me, eh? Perhaps I can make it up to you."

If you only knew... "What did you have in mind?" Jimothy was wary. The man seemed friendly enough, but who was he and why was he out here on his horse at such an obscenely early hour? He moved one arm as subtly as he could to place a hand on the hilt of the knife on his belt.

"I'm headed to Couvin. I guess that you are too."

"Why would you guess that?"

"Are we really going to play that game?" the fellow asked, surprising Jimothy into ingenuousness.

"We don't have to." He released his knife and rose, coming out from under cover into a morning still moist but blessedly free of precipitation. He stretched limbs stiffened by sleep and took the moment to observe the rider. With the sun out of his eyes, Jimothy could focus properly on him. He was slight of build and Jimothy guessed the newcomer was about four or five years his junior. His hair was a dark brown that bordered on black and his eyes were a clear ice blue. Sharp cheekbones drew the looker's gaze to a straight nose and down to a broad, smiling mouth and a narrow chin. Jimothy couldn't help but smile back. He held out a hand. "Jimothy Redwing."

The fellow reached down and shook hands. "Ricky Lennox," he replied. "I see you're a musician."

Jimothy glanced to his right where his demiguitar leaned. "I am. In fact I'm a Wand'ring Minstrel."

Ricky's eyes lit up. "Are you really? Brilliant!"

"I wouldn't call me brilliant," Jimothy jested, and Ricky laughed. Jimothy found himself unexpectedly pleased by the sound. "You said you're heading to Couvin."

"I am, and as penance for my utter bloody rudeness at waking you from your delightful dream, I'd like to offer you a ride."

It was almost too good to believe. A ride would save him hours of walking and bring him to his weighty delivery that much sooner. He didn't hesitate. "I accept."

"Good."

Jimothy picked up his pack and handed it up to Ricky, who

secured it to the saddle opposite his own satchel. Jimothy took off his cloak and slipped the strap of his guitar case over his head so the instrument hung across his back.

"So what's in there?" Ricky asked as Jimothy resettled his cloak over his shoulders. He offered a hand, which Jimothy took, putting a foot into the stirrup and swinging onto the horse behind its rider. "Lute? Mandolin?"

"Demiguitar," answered Jimothy, tucking in the long ends of his cloak.

"And that would be what, exactly?"

"It's a six-stringed instrument, not unlike a lute or mandolin. This one's half the size of a normal guitar and the back is bowed instead of flat for greater resonance. It's tuned to the same notes as a full sized one. It's just more portable."

"Handy that."

"Are you a musician yourself?"

"Oh no. I could never be a musician. I love to dance. Hold tight to me," Ricky advised.

Jimothy obediently wrapped an arm around his slim waist and held on, bracing himself. He assumed from Ricky's recommendation to hold tight that they would immediately go from standing to speed. Instead Ricky urged the horse to an easy canter—a quick pace that would cover a lot of ground, but not a jarring one.

They stopped shortly before midday for a meal and to water the horse, each sharing what provisions he had. Then they pressed on towards Couvin. It wasn't the route Jimothy would have chosen—it took them more north than northeast—but Ricky seemed to know the country and for the time being Jimothy was willing to trust his instincts about the fellow. His instincts were proved trustworthy when, as the sun began to fall in the western sky, a cluster of slate-roofed stone cabins appeared ahead of them.

"Do you know about our waycabin system?" Ricky asked, turning his head slightly in order to be heard well.

"I do, but I'm glad to see that you know more about them than I do."

"What do you mean?"

"You know where to find them."

Ricky laughed and turned his gaze forward once more. Again Jimothy took pleasure in the sound of his laughter. He smiled and ran a hand through his wind-blown hair to tidy it. Then he rolled his eyes at himself, glad Ricky couldn't see him. There was still a clear league to go; his hair wasn't going to stay neatly in place until they arrived. "Tell me more about the waycabins."

"There's not much to tell. They were established by the late Lanmere, Helene Rosslyn, about seventy years ago. She was a big believer in getting people out to see 'the natural beauty of their land'." Ricky said the last in an aging falsetto that made Jimothy chuckle. He went on in his normal voice. "Personally, I think she was a bit dotty. But they are convenient."

"If they've been around that long, perhaps you could explain to me why they're not on the map."

"They're not on your map?" Ricky sounded surprised.

"No."

"Then your map is shite."

"Ah. That answers that question. Are there always this many clustered like this? I count eight over, what, a square mile or so?"

Ricky nodded. "About that, yeah. You have a good eye for distance and size."

"I travel a lot. It sort of comes with the job."

"Which it would, of course. You must cover a lot of ground. That whole 'Wand'ring' thing." Ricky's matter-of-fact tone was tinged with humor.

In spite of having heard the age-worn joke countless times, Jimothy found it amusing rather than tiresome when it came from Ricky. It had been a long time since Jimothy had fallen into such easy banter with anyone. It was what he missed most when he was on his own.

That and a warm bed every night, and someone to share it with, and... He shook his head at the thought. He'd always been a bit of a hedonist, but when had he become so thoroughly self-indulgent? "Wand'ring is great for learning all sorts of tricks," he agreed aloud.

Ricky started to say something and then seemed to think better of it. The pair fell silent and Jimothy wondered what he would have said.

Ricky slowed the horse to a walk as they neared the waycabins. No smoke rose from any of them and Jimothy guessed them to be empty. Ricky picked a cabin apparently at random and walked the horse to it. "Off you get," he instructed, and Jimothy stiffly lowered himself to the ground. Ricky followed and handed him both packs. "If you'll take these in, I'll see to Milo."

Jimothy stopped short. "Your *mare* is named *Milo*?"

"Yeah."

"All right." It was an odd name for a female of any species in Jimothy's experience, but he said nothing more. He took the packs into the cabin, set them on the rough wooden table, and then draped his damp cloak over a ceiling beam to dry out. The single room was built of grey stone, with the door at one end and a fair-sized fireplace at the other. A rack with a few old and somewhat worn pots on it hung on the face of the chimney.

Heavy chains suspended a metal grate over the hearth and he wondered at it briefly before shrugging and turning away. The table where he'd put the baggage was under the window in the left wall. Three chairs stood around it. Looking right, he saw that the other wall was windowless. Butted up against it was a bed with folded linens and blankets atop it. He tilted his head curiously. *Do they all have only one bed?* He was probably reading too much into it, but after little things he'd observed since meeting Ricky that morning, his curiosity was definitely piqued. *Time will tell.*

He continued his observations of the cabin, but there was little more to see. Dried lavender, rosemary, sage and other herbs hung from the narrow wooden beams above his head and he wondered who had collected them and then left them behind. A sling for carrying wood lay by the hearth and he surmised it must mean there was wood to be found somewhere nearby. He picked it up, cursing the stiffness in his thighs and back. Riding used different muscles than walking and it had been a few years since he'd been on a horse for any length of time.

Outside, he circled the cabin in search of a woodpile or bin. Around the back, he found one, and he also found Ricky. There was a small, covered stable area connected to the end of the cabin where it could catch the heat of the stone chimney. Ricky was there with Milo. He had her tack off and was brushing her down. He smiled at Jimothy's approach and Jimothy nodded back.

"Wood bin is in that corner," Ricky said, tipping his head to his left.

"Thanks." Jimothy loaded the sling with logs and kindling—enough to heat water and warm the cabin overnight. "I don't suppose there's an equally handy food locker?" he asked without any real hope.

“I’m afraid not, but I have a sling if you’ve a taste for rabbit.” Jimothy couldn’t have hidden his delight if he’d wanted to and Ricky grinned. “I’ll see what I can do in that case.”

Jimothy took the load of wood back into the cabin. He layered enough in the fireplace to get it started, and then searched his bag for his flint and steel. In a few minutes he had the beginnings of a nice cooking fire. He was carefully feeding it fuel to build it up when Ricky came in with two small rabbits in one hand and a sling in the other.

Jimothy looked up from where he knelt. “That was quick.”

“I have a knack, eh?” replied Ricky a little too casually, and turned away. He set his sling on the table and put the two rabbits next to them. “I’m going to get water. There’s a rain barrel outside and it’s bound to be well supplied.” He quickly slipped back out the door.

Jimothy watched him go. He was too well trained not to recognize when someone was hiding something. If his suspicions were correct, he couldn’t blame the man. Different cultures had very different reactions to people with “a knack”, just as they had different reactions to people like himself. He found that he didn’t like the idea of Ricky hiding something from him. It wasn’t that he felt he deserved better. *That would be ridiculous,* he told himself firmly. *I just don’t want him not to trust me.* He stopped in surprise at the revelation. Why did he care? And why should Ricky trust him any more than he should trust Ricky? They’d known each other barely a day. He shook his head at himself and returned to his task.

Satisfied with the state of the fire, he rose, moaning as his muscles protested. Ricky came back at that moment, heard him and laughed. His unease of moments before was entirely gone. “Been a while since you rode a horse, has it?”

“It has.” Jimothy hauled himself to the table and sat

heavily in one of the chairs.

"Can you cook?" Ricky set an empty bucket on the floor by the table. He carried the bucket of water to the hearth, pulled a pan from the iron rack above it, and poured water into it. Setting the pan to warm next to the fire, he put the rest of the water to one side.

"If I have to."

Ricky nodded as he crossed the small space. "I'm a little better than that. How about skinning and gutting?"

"That I can manage."

"Here. You start on this one." He shoved a rabbit towards the seated man who pulled his knife from his belt and set to work. Ricky sat and began on the other. Viscera collected in the empty garbage bucket as they cleaned their dinner. Jimothy took the two fur pelts and scraped them meticulously clean. While he worked on that, Ricky took a bundle of herbs from the beams above their heads, chose a few stems of rosemary, and stuffed them into the hollowed-out rabbits. Then he skewered the little naked animals and took them over to the fire where he carefully placed them on the hanging rack Jimothy had puzzled at earlier.

"That's a clever thing," he said. "If all the cabins are this nice, I'm surprised you've not been overrun by travelers."

"With water on two sides, mountains on another, and a cautiously friendly nation on the fourth, we see surprisingly few travelers, actually. Do you have a use for those hides?" he asked, pointing to them.

"They're your kill," Jimothy replied, surprised at the offer.

Ricky shrugged. "I don't mind. They're yours if you want them."

Jimothy looked at the furry skins and thought what a nice

pair of gloves they would make this winter. He shook his head. "No." The truth was that he couldn't guarantee he would find a tanner before they went bad, or that he would have the money to have them properly cut and sewn.

"All right. I'll take them then."

Jimothy handed them over. Using the string from his pack, Ricky hung them from one of the ceiling beams like the bundles of dried herbs. They used the warm water and rough soap to wash up and scrub the table clean as they continued to talk.

"So I take it you're a native Kanbecan," Jimothy said.

"Yeah, I'm glad to say that I am."

"Have you been away long?"

Ricky stopped his scrubbing of the table to look at his companion. "How did you know I've been away?"

Jimothy shrugged. "It wasn't difficult to surmise. You were heading roughly the same direction as me and I was coming from Tesna, near the Dusit border. You're geared up for a journey—not a huge one, but more than a couple of days in the country. You knew without consulting a map—even a shite map—where to find these cabins. And, in my experience, people are most patriotic when they've been away from home for a while."

Ricky laughed out loud. "Is that so? I'd never thought of that."

"No? I've seen it a lot." Jimothy picked up the slop bucket and suddenly realized he didn't know where to dump it. Seeing his dilemma, Ricky reached for the remains.

"Keep an eye on dinner. I'll take this."

"Thanks."

Alone for a moment, Jimothy dragged a chair over to the fire and sat down. He carefully turned the spitted rabbits over the fire.

"So what about you?" Ricky asked as he returned with the emptied and rinsed bucket. "Are you most patriotic when you've been gone from home for a long time?"

"I've been gone from home for so long I don't really think of it as home any more."

"Where is home, then? And where was it before?" Ricky pulled over another chair and sat across from him.

"At the risk of sounding pretentiously poetic—"

"Doesn't your profession give you that right?"

"I try not to abuse it. My home is the open road. Or, more preferably, wherever I can find a roof and a bed."

Ricky nodded. "You want tea?"

"I'd love some, assuming you have any. I ran out and couldn't get more." In fact, there'd been ample tea sellers in Tesna. He simply hadn't had money to spare for that sort of luxury item. Ricky rose easily and Jimothy envied—and admired—the movement. "Home before that was the Sect."

Ricky opened one of the many pockets on his bag and removed a paper packet. He returned with it to the fire. "Was there nothing before the Sect, then?" he asked, taking down a kettle that had clearly seen better days. He filled it with water, shook in tea leaves, and settled it in the coals at the edge of the fire. "I didn't think people actually lived at the Sect, if you know what I mean."

"And where did you grow up?" countered Jimothy. Immediately Ricky shot him an apologetic smile.

"My mother says I'm outgoing. My father used to call me nosy. Sorry." He sat again. "Will you allow me to even the score?"

"Sure." Jimothy admitted to himself that he was as curious

about Ricky as the other man was about him. Only he didn't want to tip his hand so readily. He sat back, wincing at the movement.

Ricky noticed and offered sympathetically, "Remind me later. I have some liniment that'll help with that."

"Thanks. I will."

"So, evening the score...I've spent the last four months with those cautiously friendly neighbors I mentioned before. More specifically, I was in Torvik, Dusit. Have you been there?"

Jimothy nodded. He wasn't a fan of the city—except for a particular resident journeyman textilist—but kept silent.

It turned out Ricky didn't fancy the place either. He made a face. "Then you can understand why I'm so pleased to be going home."

"I can, yes. Is it just me or does that city stink? Literally, I mean."

"Oh, Blessed Martha, yes!" agreed Ricky emphatically. "The place smelled vile the entire time I was there. Perhaps it's better in the colder months, but I have no desire to go find out, eh?"

Jimothy chuckled. "I was there last winter. It was no better then."

"How sad for them." His regret was sincere. "I couldn't get out of there fast enough."

"And before that?" prompted Jimothy. "You need to go a little further to even the score, I think." He smiled so the other man would know it was meant lightly.

"Before that, I spent a good deal of time on that open road you mentioned. Milo and I have covered a lot of Kanbec together." It took a split second for Jimothy to remember that Milo was the inexplicable name of Ricky's chestnut mare. "Before that I was at the university in Korpi."

"I've never been to Korpi. I've heard it's beautiful."

Ricky's face darkened slightly. "Yeah, well. To look at, yeah, it's stunning actually." His expression softened. "Everything's built out of the local stone, of course. Pearlescent white stuff that catches the slightest changes in the light. The university buildings are...amazing. The university faculty, on the other hand..." He grew stern once again and frowned. He met Jimothy's inquisitive gaze evenly. "We disagreed on some fundamentals."

Jimothy nodded, accepting the ambiguity of his reply without question. "I think the tea is ready." Between the smoky scent of the tea and the fragrant herbs and roasting meat, the little cabin smelled delicious.

Ricky caught the scent of the brew and inhaled deeply. He smiled. "I think you're right. You turn the meat. I'll pour the tea." Once more Jimothy turned the spits while Ricky rummaged in his pack. He came up with a ceramic mug in one hand. He gestured with it. "I'm assuming you have one?"

"Sure. Hang on." Jimothy hauled himself to his feet and practically shuffled to his satchel. Ricky laughed and then promptly apologized.

"Sorry, sorry," he insisted as Jimothy turned a sour look on him. "You're moving like my grandfather used to move, is all. I'm sorry. I shouldn't laugh."

"You shouldn't. But I can't blame you."

He held out his mug and Ricky set it on the hearth with his own. Using his sleeve to protect himself from the hot handle of the kettle, he poured out the tea through a small, pierced metal strainer.

Jimothy sat again with a weary grunt. He took his filled mug from the other man's hand. Their fingers touched briefly and he felt a thrill zing through his belly. He silently cautioned himself against the feeling and sipped his tea to hide the sudden surge of excitement.

Ricky took his drink and looked towards the window, apparently unaffected by the brief contact. They shared an easy silence. Ricky stood watching the sinking sun while Jimothy continued to sip his tea and tried not to groan at the weight of the mug.

Eventually, Ricky roused himself. "It's nearly dark out. I should refill the water and check on Milo before it's too dark to see."

"New moon tonight, too, isn't it?" Jimothy knew some people believed the veil between worlds thinned under the new moon. He wondered if Ricky was among them.

"Yeah. It's a good night to have a roof over your head and four stone walls around you. I'll be right back." He traded his mug for the water bucket and ducked out the door.

Jimothy was glad for the time alone to stretch sore limbs and back. He was vain enough that he didn't care to have further witness to his temporary infirmity. He rolled his shoulders, tilted his head from side to side, reached up with both arms and straightened and bent each leg in turn. In short, he stretched every muscle he could without actually standing up. He couldn't quite bring himself to that point yet.

He looked sternly at the rabbits, turning them yet again and willing them to cook quickly so they could eat and he could get whatever muscle-ache remedy Ricky had. To his pleasant surprise, the little animals looked and smelled as though they might indeed be done soon. *I suppose that's the up side of being such a small dinner,* he thought wryly. He swallowed down the rest of his tea and forced himself to his feet one more time.

He pulled the last two apples and the cheese from his pack and set them on the table. It was meager, but it was all he had to contribute to the evening's meal. He was very lucky that Ricky had happened upon him that morning, because he was out of food. *How did I manage to pack and ration so badly?* He was disgusted with himself. It was a novice's mistake and he'd been at this for twelve years. He shook his head.

"Did they say something you disagree with?" asked Ricky, returning at that moment with fresh water.

Jimothy looked at him, puzzled. "Who?" *Does he think I'm hearing spirits? Is he hearing spirits?*

"The apples." He set the bucket on the floor by the hearth, at the farthest edge of the heat. "The way you were shaking your head at them, I figured they'd said something particularly foolish." He gave a small smile and Jimothy knew he was just teasing.

"No." Jimothy snorted a laugh. "Just cursing my own foolishness, but never mind. I think the rabbits are nearly done."

"Brilliant." Ricky's ready grin was back as he went to check on their dinner. "I have salt in my pack," he said, cautiously pulling one skewer from the fire. He checked the meat, put it back, checked the other. "Brilliant," he said again. "Nearly there. It's starting to rain again, by the way."

"Brilliant," Jimothy echoed sarcastically, eliciting another flash of smile.

He sat at the table and watched as Ricky dug in another pocket of his bag, found the salt, and returned with it to the hearth to season the meat. Then the dark-haired man plucked a wide, shallow pan from the rack above—"Ow!"—and quickly tossed it onto the table. He looked at Jimothy a little sheepishly. "Warmer than I thought it would be." Jimothy nodded in amusement and sliced the small block of cheese in two. Ricky pointed at the pan—"That's for the bones."—and went back for the food.

At last the meal was ready and they tore into it with gusto. The rosemary Ricky had stuffed into the rabbits had infused the meat with its flavor. Jimothy wished for a mug of ale to go with it, but contented himself with a second cup of tea.

"Shame we can't convert water into something a bit stronger," Ricky commented as if reading Jimothy's thoughts. He wiped his mouth on a sleeve. "I could go for a pint right now."

"Do you know that tale?" Jimothy asked around a mouthful.

"What? The one about that guy who turned water into wine? Who doesn't know it? It's a Magdalene standard." Ricky rolled his eyes. "As if, eh? But it sure would be nice," he added wistfully.

"It would."

Ricky sliced off a bit of the hard, yellow cheese and popped it into his mouth. He smiled around the bite. "Mm! Good cheese!"

"I thought so," agreed Jimothy. "It's held up well since I bought it in Tesna."

They continued to eat and chat about nothing in particular. Warm light from the fire softened the harsh stone walls, and the cabin grew cozy as the darkness pressed in from outside. It was a companionable silence and Jimothy relaxed into it.

Once the detritus of the meal was cleaned up, Ricky lit a lantern he'd brought in from the stable. He set it on the cleared table. "So," he began, "what can I trade you for a song or two before bed?"

Something in bed, Jimothy thought, but promptly squelched it. What was it about the man that he could get

Jimothy so heated up so quickly? He spoke before good sense could stop him. "You said you had something that would help with sore muscles."

"I do, but I'd share that anyway so it hardly seems fair to trade for it."

"Then how are you at backrubs? I'm not going to be able to reach the muscles in my back, especially when they've already tightened up." *What am I doing?* he demanded silently. Another part of his mind replied, *Nothing ventured, nothing gained.* He was pleasantly surprised when Ricky broke into one of his wide smiles. *That smile can light up a room.* And maybe, just maybe, he wasn't barking up the wrong tree.

"In fact, I'm very good at them." There was a light in Ricky's pale eyes that Jimothy sincerely hoped he wasn't misreading. Consequences could be anything from merely awkward to downright dire if he misjudged.

He smiled back, allowing a touch of suggestiveness to show. "Then it's a deal. Two songs—or stories—for a very good backrub." It might have been the light and shadow, but he thought he saw his own urges reflected in the other man's expression. "Would you hand me my guitar?"

Ricky rose and retrieved the cased instrument, passing it to Jimothy. While he tuned the small guitar, Ricky made up the bed, using lavender and other fragrant herbs hung from the beams to sweeten the mattress before layering the bedding atop it. "I hope you don't mind sharing," he said, not turning around.

"That's fine," replied Jimothy. He kept his voice carefully neutral. "Did you have a request?" he asked when he was satisfied with his tuning.

Ricky spun around, startled, to face Jimothy's anticipatory expression and ready hands. He swallowed hard and collected himself quickly. "Whatever you think would be good for a dark, wet night like tonight."

"Hmm..." Jimothy thought for a moment, and then nodded once. He began to play an upbeat song in a minor key. He'd always had a fondness for the quirky piece. The incongruity of tone and tempo intrigued him. He began to sing in a warm baritone.

"In the dark of the night
In the deep of the night
With no moon in sight
He rode alone along a street of silver
To the end of the world.

He headed out on his pale grey horse
With a destination in mind
To find a land of truth amidst a world of lies
Was his sole desire.

In the dark of the night
In the deep of the night
With no moon in sight
He rode alone along a street of silver
To the end of the world.

He turned to the east where the sun comes up
And found great beauty there.
But the shining light hid the false behind it,
Blinding him with lies."

He kept strumming and caught Ricky's delighted eyes. "You can sing along on the choruses if you want."

"I will when I get the words down."

Jimothy smiled and kept his gaze on him. He slowed his tempo the slightest bit and began the refrain again.

"In the dark of the night
In the deep of the night..."

Ricky joined in a little uncertainly.

"With no moon in sight
He rode alone along a street of silver
To the end of the world."

"Good!" encouraged Jimothy. He went on to the next verse.

"He turned to the north where the snow it falls
On the mountains so tall.
The sparkling white covered lies as cold
As the frozen ground."

He launched into the chorus again, and this time Ricky joined with more confidence.

"He turned to the south where the air it burns
And found a barren land.
But though the silence held not a whispered lie

It held nothing at all.

In the dark of the night
In the deep of the night
With no moon in sight
He rode alone along a street of silver
To the end of the world.

He turned to the west where the sun goes down
Into the ocean so blue.
But the pounding waves only told of tales
Dark and deep with untruth.

He looked to the sky and the clouds above him
And cried out in despair.
Then he turned his horse onto the silver path
Never to return."

The two men sang the refrain together one more time and Jimothy let the final chord ring before stilling the strings. There was a moment of silence, and then Ricky applauded. "That was fantastic. I've never heard anything like that before."

"I'm not surprised. It requires certain circumstances in order to be performed successfully."

Ricky tilted his head, a puzzled look on his sharp-featured and handsome face. "I don't get it."

"You have to know your audience. A lot of folks aren't fond of songs that remind them the world isn't perfect and a song like that one..." He shrugged. "Let's just say I wouldn't sing it in a politically charged crowd."

"Huh. I hadn't thought of that and I should have." Now Ricky's expression grew thoughtful. "That's really an interesting point." He fell silent and contemplative for several moments. Jimothy wondered what he was thinking, wondered too if he should interrupt with another tune. Before he had to decide, Ricky shook himself and smiled. "You said I could have two songs."

"Yes I did."

"Can I save the other one for later?"

"I don't see why not." Jimothy set his guitar down in its soft case. He stretched and yawned.

"You look like you're ready to collect your side of the transaction," Ricky said, rising from where he sat on the edge of the bed.

"I am, indeed," agreed Jimothy emphatically.

Ricky chuckled. "I thought so." He rose and went to his pack.

That bag must be bigger inside than it is outside, thought Jimothy. *I bet if I asked he could magically pull a saddle out of one of those multitudinous pockets.*

Turning around to face Jimothy again, Ricky held up a glazed pot about the size of a man's fist, its lid secured with a soft wax seal. "You're in luck. I was out, but I made myself stay an extra few minutes in Torvik just so I could restock."

"I appreciate your sacrifice," joked Jimothy.

"You should. You know how I feel about that city. I should warn you," he went on as he peeled off the seal, "it's sort of...pungent."

The moment the lid was off, Jimothy could smell the stuff. He concluded that his companion was a master of understatement. It wasn't that it smelled bad at all. In fact he quite liked the scent, detecting clove, cinnamon and peppermint oils. There was a hint of something softer underneath them, but he couldn't identify what it was. "You're not kidding. That smells like powerful stuff."

"Do you like it? I love it." Ricky stuck his nose in the pot and inhaled deeply. "Mm! Clears the sinuses a bit, too."

"I imagine it does. But all I care about is how well it works on sore muscles. I'd forgotten how hard horse riding is on my back."

"It's all that time keeping your balance. Don't be surprised if you wake up tomorrow feeling it in your gut and your thighs, too."

"I'm already feeling it in my thighs, thanks," Jimothy cracked dryly.

"I can rub those for you, too." This time Jimothy knew he wasn't mistaking Ricky's meaning or his expression, but before he could say anything, the younger man's eyes went wide. He quickly turned his back to Jimothy. "I'm sorry. That was inappropriate."

"No. Don't apologize."

"I shouldn't have said that. My mother warns me all the time that my mouth is going to get me into trouble. I'm really sorry."

Jimothy rose and came to stand a little behind and to one side of him. He cautiously reached out a hand and laid it gently on Ricky's shoulder. Ricky turned with the gentle pressure and the two men stood face to face. Jimothy looked down the short distance into Ricky's pale eyes and saw a mix of emotions he couldn't quite sort out. On impulse, he leaned in and kissed him on the mouth—a little cautiously, a little eagerly—and was thrilled when Ricky readily kissed him back.

They parted, but neither of them moved away so much as a step. There was a moment of silence until...

"Damn," breathed Ricky, his eyes alight once again. "Now that's the kind of trouble I like getting into." Jimothy laughed and they kissed again, deeper and hungrier and longer. Ricky pressed him back towards the bed until Jimothy bumped into it and sat down, abruptly breaking the kiss. He looked up at the other man and smiled salaciously.

"Nice bed."

"Blankets are soft, too. The linen sheets are nice on bare skin."

Jimothy ran a hand over them. "Mm-hmm."

Ricky stood close, legs spread just enough to squeeze Jimothy's knees between them. "I like to be on the bottom," he said, his voice daring a challenge.

"Then what are you doing up there?" Jimothy's words were met by a wide smile.

Ricky stepped back. Jimothy leaned forward to pull off his boots and moaned inadvertently as his back protested. Ricky laughed and knelt in front of him. "Let me do that," he offered. Jimothy was happy to let him. He held out each foot in turn and Ricky quickly removed Jimothy's boots and chucked them aside. They were soon joined by Ricky's boots and clothing. He pulled Jimothy to his feet and helped the aching man undress.

Standing naked together, each took time to look the other over appraisingly—flat bellies, sharply defined calves and thighs, strong arms. Jimothy smiled at the dark hair that curled over the other man's chest and the thin line of fine hairs that led down to his groin and his engorged penis. It was bigger than he'd expected and his own cock jumped eagerly in response. Ricky saw and grasped it, winning him a wordless grunt of excited surprise. He massaged the silken skin with strong fingers and Jimothy moaned and thrust his hips forward into his touch. Ricky trailed the fingers of his free hand over Jimothy's smooth chest with a feather-light touch that caused the taller man to shiver slightly. Leaning in, Ricky tilted his head to nip at Jimothy's ear and murmured, "That liniment is good for more than treating sore muscles." He looked into Jimothy's dark eyes, his own as blue as the center of a candle flame.

Jimothy met his gaze steadily. "Then let's put it to good use."

Ricky didn't release his hold as he used his other hand to grab the open pot from the table where he'd left it. He held it out and Jimothy took it in one hand. Then Ricky dipped in his fingers, drawing out a small dollop, which he rubbed between thumb and fingers before wrapping that hand around Jimothy's erection.

Jimothy gasped, his eyes wide at the unexpected sensation of hot and cold all at once, and Ricky's smile broadened a little wickedly. "It's even better on the inside. Want me to show you?" Jimothy only nodded, senses temporarily overwhelmed. This time Ricky dipped a single finger of his other hand, and then reached around to Jimothy's anus. Gently, he slid the slippery digit inside.

Jimothy thought he couldn't feel more than he already did, but the slight movement of the coated finger in his ass proved him wrong. Hot and cold, inside and out. The sensations were too great. "Take it out," he gasped and immediately Ricky obeyed, releasing him from the back and front at once.

"Are you all right?"

"Yes." He breathed deeply, gathering his control. "I just don't want to come yet, and that..." He trailed off, words escaping him.

"I've made a Wand'ring Minstrel go speechless," quipped Ricky. "I think I'm proud."

"You should be," Jimothy confirmed with a giddy laugh. "My turn." Quick as a flash, he spun the other man around and shoved him onto his back on the bed. Ricky landed with a surprised thud and laughed.

"Done wasting time, eh?"

"I think so. Don't you?" It had been several months since Jimothy had had a partner in pleasure and he was more than ready.

"Oh yeah." Ricky stretched out on his back, knees bent and legs spread, his tumescent cock a hot, red contrast against the pale skin and dark hair of his belly. Jimothy gave him a mildly surprised look, but made no complaint. "It's hotter when I can see your face when you come."

"No argument here." Taking a bit of the liniment in his hand, he set the pot aside on the floor—out of the way, but not out of reach. He knelt on the bed facing the waiting man. Using two fingers to ready him, he found him easy to prepare. If Jimothy had needed any more proof that Ricky was accustomed to this sort of thing, he had it now. Removing his fingers, he got his hands under Ricky's hips. The slighter man raised them readily, slipping a pillow underneath to help him get the angle that would most benefit them both. Jimothy needed no hands to slip his hard, throbbing prick into Ricky's ass. The fit was pleasantly tight and the salve made him slide in and out with ease.

He used one hand to support himself against the mattress, not wanting to force the smaller man to take all his weight. With his slicked up hand, he grasped Ricky's cock, pressed between their bodies. He began stroking hard in time with his thrusts.

"Yeah," gasped Ricky. "You've got it." Their eyes locked and Ricky issued his command. "Fuck me hard."

Jimothy obeyed gladly, increasing his speed and pressure until his pubic bone pounded against the supine man's ass. The heat and chill of the ointment combined with the tightness around him and the feel of flesh on flesh was delicious. Soon all the sensations were too much and he came, groaning and gasping his pleasure. He felt Ricky come a split second later, semen spurting up and over the tip of his penis to slide down over Jimothy's fingers and onto Ricky's muscled stomach. Small spasms shivered through them both until at last they calmed to stillness. There was a frozen moment before they relaxed enough to release one another. Jimothy slipped his softening cock from its hot mantle and released his hold on Ricky's equally flaccid penis. He sank heavily to the mattress beside him. "That was..." His stunned brain sought the right word.

"Amazing?" supplied Ricky a little breathlessly.

"Mind-blowing."

He laughed. "I've never heard that term before, but yeah, I have to agree. Mind-blowing. You're incredible."

"Thanks. You're damned fantastic yourself," answered Jimothy with the utmost sincerity.

The pair lay there for several minutes and Jimothy had to fight not to doze off. Eventually he forced tired eyes to open and sat up enough to lean on one elbow. He started to speak, but realized Ricky had in fact fallen asleep. With knowing self-indulgence, he watched the dark-haired young man sleep, his furred chest rising and falling gently with each breath. *Enough.* He nudged Ricky's shoulder, gently prodding him into wakefulness.

Bleary blue eyes looked up at him. "Huh?"

"We should clean up." Jimothy looked pointedly at the

residue drying in the hair of the other man's belly. Ricky's eyes followed the gaze.

"Huh." He chuckled. "Yeah." Then he looked into Jimothy's eyes. "Worth it, though."

"Definitely worth it."

Chapter Two

The next morning dawned clear. Blue skies sported white puffball clouds that scudded across the heavens as if running from the painful clarity of it all. Jimothy woke first and stole a moment to watch Ricky sleep just as he had last night. Then he crept from the bed, careful not to wake him. Naked, he claimed the slop bucket-cum-chamber pot and stepped outside. He inhaled air that was rich with the clean scent of a morning after a hard rain and then padded to the back of the cabin where a tiny outhouse stood. He emptied first the chamber pot and then his bladder, and then returned with the empty bucket to the cabin.

Ricky was up and halfway dressed when he entered. "I figured you couldn't have gone too far," Ricky said with that perpetual smile. "Seeing as your clothes are still here."

"Actually, it's the guitar that's the true tell. A Wand'ring Minstrel might be robbed naked, but he'll never give up his instrument without a fight."

"I'll keep that in mind. Want your pants?"

"If I have to." They both chuckled and Ricky sighed as he handed over the garment in question.

"I'm afraid so. We need to sort this place out and hit the road if we're going to make it to Couvin by lunch."

"That's the goal?"

"It is. I have obligations waiting for me and they don't appreciate tardiness, eh?"

Jimothy nodded in understanding. "It's all right. I have some obligations of my own." He thought of the letters he carried and thanked the small gods of fortune for the chance encounter with Ricky and his generous assistance since then.

"Heya, how are your muscles this morning?" Ricky asked as they dressed.

"Surprisingly not sore."

"Yeah? Good. You never did get that backrub I promised."

"And you never got your second song."

"I guess we'll both have to collect another time."

While Ricky went out back to see to Milo, Jimothy brewed a fresh pot of tea. They shared a brief breakfast of sweet pastries—once again produced from one of the numerous pockets on Ricky's pack—and put the cabin back together as best they could.

"Who cleans up the rest of the mess?" Jimothy asked, a little guilty over the pile of dirty bed linens heaped next to the slop bucket.

"The tenders. Their job is to ride from waycabin site to waycabin site and maintain the facilities."

"What, like chambermaids on horseback?"

Ricky chuckled. "Something like that, but more, too. They do everything from laundry to chopping wood to retiling the roofs. There's a locked maintenance cabin at the center of each site where their gear is stored."

"Ah!" Jimothy had noticed the little building as they'd rode in, but had assumed it was just a small waycabin. He nodded as he mentally placed this latest piece of the puzzle. "So they don't have to haul everything from one site to another. That's clever."

"Here." Ricky handed him a wooden disk on a leather thong.

"What's this?" He turned it over in his hands. One side was plain wood while the other was painted bright yellow.

"A sign for the tenders and any travelers. There's a little hook outside to the left of the door. Hang it there with the yellow side out to indicate that this cabin was used and needs tending."

"This is quite a system you have. And everyone actually abides by it?"

Ricky shrugged. "I don't really know. I've never heard of any problems beyond the odd missing pot or blanket. That's why everything in the cabins is second-hand. Nothing is new, you might have noticed. It's all stuff that's still useable but the previous owners didn't want it any more for whatever reason. There was even a man—a baker, I think—who willed his pots and pans to the waycabins when he died."

"Didn't his family or his journeyman have something to say about that?"

"They may have, but a will is a will and if it's legally in order, what can you do?"

Jimothy nodded at the logic. It was a bit callous, but then that was the way of most laws. Then, shaking himself into movement, he quickly ducked outside, found the hook in the wall and placed the little wooden sign on it.

"Ready?" asked Ricky as he checked to be certain the fire was out in the hearth.

"Almost." Jimothy cased his guitar and slung it across his back, then pulled his cloak on over top. "Ready." As much as he'd enjoyed their night in the waycabin, he was eager to be on his way.

They settled their baggage on Milo, who protested with a whicker. “Hush, you whiner,” Ricky scolded the mare. “You've carried more and been none the worse for it.”

Jimothy remembered something from the previous evening and chanced a question clothed in lightness so as not to cause suspicion or upset. “Does she ever answer back?”

Ricky looked at him intently, reading the question right despite its tone. “Not to me. But I once knew someone who said this horse had the foulest vocabulary she'd ever heard outside a sailors' bar.”

Jimothy shook his head, amused. “I can't even begin to imagine.”

“Blessed Martha,” exclaimed Ricky in mock horror. “Who would want to?” They both laughed. Then he climbed up into his saddle and reached a hand down to Jimothy. “This is familiar.”

“I was thinking the same thing.” *And thinking I could get used to it,* his mind added, but he shoved it aside. He silently chided himself for the maudlin line of thought. This was nothing more than a particularly fortunate and pleasant one-off. No strings. No promises.

He found the conclusion intensely disappointing.

“You coming?” asked Ricky.

Apparently he'd stalled too long. “Sorry. I was just thinking.” He took Ricky's hand and, tucking foot into stirrup, climbed up on the horse. He took hold of the smaller man and braced himself to ride.

“About what?” Ricky nudged the horse to a walk, expertly angling her out of the covered stable.

“I was thinking I should thank the lanmere who had the

waycabins built."

"She's dead."

"I know, but they say the dead can hear us if we speak to them."

Ricky glanced back at him over one shoulder. "Who says that?"

"An old friend of mine. A Northerner who was my roommate at the Sect."

"Huh. I suppose it's not unreasonable. I mean, what else do the dead have to do until they reincarnate?"

Jimothy looked up at the sky and spoke stentoriously, his voice carrying over the green countryside. "Lanmere Helene Rosslyn, you have my thanks."

"You've got some lungs on you," commented Ricky, rubbing one ear dramatically.

"It comes with the job," the Wand'ring Minstrel replied, chuckling.

Ricky clucked his tongue at the horse and urged her to a quick walk. As the morning wore on, the landscape around them changed. The hills had been wild and scattered with boulders, but as they drew closer to Couvin, the gently rolling land was divided into farmland plots that had been cleared of the erratic stones. They passed fields of wheat, barley and mint that bordered rows of old hoary pear and apple trees, towering hop vines and acres of berry and grape vines. Interspersed was pasture land dotted with livestock too distant to identify. Jimothy guessed they were sheep—but that could have been wishful thinking. He was growing hungry and lamb sounded good. Occasionally they passed an empty square acre or two, left fallow for the land to recover. There was never anyone within hailing distance, but Jimothy could see people picking out in the berry patches when the angle between the rows was right.

True to Ricky's word, it was nearing midday when the city walls of Couvin came into view in a lush, wide valley. Ricky slowed Milo to a walk and then a full stop atop a rise. "We're still a fair distance out," he said unnecessarily.

When he didn't continue, Jimothy asked, "Do you want to drop me off here?"

"What?" Ricky seemed genuinely shocked. "No. Why?"

Jimothy shrugged. "We Wand'ring Minstrels aren't always popular, in spite of the services we can provide." He thought of the eight written letters and three more he'd memorized, all for delivery from citizens of Tesna for friends or family in Couvin. And the one special missive, sealed with a wax crest. The sooner he delivered the mail, the happier he'd be. He wanted that official letter off his mind and conscience. More than that, he wanted it out of his sphere of responsibility.

"You won't have that trouble here. We've had Wand'ring Minstrels through Couvin for generations, although it's been a while since I met one. Still, it's policy to make them welcome."

"That's good to hear."

"In fact, you should come up to The Heathers once you've settled into a place in town," Ricky said eagerly.

"The Heathers?"

"The lanmere's estate. I'm willing to bet the house musicians there would love the chance to play with a real Wand'ring Minstrel."

It was more serendipity and for the second time in as many days, Jimothy silently thanked the small gods of fortune for it. "I'll do that."

There was that grin again. "Good." Ricky once more picked up the pace and they headed down into the valley.

Jimothy studied the city as they approached it. The wall around it was at least twenty feet high, built of the same stone he'd seen littering the landscape. Clearly it had been intended to be a defended stronghold. He could see narrow slits high up where archers could stand to ward off attackers. There was one major entrance to the southwest, and at least one smaller one around the wall towards the north side. A wide road led off from the larger gate, weaving over and around and out of sight beyond a high ridge.

"So do you know much about Couvin?" asked Ricky.

"Only what I've read in the Archives at the Sect, and that was pretty dry. Why don't you tell me about it?" Jimothy had long since learned that when you wanted to get to know a place, your best bet was to ask the locals. They tended to have the most pride while at the same time being the most critical, and so you got a lot more interesting information than could be found in any book. Besides, he liked listening to the sound of Ricky's voice.

"You're not afraid I'll bore you to death?"

"No. I enjoy history."

"All right, but if you start to doze and you fall off the horse, don't go blaming me." Ricky began to recite, a little like an apprentice at his lessons—a bored apprentice. "Generations ago, before the city was built, the land around here was all owned by one family—not the family that rules now. They parceled out the land around their estate to resident farmers. Over time, the usual drama ensued: unscrupulous lord, angry indentured farmers and the inevitable rebellion. Once they overthrew the overlord, they elected a new ruler. The first lanpere."

"That's the most interesting bit, at least to me," put in Jimothy. "They chose to have a monarchical government. That's really unusual."

"Is it?"

"Of course. I mean, they won their freedom and then turned around and essentially elected a king. Don't you think that's odd?"

"I'm hardly one to ask."

Jimothy chuckled. "Right. You grew up with it, so of course it's normal to you."

"Something like that." Ricky directed the horse to the smaller of the two visible entrances. The ground went from hard-packed dirt to cobblestones as the pair rode unchallenged through the stone archway. Looking down, Jimothy saw where a portcullis would have landed between dirt and cobbles. It had long since been filled with a sunken wooden beam to level the ground and protect against injury to human or beast. Looking above him, there was nothing but stone. Not even the mechanisms that would raise and lower a gate were left, though he could see where they should have been.

"Was there never a gate here?" Jimothy asked.

"No."

"Why not? Did they run out of funding?"

"No. We've just never needed any."

"How did you manage that?"

"Do you really want to hear more of our history?" Ricky sounded doubtful.

"I'm a Wand'ring Minstrel," replied Jimothy matter-of-factly. "Recording history is part of what I do. Please, go on."

"All right. Well, there was about a century of peace when the farmers moved out farther from the central area. A city core grew up in the area they'd left. And when I say grew, I mean *sprawled*. There's not a straight street in town."

Jimothy made a mental note to buy a map at the first opportunity.

Ricky went on. "A merchant class developed at that point. Are you sure you want to hear this? It's a pretty ordinary story."

"There's something to be learned in every story. Please, go on."

"If you say so. The wall was built to protect from an outside threat. The agricultural class took refuge everywhere within the city—inns, taverns, private homes. The ruling family—the Rosslyns—opened their estate, too. There were farming families staying in the house, the chapel, the stables and even camped out on the grounds. Plans were made to complete each of the five gates, but in the end they didn't need to. The threat...went away."

Ricky's tone grew proud as he talked about the ruling family's actions during the crisis. And rightly so, in Jimothy's opinion. He knew of plenty of governments—past and present—that weren't so concerned for their citizenry. But it was Ricky's more conspiratorial note at the end that really caught his ear.

"I read something about that in the Sect's records, but they were a bit vague on the point." Jimothy chose not to add that the suspicions of the Sect's Historians were easily read if one knew how to read between the lines. He hoped he would get a bit more detail from his ad hoc tour guide. He was disappointed.

"Work's being done to complete the defenses now."

"It is?" It wasn't what he was looking for, but it still piqued his curiosity. "Why now?"

Ricky's enthusiasm came through as he talked of the current project. It was obviously more interesting to him than ancient history. "Couvin's tercentennial is just two years away. The lanmere and much of the city council want the city looking its best for the festivities, and that means finishing whatever was left unfinished in the original construction or has since been damaged. They've completed repairs to the outer wall and installed two gates already. The one we just passed through and two others are left."

"And they'll have them done in just two more years?"

"You'd be surprised what bureaucrats and laborers can get done when the lanmere and a big anniversary are staring them down."

Jimothy nodded at his wry tone and filed the information away with everything else he'd learned from the other man since their unusual meeting yesterday morning. It was quite a collection, and he wondered if Ricky knew just how much he'd shared. *Some of it's probably only news to me, of course,* he reminded himself. Any citizen was bound to know about the upcoming celebration and the preparations for it. After all, a lot of work had already been done and the money to complete that work had to come from somewhere. What were taxes for but to fund community services and maintain public properties?

The street on which they'd entered the city was surprisingly quiet considering the hour. They turned left and Jimothy caught a glimpse of more activity. Judging by the direction, he guessed the people and horses were moving towards the town center. Like any place that had grown instead of being planned, the streets were narrow and winding, and logic was entirely lacking. He looked around another corner only to have that street bend a mere twenty yards farther along.

Ricky reined Milo to a stop at the next crossing. "I have to leave you here," he said apologetically. "We're headed different directions at this point."

"We are? You know my plans better than I do," Jimothy said, but he threw a leg over Milo's back and slid to the ground.

"What direction am I heading, in that case?"

"Naturally you're headed to the Cat and Turtle," replied Ricky with a matter-of-fact expression.

"I am?"

"Yeah." He nodded and handed down Jimothy's satchel.

Jimothy took off his cloak and slung the pack over one shoulder, and carried the cloak over one arm. It was too warm for it that afternoon. "I see. So, what direction am I going in order to find the Cat and Turtle?"

"You're going to start that way." Ricky pointed across his body towards the right branch of the road. "It's going to curve left, as you can see."

Jimothy looked around Milo's head. "I can see."

"At the second cross street, you're going to turn right. You're going to follow the road—it'll curve a lot, but just keep going—until you reach a five-way intersection."

"Five-way. All right. And what am I going to do when I get there?"

"You're going to stop, find the sign with the black cat and the turtle on it, go inside and ask the woman at the bar for a room. Her name is Maeve. The second floor off the back is the best."

Jimothy considered everything and nodded. "All right. It's a good plan."

"You'd never come up with a bad one."

"If only it were true." They laughed. "Thank you," said Jimothy sincerely.

Ricky's face grew thoughtful. Jimothy would almost have called the expression caring if he hadn't warned himself against over-sentimentality that very morning. "You're welcome." Then he flashed a grin. "But you still owe me a song."

Jimothy burst out laughing. "Fair's fair. I'm holding you to your part of that bargain, remember. I want that backrub."

Ricky leaned down so his face was inches from Jimothy's. "You can hold me anytime," he practically purred. "And I can't wait to get my hands on your back, your front, and your everything else."

Jimothy felt the heat rise in his gut. *Not just a one-off, then.* He smiled slyly. "I look forward to it."

"So do I." A sonorous chime rang at that moment, disrupting their banter. Jimothy's trained ear detected at least three bells ringing within a split second of one another and was pleased they were all in tune.

Ricky's reaction was less genial. "Bollocks!" he snapped, abruptly sitting up straight. "I have to go. I'll see you later." He kicked into Milo's sides and the mare snorted in what sounded for all the world like annoyance. But she began moving again, her hooves clomping noisily on the cobbled street. Turning back, he called over his shoulder. "Go to The Heathers tomorrow about mid-afternoon. Ask for Gretta." He was practically shouting now across the growing gap. "And shave first! Bye!" He waved one hand and moments later followed a bend in the road and vanished from sight.

Jimothy took the right-hand route—that promptly curved to his left—as he'd been instructed. One- and two-story buildings lined either side of the street. Most were obviously people's homes. He turned right at the second cross-street and soon private homes gave way to small shops selling anything from woolens to vegetables to—*What the...?* He paused in front of a narrow two-story building and blinked. A low stone fence with a whitewashed gate surrounded a small garden where herbs and flowers mingled in riotous abandon. The structure itself was obviously old but had been well maintained. There was evidence of recent repairs to the façade. A middle-aged woman in an embroidered robe lounged on a beautifully carved wooden bench to the left of the doorway. She was smoking a pipe. She smiled at him and gestured up at the sign. "I just had it repainted. What do you think?"

Yes, I saw that right, Jimothy thought, taking a closer look. The freshly painted sign over the door depicted two people of unclear gender in a contorted position that was so intriguing it forced the looker to stand there and puzzle it out. When he did, he smiled. *I wish I were that flexible.* "I find the artistry and the subject matter to be exquisite," he replied.

The woman nearly choked with laughter and slapped a palm on her knee. "That's the best answer I've ever heard," she guffawed. "Can I interest you in my wares, stranger? I'm sure we can find someone to suit your fancy."

A man and two women had moved into the open doorway while he was examining the sign. He looked over the trio appraisingly. None was more than half-clothed, and what they did wear was clearly meant to be removed with ease and speed. "Your wares appear most excellent, madam, but I'm afraid I must attend to business before pleasure." He bowed his head apologetically at the woman and her employees.

"You come back after your business is done," she recommended. "Polite fellow like you could make lots of friends here. Good price for you, too, if that pack on your back is what I think it is...Minstrel?"

"You're not wrong, and I thank you. I'll keep your fine establishment in mind." He let his smile show his appreciation for her wares and for the sign in which the woman took such pride. She chortled and nodded, waving a hand in farewell.

Jimothy continued down the street, which curved as much as Ricky had warned. He began to wonder if he'd managed to turn off accidentally when he suddenly came around a bend and found himself at the intersection of five roads.

The bustle of the city's center was an assault on his senses after the quiet and solitude of the country. He took a moment at the edge of it all to let it wash over him. People hurried along in every direction, seemingly in a great rush to get somewhere else. Vendors stood in front of their shops, wares out for shoppers to examine while the shopkeepers examined the customers. A young woman bumped Jimothy's arm in passing and muttered an apology as she hastened on. He simply smiled. The pickpocket was out of luck and they both knew it.

How to negotiate the five-way intersection held him stymied until he began to see a pattern in people's movements. They were taking turns, but he couldn't see any indication of who or what determined right-of-way. It was one of those phenomena where people simply behaved a certain way because that was the way to behave. It was impressive.

He searched the area's many signs and promptly found the one he sought—a fluffy black cat huddled with its tail protectively curled around a grey-brown turtle with disturbingly wise eyes. The artwork was incredibly skilful and he wondered if the same person had painted it as had painted the one for the brothel. The door over which it hung was dark wood with a small window at about eye level. To either side were more small-paned windows of clear glass, filling spaces nearly as large as the door. He was surprised to see that it was a full three stories tall with what looked like another half story above that.

Deeming himself as ready as he could be, Jimothy stepped into the barely controlled chaos. He fit himself into the traffic pattern very carefully and crossed the intersection towards the Cat and Turtle, glad there was only one road to cross between him and it. He reached the door without incident and went inside.

The place was busy but not overly crowded and he breathed a small sigh of relief. The room he'd entered was as wide as the shop front. A large fireplace dominated the wall on his left and a long bar ran nearly the length of the wall directly opposite the door. Booths, tables and chairs filled the rest of the room, about a third of them occupied by customers. He wove carefully through the space to the bar. The petite woman behind it nodded at him, her expression friendly. She was dressed in a simple brown dress that was embroidered along the neckline, and a clean white apron. Short dark hair framed her face and set off bright green eyes, and her smile showed straight white teeth. She was charming and Jimothy smiled back. *This must be Maeve,* he thought.

"Welcome, Minstrel," the woman said, recognizing him from his accessories just as the madam had. "What can I get for you?"

"A room, I hope, and some lunch."

She nodded once. "I can do that. What currency are you carrying?"

"Sadly none of the solid kind," he replied. "But with your permission, I'll ply my trade in your fine public room and you will have first claim to what I earn."

"And having you here will bring in extra custom, so we'll both benefit. I know how it works, and I'm happy with the arrangement." She rose up on her toes to reach a hand over the bar. Jimothy shook it. "You said you wanted a room and lunch. Which do you want first?"

Jimothy's stomach growled quietly but he ignored it. "The room first, please."

"All right. My husband will see you up." She turned and it was only then he saw that she was pregnant, further from due than from deed, but well on her way. She called out to be heard through the curtained doorway behind and to her right. "Japheth? Guest!"

"Just a second," a male voice responded.

She turned back to face Jimothy. "Are you sure you wouldn't like to eat first?"

His stomach growled again, a bit louder this time, and he and the hostess exchanged amused looks. "I can wait a little longer, thanks."

"If you say so," she said with good humor.

"I wonder if a second floor room is available. Preferably off the back."

She looked at him curiously. "You've never been here before. I'd remember you."

"It was recommended to me by a friend."

"Any friend who recommends the Cat and Turtle is a friend of mine," she said with a satisfied smile. "I expect we can manage that."

At that moment, a dark-skinned man with warm brown eyes and tight, short, brown curls appeared from around the curtain. "What was it you wanted?" he asked the hostess a little distractedly. "I didn't hear you."

She gestured to the waiting man. "Guest," she repeated, a hint of amusement and impatience in her voice. Jimothy got the impression this was a habit well worn over years. "He needs a room."

"If possible, something on the second floor off the back," Jimothy added.

"I think we have one open. Japheth?"

"Huh? Oh, yeah. Room eight is occupied but number six is available. I'll get the key." He disappeared briefly and returned with a key in one hand. Jimothy noticed that a ring of keys hung from his belt, jingling slightly as he moved. Then Japheth looked at Jimothy directly for the first time and smiled at him. "If you'll follow me?"

"Thanks." He nodded to the hostess and followed the man through the curtain and immediately up a narrow stairway to their left. Jimothy reached behind him with his free hand to keep his guitar from bumping into the wall.

"Will you be staying long?" Japheth asked.

"A week at least, possibly longer."

"Did Maeve give you the lowdown?"

I was right. "No. We only discussed basics."

"There's a discount if you pay for a full week in advance. Breakfast is included with the room. There's cold water from the well and you're welcome to help yourself, but if you want someone to bring hot water up for washing it's an extra copper a day. You can also get a brazier brought up. That's another two coppers a day." They paused at the first floor landing and he pointed out a small window to the back garden. There were several fruit trees and small plots of all shapes and sizes with everything from coriander to carrots planted in them. But it was the well in the center and the privy at the far end that Japheth pointed to, and Jimothy nodded.

"I see."

They continued up to the second floor. "There's a chamber pot in each room and you can empty it in the outhouse in the back of the yard. If you want it emptied by the staff, that's another two coppers a day."

"That seems more than fair." It wasn't a job he'd want to do even for money and he was glad for the chance to pay someone else to do it for him. *Assuming I can make a bit of cash in a hurry.*

"Are you sure you want the second floor?" Japheth asked him as they ascended. "It's a long way from the facilities."

"It was recommended to me. I'm guessing because of the view of your garden." Jimothy was surprised to see such a large garden in the heart of the city.

"There is a good view from up here," agreed the host. "It's even better from up top, but those rooms aren't as nice." They reached the second floor landing and he opened a door to a hallway as narrow as the stairs. There were two doors on either side of the hall, and Japheth stopped at the first one to their left. There was a neatly painted number six on it, adorned by the artist with blackberry vines heavy with ripe fruit. Japheth used the key in his hand to unlock the door and swung it open for his guest.

Jimothy stepped inside and assessed the place. A small round table and a chair stood in the center, a bed against the left wall, a trunk in the near right corner and a chamber pot in the far right. Between the pot and the bed, and beneath a four-paned window, stood a wash table with a bowl and pitcher on it.

"The chest is there if you want to unpack properly. Linens are cleaned once a week unless you arrange for more. You can speak directly to the staff about that. Fuel for the brazier is included in the cost. Do you want one?"

"Yes, please." It was warm for the moment, but the weather could change suddenly with the vagaries of the oncoming autumn.

"I'll have someone bring it up for you."

Jimothy set pack, guitar and cloak on the bed and went to the window. The view of the garden from above was indeed lovely, but it didn't compare to the view out over the city.

Japheth went on. "This room's east facing, so you'll get the sun in the morning."

"That's fine. Can you tell me...?" Jimothy glanced over his shoulder at his host and then pointed at something out the window. "That big building on that hill there—what is it?" He had a guess, but wanted it confirmed.

"That's The Heathers. The lanmere's estate."

"I assume the family resides there."

"That's right."

He turned to face Japheth. "Thanks."

The host handed over the key. "This will get you into this room, but it won't get you in the front or back door. We close the kitchen at ten, the bar at midnight, and the doors at one o'clock. If you're out past that, just ring the bell and the night keeper will let you in."

"How will the night keeper know I belong here?" Jimothy didn't expect high security, but he did want some assurance of the place's general safety.

"She'll have a list. You're one of only two guests at the moment, so the list is short. Just introduce yourself to her this evening so she recognizes you. She's easy to spot," Japheth added before Jimothy could ask the question that was on the tip of his tongue. "She'll be at the bar and she looks like someone you don't want to get in a fight with."

"I'll keep that in mind."

Japheth turned to go, and then stopped in the doorway. "I should warn you, she has a thing for musicians." He tipped his head at the guitar.

"I'll keep that in mind, too," said Jimothy with a chuckle. "Thanks again." He shut the door behind the host and locked it. He went again to the window and looked out at the stately home atop the hill. "So that's The Heathers," he muttered. "Why do I think getting to it won't be as easy as it looks?"

Chapter Three

By the time he made it back down to the bar, it was closer to dinner than lunchtime. Only three people occupied the main room: an old man nursing a pint at the end of the bar who looked like the sort of regular every good public house could boast; a dark-haired girl in a simple green dress and white apron wiping off the many tables, cleaning up after the departed lunch crowd; and Maeve. Jimothy sat down at the bar and she brought him a wedge of soda bread and a bowl of hearty soup laden with kale and tomatoes that he guessed were grown right out back. “Ale or wine?” she asked.

“Which is cheaper?” he answered question with question.

“Depends on how good you want it to be,” the hostess remarked wryly. Then she went on, “I’ll get you a bit of wine. It’ll be better with that soup than beer would.” Reaching up she pulled down an earthenware goblet from a rack, and then bent down to reach under the bar for a green glass bottle. She poured out a generous measure of the dark red vintage and placed the cup before him. “Tell me what you think.”

Jimothy set down his spoon and picked up the goblet. He swirled the wine and sniffed it, then slurped a small amount, rolling it about in his mouth. He swallowed and smiled. “That’s delicious. Blackberry, some raspberry and a hint of pear, I think.”

"You're very good!"

"Not really. Those are all crops I saw on my way into the city."

Maeve laughed. "I'm disappointed! I was ready to be incredibly impressed. I'm Maeve Linden, by the way."

"Your husband said. Jimothy Redwing," he introduced himself.

"It's a pleasure to meet you, Jimothy Redwing." They shook hands as they had earlier.

"I wonder if you could help me with something."

"What's that?" She leaned her elbows on the bar in a casual manner.

"I need directions to your market square. Or better yet a guide to get me there. I have letters to deliver, and the public market is usually the best place for it." He took a bite of his soup and followed it with one of bread.

"Five Corners is the closest you'll find to a public market in Couvin, eh?"

Jimothy was surprised. "You mean there's no open square or park where people go?"

Maeve shook her head. "No. There are parks and squares all over, but nothing you'd call central. But I can help you out another way. We'll send a crier at our expense to spread the word you're here. That way people who are expecting mail can come to you."

"Bringing you even more business," commented Jimothy, wondering if she was lying about the city's lack of a public square. He decided she was telling the truth. From what he'd seen of the city thus far, it was likely there really wasn't one. Everything was just too scattered and haphazard for it.

"I won't deny it," she agreed good-naturedly, "but it will get you what you need, too. There's really no better place than here for you to be, and I don't think you'd enjoy busking out in front of the tavern." Her eyes slid to look through the front windows to the street crowded and noisy with humanity, and his gaze followed.

"You make an excellent point, hostess."

"Call me Maeve, Minstrel."

"Call me Jimothy."

"It's a deal. When would you like me to send a crier?"

"As soon as is convenient," Jimothy said.

Maeve nodded once and looked over at the girl who had gone from wiping tables to sweeping the floor. "Nita, go find Japheth and ask him to send for a crier. Tell him our Wand'ring Minstrel needs some advertising if any of us are going to make a profit."

"Yes, ma'am." Nita quickly swept the pile of dirt she'd collected into the banked coals of the hearth fire and then disappeared into the back.

"That'll get him moving quicker," Maeve said to Jimothy, a smile quirking her delicate mouth. "Japheth is never one to turn down something that will bring an honest profit. Let me know if you need anything more."

"Only your charming company," said Jimothy gallantly.

She laughed. "The last one of your lot that we had here was just as good at the shallow flattery," she said without malice.

"Madam, you wound me!" Jimothy placed a hand dramatically over his heart. It only made Maeve laugh harder, and he grinned back. "You caught me. I need directions."

"To where?"

"The Heathers." Maeve made a face. "That bad?" he asked.

"Have you been to Couvin before?"

Jimothy shook his head. "No."

"I'll draw you a map." She rose and ducked into the back, returning moments later with a rectangular sheet of parchment, ink and a quill. She pulled over a tall stool that must have been tucked out of sight and out of the way under the bar and sat down to draw. In a few minutes she had a detailed map with a clear indication of the route from the Cat and Turtle to the estate on the hill. "Here." She turned it to face him and slid it across the bar. Jimothy pushed aside his empty bowl and picked up the drawing by the edges. He blew on the ink to finish it drying.

The map was a small work of art in sepia and black. The Cat and Turtle and surrounding businesses at Five Corners were easily identifiable at the left side of the map, while The Heathers and its grounds were clear on the right. The twists and turns of the city's streets were like endless writhing snakes caught frozen in a moment as they curled around buildings and trailed off into the unfinished.

"What's this?" Jimothy pointed at a circle with what might be a person on it.

"That's a statue of the first lanpere, Byron Rosslyn. It was erected by the citizens after his death. He wouldn't allow it while he was alive, but his daughter caved to popular pressure after he passed away. You should see it. His expression is priceless."

"What do you mean?"

"It's on your way to The Heathers. Stop and see if you can see what I mean," answered Maeve cryptically.

Jimothy eyed her, an intrigued smile on his face. "I'll do that." Sure that the map was dry, he folded it twice despite the twinge of regret he felt at creasing such beautiful work. "So you're an artist, too."

"Huh?"

"This." He held up the map before tucking it into his tunic's inner pocket.

"That's just scribbling," Maeve said dismissively. Then she asked with some pride, "Did you take a good look at the sign over the door?"

"Is that your work? It's beautiful."

She beamed. "Thanks. If you keep your eyes peeled, you'll see similar work all over the city. It helps pay the bills in the lean seasons."

"I think I've seen one already," he said, remembering the sign over the brothel.

Maeve walked to the far end of the bar where the old regular sat and took his empty pint mug. She pulled a fresh one without even glancing as she spoke. "Really? Which one?"

"I'm afraid I never learned the name of the establishment," he answered a little awkwardly.

But the hostess's smile turned sly and knowing. "Now I know which one it was. Did you sample the product?" She set the beer before the man and returned to the stool opposite Jimothy's seat.

"I only arrived today and came directly here on the advice of that friend I told you about."

"Well you're missing a treat," Maeve informed him matter-of-factly. "That's where Japheth and I met." Despite his best effort, Jimothy couldn't quite hide his surprise. She laughed. "Neither of us was working there."

"I would never assume one way or the other," he said diplomatically.

Nita returned then and cleared her throat.

"You're not subtle, Nita," said Maeve. "What is it?"

"Crier's come and gone, ma'am," the young woman said.

"Excellent. Thank you." The girl dropped a tiny curtsey and disappeared to the back again. "I hope you're ready to work. The first dinner customers should start coming in fairly soon, and if the crier does his work right, we'll be busy tonight."

"In that case I'd better get ready." He swallowed the last of his wine, thanked her for the meal and the map, and headed upstairs for his guitar and the letters. He collected everything he needed and was back down in ten minutes. A short stool had been placed to one side of the hearth and he shot Maeve a questioning look, which she returned with a single nod. He nodded his thanks back and sat down, placing his pouch of letters under the stool and his trusty misshapen mug near his left foot.

In the short time he'd been upstairs, half a dozen people had arrived in the bar. A table of four looked up curiously and turned back to their dinners. One well-dressed woman leaned across a small table and spoke secretively to her equally stylish companion. Both women looked at him, and then at each other, and giggled.

If I were the self-conscious sort, I'd be worried, Jimothy thought. He did steal a moment while tuning his guitar to make sure his breeches weren't undone or something equally unfortunate. All was well. He glanced over at Maeve behind the bar, who gave him a small nod and smile. He began to play a quiet melody, something simple and unobtrusive. The pair of women sipped at their goblets of wine and shot him furtive glances as he played. The others in the place simply went about eating and talking amongst themselves. *I guess we know who came for the show.*

He finished the first piece and stilled the humming strings. The women clapped a bit more eagerly than simple politeness dictated. He smiled appreciatively and nodded towards them. One woman bit back a squeal and was promptly shushed by her friend. Jimothy cleared his throat to hide a laugh and began another more intricate piece full of quick arpeggios and syncopated rhythms. Another five people, all in a group, came in as he played. They took a booth in the corner by a window and waved Nita over. Jimothy watched her take the orders and then come back shortly with food and drinks for the table. The pair of women caught her as she passed, and it wasn't long before Nita returned with a green bottle and refilled their goblets. One of the women pressed something into her hand and whispered to her. Nita smiled politely and said something quiet in reply. On her way back towards the bar, she stopped in front of Jimothy and dropped two coins into his mug, keeping a third for herself. They exchanged a look and Nita tipped her head to indicate the table. Jimothy smiled again at the two women and was rewarded with another swiftly stifled squeal. *I will not laugh,* he told himself firmly. It didn't pay to bite the hand that fed him. Then he caught sight of Maeve pulling a pint and hiding her own mirth and it was all he could do not to lose it. Fortunately, people continued to arrive and partially obscure the giggling pair. By the end of his third piece, the place was crowded and lively, and tips flowed as readily as drink.

Someone called out for a song and Jimothy obliged with an old folk tune that never failed to engage an audience. Then he began a slightly bawdy song with a good chorus for a crowd to join in on—simple, obvious lyrics anyone could pick up after one or two repetitions. By the end, the whole place was packed and singing. Folks applauded and cheered.

"My thanks! My thanks!" called Jimothy over the din. He raised a hand to shush them and they quieted enough for him to speak without shouting. "If you'll grant a poor fellow pause, I have another task to perform. I have mail!" That got the notice of the few whose attention had wandered or simply failed to focus due to too much good drink. He called out eleven names and received scattered responses, including one very familiar squeal of delight. "I'm going to take a short break to deliver the post and get myself a drink from our fine hostess, and then I'll be back to entertain you good people further." There were a few more cheers at that announcement. "If I called your name, please come and collect your mail at your leisure during the break." Gradually people returned to their meals and conversations. Chatter filled the place comfortably.

Jimothy carefully leaned his instrument against the wall behind him. A few people wound their way through the crowd to his post by the hearth. Each gave his or her name and he handed over their sealed letters. Most dropped at least a copper or two into his mug in thanks; actual payment for the deliveries was made by the senders. An older man received a memorized letter that recounted news of the successful birth of his granddaughter. He listened to each word intently as Jimothy spoke, then shook his hand and pressed a copper crown into it gratefully. Jimothy saw him wipe a tear of joy from the corner of his eye with a hand that seemed too thick and heavy for such a delicate motion.

He reached the end of the line and met the excited gaze of the squealing woman. "Lynette Larch," she said breathlessly. Jimothy dug into the pouch and pulled out a letter that had been folded three times and sealed with wax pressed in the shape of a heart. The young woman's name and the city were written above it in a flowing, feminine hand.

He gave her his most charming smile. "I wondered who the lovely lady would be to receive this missive," he said as he handed it to her. She practically vibrated with anticipation.

"Was there any spoken message to go with it?" she asked, her eyes wide and hopeful.

"The lady who gave me this letter said such things were only to be spoken in private, and so she sends silence and the written words of her heart."

She squealed again, dropped a silver penny into his cup, and practically bounced back to the table where her friend waited. This time Jimothy allowed himself to laugh. He enjoyed seeing people so happy to hear or to read what he delivered. Not all messages were so pleasant. In fact there were still two in his mind and two in the bag, and he knew at least one of each bore bad news. Then he thought of the sealed letter locked in his room upstairs. *That one isn't going to bring any joy, either,* he thought. He would have preferred to deliver it right away, but had decided against it. *Better to wait until tomorrow when I'll be expected than to appear unannounced with unpleasant news.* He hadn't expected to have the option and was very glad he did. He would have to make a proper offering to the small gods of fortune if his luck continued to hold like this.

Taking the letter pouch and his mug of earnings, he wove his way to the near end of the bar. Maeve glanced into the mug. "We're all doing well tonight," she commented happily. Japheth had joined her pouring wine and pulling pints. He smiled at Jimothy.

"I hear we were recommended to you. You'll have to thank your friend for us," he said.

"I'll be sure to do so the next time I see him. Now, I could use a drink, please." He poured his cash into the pouch with the remaining letters and then put the mug on the bar. Maeve filled it with the wine he'd had earlier.

"It's on your tab," she quipped.

He nodded and thanked her, raising the mug in toast to hostess and host. They returned to work and he leaned against the bar to survey the crowd and have his drink. The failing light outside the window heralded the fall of night. The place was warm and stuffy and Jimothy was thankful the fire hadn't been stoked up for the evening.

The crowd was boisterous but not yet rowdy, and he hoped it would stay that way. A flash of coral fabric caught his eye and he turned his head to look at the woman who sat in the far corner booth. She had large eyes and ginger hair under a hat as bright as her gown. She stood out amongst the browns, blues, greens and greys of the rest of the crowd. He let his gaze continue on. There were universally cheerful expressions on every face. Thus far he'd been fortunate with everyone he'd met in Couvin. He knew it couldn't last his entire stay, but for now he was glad of the pleasant atmosphere. It allowed him to relax a little. *And the wine's probably helping,* he thought wryly. He finished the drink, wiped the mug dry with a rag borrowed from Maeve, and returned to his post.

It was a long night of work, and despite training and years of practice, Jimothy's voice was tired by the time the last of the patrons shuffled out into the night. Japheth locked up, pulling heavy shutters over the front windows, while Nita and Maeve cleaned up. Only one other person remained and Jimothy guessed she must be the night keeper Japheth had mentioned. He'd noticed her earlier, but this was the first chance he had to really look at her. She certainly fit the limited description he'd been given. She was tall, almost as tall as Jimothy, and had broad shoulders and strong hands. She wore a knife at her belt and she looked as though she knew how to use it. Her long dark hair was pulled back into a thick rope of a braid, but a few ringlets escaped around her face. Despite their softly feminine effect, he agreed with the host's assessment: she definitely wasn't someone he wanted to get in a fight with. Jimothy left his guitar by the hearth and brought his mug and letter pouch over to the bar once again. He set them down and reached a hand out to the dark-skinned woman.

"I'm Jimothy Redwing," he said. "You must be the night keeper."

She took his offered hand and shook it firmly. She was just as strong as he suspected. "Vashti Linden," she replied.

"Linden? Coincidence or family?"

She smiled and it was the same smile he'd seen on Japheth's face. "Family. I'm Japheth's little sister." There was amusement in her tone at what was undoubtedly a family joke. She had to be nearly six inches taller than the host.

"It's a pleasure to meet you."

"And you." Her smile turned slightly coy and Jimothy remembered the warning that had accompanied the description: "She has a thing for musicians."

He smiled back, assessing her in ways other than combative, and found her quite appealing. Strength and beauty were a combination he appreciated in either sex and Vashti had both in abundance. She saw him looking and her smile grew. Not ready to go any further at that moment, Jimothy simply nodded his acknowledgement of her offer and took a seat. Carefully, he poured out his take for the night onto the bar, which was still slightly damp from the cleaning Maeve had given it. The hostess emerged from behind the curtain and gave Jimothy a weary smile.

"Good night?" she asked.

"Good indeed," he replied.

"You met Vashti?" She nodded towards the night keeper.

"I did, thank you." He smiled again at the tall woman and she gave him that same coy, enticing look she'd given a moment before. Jimothy focused on counting his cash. He portioned out the total for the week's stay plus the additional five coppers per day for amenities, and then added in the cost of the food and drink he'd consumed. Maeve set a goblet of wine in front of him as he tallied.

"This one's on the house," she said. She looked at the two piles of coins Jimothy made. "Meals for staff are half what the public pays. You worked hard tonight, eh?" She counted back a number of coins from the smaller pile and dropped what remained of it into her apron pocket. "You're really good."

"Thanks." He collected his earnings, pleased with the result even after paying his bills. He raised his goblet in toast to the hostess. "Cheers." He took a drink.

Japheth came in from the back then. "We're locked up for the night," he announced. Maeve removed the cash drawer from under the counter. She took off her apron, careful not to spill its pocket as she set it atop the drawer, and handed the pile to her husband. She kissed him on the cheek. "Thanks, honey." He took the stack of stuff, nodded goodnight, and disappeared behind the curtain.

"I should turn in as well," Jimothy said. He took another sip of wine and was about to leave the rest when Maeve stopped him.

"Take it with you. You earned it and I can't resell it, so enjoy it."

"Thanks," he said again. He gathered goblet, mug, pouch and guitar. It was a bit of a juggling act, but he managed to balance it all. "Good night, ladies."

"Good night, Jimothy," said Maeve, holding the curtain open for him. "And good work."

"Sleep tight, handsome," Vashti called after him as the curtain fell closed behind him. He could just hear her added, "Nice ass," as he headed up the stairs.

Jimothy shook his head in flattered amusement. If he

weren't so tired, he might have invited her up. But he was exhausted and she had work to do.

Safely locked in the privacy of his room, he set down his things and rummaged in his satchel. It was a challenge finding what he sought by the limited starlight that trickled weakly though the window, but eventually he came up with his small lantern and flint and steel. He lit the wick and opened the lantern to get the fullest light. He considered the waiting clothing chest but he didn't have the energy to unpack into it just then.

A quiet knock on the door startled him and he called out, "Yes?"

"Brazier for you, sir."

He opened the door and a boy he'd seen off and on that evening came in bearing a small brazier with a punched-metal grate on top.

"Just put it over there." The boy carried it to where he pointed, near the window and the wash table, and set it down, then hurried back towards the door.

"It's fuelled already, sir. Do you need a starter?"

"No, thanks. I have my own."

"I'll be right back with your hot water, sir." True to his word, he returned soon carrying a metal bucket of steaming water. Both of his small hands were wrapped tightly around the handle.

"Just set it here, next to the brazier."

"Yes, sir." He put down the heavy bucket and hurried to go once more.

"What's your name?" Jimothy asked before he could vanish.

"Aren, sir."

"Thank you, Aren. Good night." He locked the door behind the boy, hoping there would be nothing else that night.

Jimothy put his guitar away properly; everything else could wait for morning. He used the pitcher to scoop hot water from the bucket and tipped it carefully into the waiting bowl. Then he scrubbed his face with the soap from his pack. *Ricky was right. I really need to shave.* Thinking back he realized it had been three days since he'd last had his razor out. It was a wonder Maeve hadn't shooed him off as a vagrant. He certainly looked unscrupulous enough that he wouldn't have blamed her. Next he stripped down and took a sponge bath, scrubbing away the residual funk of his travels. He would have to find a bathhouse tomorrow, and probably a launderette. But he would worry about all that in the morning. Content that he was clean enough for the time being, he debated his options. Unless he lit the fire in the brazier, the water would be cold by morning, but did he really want to add heat to the room overnight? He slept better in cooler air. In the end he lit a small fire, banked it carefully, and set the metal bucket as close to the brazier as possible. If he'd done it right it would stay reasonably warm until he rose in the morning.

He dumped the dirty water from the bowl to the chamber pot and used the pot himself. As a last thought before climbing into bed, he opened the window a couple of inches to catch any breeze in the night. His eyes caught sight of the twinkling lights of The Heathers and he thought again of Ricky. *I wonder where he is tonight. I hope he made it to wherever he needed to be on time.*

He continued to stand looking out the small window. Then he closed his eyes, breathing in the cool night air. It felt good on his clean, bare skin. He called up images of Ricky in his mind's eye, remembering the two pleasant days and the one fantastic night they'd spent together. His penis grew hard at the memories and he took himself in one hand. He began to massage his erection, picturing Ricky's sharp features and broad mouth. *I wonder what that mouth would feel like.* His prick jumped in his hand at the thought and he rubbed his thumb over the tip, feeling the pre-cum that leaked out. He wished he had a little of that spicy salve right then, but contented himself without it.

He grasped himself tighter, moved his hand up and down his shaft with increasing speed. He thought of Ricky's muscled chest and its covering of dark hair that led his inner eye downward to the hard, red cock he'd held just last night. He remembered the feel of it, hot and silky in his hand. He remembered the tightness of Ricky's ass, slick with lubricant that made it both hot and cold around him. The sensation had been amazing and exhilarating. His hand moved faster and faster until he gasped and came, his gut clenching and unclenching with the spasms of pleasure.

Several moments passed as he stood there holding himself and letting the intensity of feeling fade to a manageable level. Soon enough his cock softened and he released it, opening his eyes. A small pool of semen had collected at his feet. Remembering the power of his release, he looked around for evidence of more. The force of his orgasm had spurted it several inches away. He sighed heavily, both satisfied and tired, and shook his head at himself. *Careless, Jimothy,* he scolded silently. Using the hand not covered with ejaculate, he dipped warm water and poured it into the bowl as he had before. He used his soap and small towel to wash himself and then another towel to wipe up the floor. He had to refresh the water again to rinse out the towels to his satisfaction. Finally, he was ready to fall into bed, and did so. He slept very soundly that night.

✧

Jimothy spent the next morning exploring the neighborhood around Five Corners. He'd decided over breakfast to allow himself a little time just to look around. He found what he saw of Couvin to be much like other large cities he visited, although this one boasted more color than most. There were the usual painted signs over shop doors—he counted four more that he expected were Maeve's work—but unlike most cities he'd seen, the buildings themselves were often painted in bright colors. He couldn't blame the citizens for wanting to paint them; nearly all the structures he saw were constructed of the local grey stone with tiled roofs and occasional wooden additions or outbuildings. Without paint it would have been drab and tiring on one's eyes. *Not to mention making it that much harder to find anything.*

He enjoyed his morning of anonymity. Without his guitar on his back, there was nothing to identify him as a Wand'ring Minstrel. He would rectify that tomorrow. He still had mail to deliver, after all, and with nothing more than a name there was little he could do to find the recipients other than spread the word that he was there. If that failed, his next step would be to find the city clerk's office. In the meantime, he simply tried to relax into the rhythm of Couvin. It was a challenge after days in the country, but he'd grown up in a large town and found the pace familiar.

He bought himself lunch at a street vendor selling fried vegetable pies and pear cider. He ate as he walked, strolling in the general direction Maeve's map indicated The Heathers to be. He turned a corner and came upon an intersection with a statue at its center, forcing traffic to circle around it.

"By all the smaller gods!" he exclaimed aloud before he

could stop himself. He looked around to see if anyone had heard his outburst, but no one paid him any mind. He was glad. It wasn't that the statue was badly carved or offensive. It wasn't even particularly oversized. It was just...

I can't think of the words, he thought, stymied, *and that's something I do for a living!* He crossed the street to the statue. Several people were there, seated on the low stone wall that surrounded it. Some of them were enjoying a lunch in the late summer sun. One woman had even pulled up her skirts to above her knees, baring her legs to the sun's rays. Jimothy found a spot to sit and finish eating while he contemplated the statue's profile. The figure was a man roughly eight feet tall and who stood atop a stone pedestal of perhaps two feet. There was nothing written on the side of the base, but Jimothy had seen something carved on the front. He would read it later, after he'd eaten. It was easy to guess who it was—the first lanpere, Byron Rosslyn. He wore no mark of office that Jimothy could see, but he had no doubt it was him. There was a certain nobility of stature that was only ever applied to the artistic depiction of monarchs.

Maeve said to look at his expression. Jimothy finished his pie and wiped his fingers on his breeches. Misshapen mug of cider in one hand, he strolled slowly the long way around to the front of the statue, uncertain of what he should expect. "Priceless" wasn't much to go on.

He reached the front and looked up—and had to bite his tongue to keep from laughing out loud. It was just as amusing from below as it had been when he first spotted it from across the street. Not knowing just how seriously the average citizen took the thing, he didn't think it prudent to openly mock it.

But by the little goddesses of art and irony...

The sculptor was a master of his or her craft and clearly

someone with a wicked sense of humor. The statue's face was upturned just slightly, not so high that one couldn't see it from below, but high enough that to see it truly well one had to cross the street. So he did, crossing back the way he'd come. He couldn't stare directly up at it as it faced the street rather than the corner. *Was that intentional, too, to keep people from looking too closely?* Not that he could get very close and still see it. He decided it *was* intentional and terribly clever. There was a chance that someone who took the local aristocracy too seriously could take offence.

The statue's expression was one of benevolence; carved eyes gave the illusion of softness, gentleness. But there was also a hint of wry amusement in them, and the corner of the mouth was turned up in what Jimothy could only describe as a tolerant but annoyed smile. In short, he looked like he was only standing there to humor a dull-witted, idol-worshiping, ignorant populace.

He took a long swallow of his cider to also swallow his mirth and drained the mug. It wasn't enough. He forced himself to look away and walk back down the street he'd come up. Two blocks later, with the statue firmly out of sight, he burst out laughing, startling a small cluster of women as they passed him. He apologized profusely and hurried on his way, leaving them chattering in mild consternation.

The city clocks he'd heard off and on since his arrival struck half-past one and he realized he needed to get back to the Cat and Turtle if he was going to make himself presentable before heading up to The Heathers as Ricky had instructed. It was too late to visit a bathhouse, but he could at least shave. He carefully checked the money in his pouch and decided there was plenty left of what he'd rationed for the day for him to splurge on a haircut and a professional shave. He'd seen two barbers' shops on his walk and chose the one closest to Five

Corners.

The clock at the nearby hospital chimed half-past two by the time he was done at the barber's, which was why he'd chosen one so close to the tavern. He hurried back to the Cat and Turtle, waving hello to Nita and Maeve as he headed up to his room.

He stripped down and sponge bathed quickly, wishing he'd had enough time to find and utilize a launderette. He dressed in his cleaner pair of breeches, which fortunately happened to be the less patched of the two. He donned a clean shirt and pulled his better tunic over top of it. He could wash his traveling clothes himself that evening and hang them to dry by the brazier overnight if he had to. He slipped his feet into his boots and adjusted his belt, then wetted his hands and ran them through freshly trimmed waves of golden brown hair. Deeming himself as ready as he could be to meet the lanmere's leading house musician, he tucked his map into his tunic's inner pocket, hung his cased guitar across his back and grabbed his cloak. It was warm for the cloak, but it kept the instrument out of sight to some extent. This wasn't the time for him to be stopped on the street by people hoping he had a letter for them.

He locked the door behind him and then had to wait at the top of the stairs as a fellow guest ascended. They nodded at one another pleasantly. Jimothy immediately recognized the woman from the bar the previous night. Redheads were rare in Kanbec, and the bright coral color of her gown set her apart in any workaday crowd. She stopped at the door to room eight and Jimothy made himself turn away and head down before anyone else chanced to come up. The stairs were too narrow to pass anyone except at the landings, and with his demiguitar even that was a challenge.

He made it down without further interruption and stopped at the bar briefly to speak to Maeve. She looked tired today, unlike the bright smiling presence she'd presented yesterday. "Are you all right?"

"I'm fine, thanks." She sat on the stool she kept behind the bar. "Just tired. The kid kept me up all night."

"Kicking?" he asked solicitously. This was something he'd heard pregnant women complain of in the past.

"Sitting on my bladder," Maeve said.

His experience with expectant mothers wasn't enough to tell him how to respond to that, so he simply said, "That's unfortunate."

"It is. I see you're going out again, working it looks like."

"I am. I will be back before dark to work here," he assured her.

"That's all I needed to know." Her warm smile was back. "Have fun. Earn lots."

"Thank you." He grinned and headed outside.

Finding The Heathers proved to be a simple matter thanks to Maeve's map. He reached the front gate of the estate without any trouble. A stone wall, similar to that which surrounded the city but on a much smaller scale, surrounded the grounds. This one, though, had a portcullis and guards at the gate.

"Greetings," said Jimothy, sketching the polite bow of an equal. "I'm Wand'ring Minstrel Jimothy Redwing. I'm here to see Gretta."

The guard on the left nodded at him. "We were told to expect you." He gestured to the fellow on the right, who hauled on a pulley chain that opened the gate. It wasn't until it moved that Jimothy realized it was there for show more than security. It was wood painted to look like steel, rather than the genuine article. The first guard spoke again. "Follow the road to the house and take the right fork around to the south side.

Introduce yourself to the porter there. He'll see you where you need to go."

"Thank you." Jimothy passed under the gate and began the long walk towards the house. He looked around him as he walked. Rolling lawns led into neatly tended gardens of flowers. Farther off to either side he saw fruit trees—pears and cherries, he thought. As he curved around the house to the south, more fields came into view. These were clearly crop-producing, evidence of the region's agricultural history, and he squinted into the mid-afternoon sun to make out what they were. There was a grain he couldn't identify at a distance and a patch of even rows he guessed might be vegetables of one kind or another. The estate looked to be almost self-sustaining, assuming there was livestock somewhere on the grounds.

The house itself was three stories tall, putting it higher than most of the city even if it weren't atop a hill. It had three wings, one in the center and one each on either end at right angles to the first. It was to the one on the right that he headed.

Ringing the chime at the south entrance, he studied the little porch area as he waited for the porter to answer. The door was heavy wood, carved with intricate pastoral designs. The stone step on which he stood was bordered on either side by trellises of rose vines that reached up to a small roof overhanging the entryway. Minutes passed and he wondered if he should ring again, but then the door opened and he found himself facing a short, aged man with a bushy white moustache.

The fellow looked him up and down twice and Jimothy was glad he'd made the effort to clean up properly. It might be policy to make Wand'ring Minstrels welcome, but that didn't mean he should push his luck. "May I help you?" the man asked, his voice as wizened as his face.

Jimothy introduced himself as he had at the gate, adding, "The guards directed me here to speak to the porter."

The little man nodded. "That's me. You must be looking for Gretta."

"That's right."

"Follow me." He turned and led the way inside. Jimothy bemusedly shut the door behind them, as it seemed the fellow wasn't going to stop to do so himself, and followed him.

Heavy rugs lined the center of the hallway, muffling their steps. The porter turned right and the rugs stopped abruptly; they stepped off onto stone worn smooth by years of traffic. The old porter led him through a number of large, open rooms—servants' dining room, laundry, kitchen. The kitchen was the busiest, as Jimothy knew it would be. There was rarely a moment in a house this size that there wasn't a meal being prepared, eaten, or cleaned up after.

A grey-haired woman as short as the porter but twice as big around looked up from chopping vegetables. "Who's that you're bringing through here, cluttering up my kitchen, Paul?" she demanded, although her tone was less adversarial than the words suggested.

"He's the Wand'ring Minstrel the master said to expect, Sarah. You remember," he answered without stopping.

The woman's eyes lit up. "Oh! In that case, welcome to The Heathers, Master Minstrel."

"Thank you." Jimothy smiled, pleasantly surprised by the formal address, and continued after the porter.

They reached another hallway, turned left, and stopped in front of a door. Paul knocked and then opened it without waiting for a response. He poked his head inside. "Is Gretta around?" he asked.

"Yes," a woman answered. "I'm right here. What is it?" She sounded a little put out to Jimothy's ears.

Paul swung the door open so Jimothy could see in. Five musicians sat in a semi-circle, their instruments in their hands. The nearest was a woman with pale blonde hair pulled up into a slightly skewed bun, practicality rather than vanity clearly prompting the style. The sleeves of her shirt were tied up above her elbows and she wore breeches, giving her the freedom of movement she needed to play the cello that rested between her knees. He saw that this room, like the first hallway, was carpeted and he wondered if it was for the sake of the instruments or the musicians. Either way, he was impressed. Not all landowners took such good care of their house entertainers.

"It's the Wand'ring Minstrel," Paul said simply. Then he turned around and shuffled off, his task complete.

The woman rose, carefully resting her instrument on its side on the floor. "Gretta Bergen," she said, holding out a hand. Jimothy shook it and introduced himself. "You've undoubtedly gathered that we were expecting you."

"So I was told, and told, and..." he said with humor.

"I must say I'm really pleased you're here. Let me introduce the group." She turned to the four seated musicians. "Cita Fisher plays the various bowed instruments, like me." A petite, auburn-haired woman raised a hand in greeting, her viola on her lap. "That's Liam Halsey, our lead male voice and percussionist. Next to him is Jenna Howard—winds, reeds, and lead female voice. And finally Linnie Smies, who is a wizard on any instrument with a keyboard."

"Hello," Jimothy said, taking in the group with a smile and nod. "It's a pleasure to meet you all."

Gretta turned to the heavy-set woman seated at the

harpsichord. "Linnie, grab him a chair, would you?"

"Sure." She nodded and went to pull a chair from a row of them along the wall behind her.

"So what have you brought with you?" Gretta asked as Jimothy took off his cloak and hung it on the coat stand by the door.

He thanked Linnie for the chair, and she smiled and retook her place. Then he turned to Gretta. "I travel with my demiguitar," he said, pulling the cased instrument over his head. "But if there's something else you have that you'd like me to play, just ask." He uncased the small guitar and the others leaned forward for a closer look.

"I've not seen one of those," said Cita, eyes wide with eager delight. "I've only heard about them."

"Leave it, Cita," recommended Gretta, and the other woman looked deflated.

"I'm happy to teach you some later. But right now..." Jimothy glanced at the group's leader for confirmation, "...I suspect you'd like to learn some new material."

Liam nodded emphatically. "That we would, Master Minstrel."

Jimothy opened a pocket on the inside of his guitar case and pulled out several sheets of parchment. He thought the musicians' eyes were going to bug out of their sockets. "They're not divided into parts, of course. But I assume you have the facilities to do that."

Gretta gave him a wry smile. "If by facilities you mean me, ink, parchment and a lot of long hours, then yes. We have the facilities. For now though, slap those up on Linnie's harpsichord. We'll gather around and see what we find."

The group rearranged itself to best effect and started on the first of the three pieces Jimothy had brought. Jimothy led Liam into the lyrics before switching to a harmony line of his own invention to allow the fair-haired young man the lead. When they reached the end of the first piece, he replaced the sheet music with the second piece. The others looked it over and Gretta traded cello for violin while Jenna set aside her wooden flute and picked up her oboe. She wetted the reeds quickly, then nodded that she was ready.

When they reached the end of the second piece, they were surprised by the sound of applause. A man stood in the doorway, clapping and grinning. He was dressed in a rich burgundy tunic and brand new breeches, and his boots were impeccably polished. Despite the expensive garb, Jimothy recognized him immediately. A warm smile spread across his face.

"Well done!" Ricky exclaimed, stepping into the room.

Before Jimothy could reply, Gretta spoke up. Her tone was surprisingly deferential after the authoritative way she'd spoken before. "Our thanks, sir." She bowed her head courteously.

"How long were you working on that before I wandered in?"

"That was just sight-reading, sir. We'll play it much better once I've copied it out and we've had time to rehearse properly." She gestured to Jimothy. "Thank you for sending Jimothy to us. It's a joy to have new music from outside of Kanbec."

"I knew you'd be pleased. Now," Ricky went on, "I hate to interrupt you all, but I'd like to borrow him for a little while if I may."

"Of course, sir."

Jimothy looked at her. "There's one more piece." He handed it to her. "You'll be fine without my help. You're all very skilled."

"Thanks." Gretta smiled proudly, her brown eyes alight with pleasure at the compliment.

"Get your stuff," Ricky instructed Jimothy. "You can come back tomorrow if you want, but I'm sure you have to return to your lodgings this evening. Right?"

"That's right," Jimothy confirmed. He packed his guitar and put on his cloak, thanking the musicians once more. He joined Ricky at the door.

"Thank you again, my lord," Gretta called after them, and Jimothy nearly missed a step. He held on and kept going, following Ricky along the hallway.

He led him past rather than through the kitchen towards the front of the house. "Where are we going?" Jimothy asked.

"To the gardens," Ricky answered. "It's a gorgeous day. I thought you'd like a tour of the grounds."

"I would." Jimothy fell silent until they were outside, but his mind spun. Once they were away from the house, walking along a path between beds of chrysanthemums and dahlias, he finally spoke up. "Gretta called you 'my lord'."

"Huh?" Ricky stopped and turned to him.

"Gretta. She called you 'my lord'." Suddenly all Jimothy's assumptions were shattered and he found himself with answers to questions that it had never occurred to him to ask. Things Ricky had said suddenly coalesced into a trail of clues he'd completely failed to follow: his instructions to come here; his knowledge of whom to ask for; the ease with which Jimothy had entered the grounds and the house; the fact that everyone he'd met here had known who he was and were expecting him. It all added up to one thing, but he dreaded hearing it confirmed. "Who are you?"

Ricky opened his mouth to reply when a woman's voice came to them over the afternoon breeze. "Patrick? Patrick, are you out here?" The woman appeared a short distance away, striding towards them. Her dark, almost black hair trailed out from under her wide-brimmed straw hat. She wore lime-green gardening gloves, and a heavy apron that looked like it belonged on someone twice her size covered the front of her amber dress. One hand held a trowel, well worn with use. But despite the tool and her attire, Jimothy had the sick feeling that this was not the groundskeeper. "There you are," she said a little breathlessly as she reached them. She turned sharp brown eyes on Jimothy and looked him up and down. "You must be the Wand'ring Minstrel that my son has been talking non-stop about ever since he got home yesterday."

"Mother!" protested Ricky, blushing. The woman just smirked at him, knowing she'd embarrassed him and taking motherly delight in it. He tried to regain his composure. "Wand'ring Minstrel Jimothy Redwing, I'd like you to meet my mother, Lanmere Fallon Rosslyn."

She pulled off a glove and stuck out a pristine, well-manicured hand. "Pleasure to meet you, my boy."

To his credit, Jimothy kept his expression friendly and unruffled. He shook her hand, bowing over it respectfully. *This has got to be the oddest situation I've ever been in.* He tried to think of anything stranger than this, but his memory came up blank. "Lanmere, the pleasure and honor is mine."

Fallon looked over at her son, who shot her a knowing grin that said as clearly as spoken words, 'See? I told you he was fantastic.' Her answering smile was warm but cautious.

Jimothy looked from one to the other, releasing the lanmere's hand. *I'm missing something.* It was annoying, especially when compounded with how much he had missed up until this moment.

Fallon turned her smile on him and he knew it was provisional. "Welcome to Couvin."

"Thank you, Lanmere." He suddenly remembered

something more important than these revelations and introductions. He glanced at Ricky and then back at the lanmere. "I have a letter for you, Lanmere."

Her dark eyebrows rose. "Let's see it, then." She removed her other glove and tucked the pair into an apron pocket.

Jimothy set down his guitar and reached into a narrow pocket along one side of the case. He pulled out the wax-sealed parchment he'd carried so diligently since leaving Tesna. "It was given to me by another Wand'ring Minstrel in Tesna who had recently come from Korpi."

Fallon took it. Her gaze was keen. "Do you know what it contains?"

"Only in general terms, your highness."

"I see. Thank you." She turned to Ricky and there was a silent moment when Jimothy felt once again that he was being deliberately left out of something. Then she said, "See that he gets compensation for this, Patrick." She held the letter up, and Ricky nodded. "I'll see you at dinner. Master Minstrel, come back tomorrow morning. I'll tell Gretta to expect you at nine." She nodded once to Jimothy and then headed at a quick pace towards the house.

Left alone in the garden once more, Ricky smiled at Jimothy. "She liked you," he said.

"How could you tell?"

"I know my mother." He stepped closer to Jimothy, letting his hands rest on the taller man's hips. "She said to make sure you were compensated. She didn't say what form that compensation should take." He leaned in to kiss him, but Jimothy took a step back, forestalling him.

"Why didn't you tell me?" he asked in a strained voice.

"Tell you what?"

"That your mother is the lanmere of Kanbec, of course!" Another thought struck him and he took a deep breath, bracing himself. "Please tell me you have an older sibling. Tell me you're not the lanfis."

Ricky shook his head. "Sorry," he said, although he hardly seemed it. He frowned. "What's the matter? Nothing's changed."

"For you maybe, but I just found out that I fucked the heir to the throne!" Jimothy's voice rose and he immediately brought it down to a near-whisper. "There are places where that's punishable by death—or worse!"

"Kanbec doesn't have a throne and capital punishment is reserved for murderers and rapists. Since neither of us is dead and everything we did was consensual, I can assure you you're perfectly safe." He grinned, but for once Jimothy didn't find the expression contagious. He couldn't take the situation so lightly.

"Why didn't you tell me who you are before this?"

Ricky's smile vanished in a blink and there was a defensive anger barely hidden in his voice. "I did tell you who I am. My title isn't me. And what difference is it if I go by Ricky when my name is Patrick? My mother's the only one who ever calls me that."

"And your family name?" persisted Jimothy.

At that Ricky looked chagrined. "I'm sorry. I use my middle name when I'm not trapped in politics and affairs of state." Then he grew defensive again. "But it's still my name. I haven't lied to you, Jimothy. Not about anything." His blue eyes were as intense as firelight and he stepped towards Jimothy again. "Do you understand?"

Jimothy was silent for several moments, and then nodded. "I understand," he said. "I just need time to think."

"What's there to think about?" Ricky moved closer, once more placing his hands on Jimothy's hips. "I'm still the same person I was when we met," he said in a low, warm voice. "The same person who shared music, food and bed with you." This time when he leaned in, Jimothy didn't stop him. The kiss was long and intense, stealing the breath of both men as their passion rose. They pressed close and Jimothy could feel himself growing hard as Ricky rubbed a thigh against his crotch. Then he felt a hand in place of the thigh and he heard Ricky chuckle in his throat. The lanfis broke the kiss and flashed a lustful grin as he undid Jimothy's breeches and slipped his hand inside their front. Jimothy gasped as Ricky grasped him, tugging on his hardness. He slipped another hand in to fondle Jimothy's scrotum and for the second time that day Jimothy found himself without words.

Ricky kissed him again. *You don't need words.*

Jimothy's eyes widened at the voice in his head, but Ricky continued to smile. Then he sank down to his knees, pulling Jimothy's breeches down just far enough to release his tumescent cock.

"Ricky!" he gasped as the man licked slowly around the tip. "We can't. Not—" Not in the open. Not in view of the house. Not where someone might see us. All the arguments in his mind were eclipsed in a single act. His breath caught and he couldn't go on as he felt Ricky take him in his mouth. The warm wetness made his gut clench with pleasure. He'd been sucked before, but never quite like this. The open sky was no stranger, but standing there in a formal garden on a royal estate with the heir to the ruling seat on his knees before him was potentially dangerous for so many reasons. His heart raced at the thrill of that danger and at the thrill of something so private happening somewhere so public. He opened himself to the feeling.

Ricky released him for a moment and Jimothy looked down to see the dark-haired man looking up at him and licking his fingers. They smiled hungrily at one another, and Jimothy gave a single nod of assent. Then, as he took Jimothy's erection into his mouth again, Ricky reached spit-slicked fingers around behind Jimothy and slid one carefully into his ass. The situation, the sensation... It was too much and Jimothy came right then and there—in the lanfis's mouth, in the royal flower garden, in full view of anyone who might glance out a window in their direction. Ricky swallowed down his warm discharge, sucking gently until Jimothy's tremors had slowed to no more than a shiver of residual pleasure. He slipped his finger from Jimothy's ass and rose to his feet, pulling his pants up and tying them while Jimothy just stood there, helpless with satisfaction.

Ricky grinned again—an expression that he used in so many ways. This time it was sly, knowing and lascivious all at once. "How was that?" he asked in a husky voice. "Was that fair compensation?" He drew a handkerchief from his pocket, wiped his chin and his hands as he spoke.

Jimothy nodded. He knew he'd have to think things through, to deal with everything he'd learned. Later. "More than fair," he agreed.

"I'm glad to hear it. Will you come back tomorrow?"

"I will."

"What if I don't want to wait until tomorrow?" Ricky added coyly. "I know where to find you, after all."

"I—" The idea appealed strongly, but a sliver of common sense poked through his sex-numbed mind. "Is that wise? Surely you'll be recognized in town."

"Maybe. Maybe not," Ricky replied evasively.

"But surely there's the chance of it." Jimothy shook his head. "Shouldn't you be more...discreet?"

Ricky laughed out loud at that. "Do you think this was discreet?" he asked, gesturing to the flower-laden landscape around them.

"This was at your home where even if someone saw us they would be unlikely to criticize their master."

"That's true, but only up to a point. You know more about courtly politics than that," he chided. "Trust me. Maeve and Japheth are good friends of mine."

Jimothy's gut clenched again—not in enjoyment this time, but at an unpleasant thought. He knew his jealous reaction was out of line; he had no claim on this man beyond the moments they shared. Anything more was preposterous and impossible—especially given what he'd just learned of Ricky's rank and position. "Is that where you've sent your other dalliances?" he half-joked, trying to sound casual.

"A few," admitted Ricky. He gazed deep into Jimothy's eyes, and again Jimothy heard his voice in his head. *But none of them has had quite the effect on me that you do.*

Same here, he thought, and was surprised to see Ricky's lips turn up into a tender smile.

"I'm glad. I'll walk you to the gate."

"All right."

They strolled in companionable silence to the estate's guarded front gate, but before they reached it Ricky pulled Jimothy into a quick kiss. "Expect me after ten o'clock," he said softly.

"I will."

"Oh bollocks!" exclaimed Ricky suddenly, startling him. Ricky immediately looked apologetic. "I can't come tonight. Affairs of state." He rolled his eyes.

"That's all right," said Jimothy. In truth, while he would have welcomed Ricky's presence, he was just as glad he would have the evening to think about things. "I'll be back here in the morning. I expect I'll see you."

"I promise you will."

They parted at the gate, and Jimothy walked slowly back towards the Cat and Turtle. His mind was in a fog, but it was a comfortable, warm fog and he didn't force it away. Instead he allowed it to carry him to his destination, his feet barely touching the cobbled streets all the way back to the tavern.

Ricky stood at the gate watching Jimothy until his long-legged stride took him around a corner and out of view. Ricky was more than sorry to see him go, even if it was only until tomorrow. He turned and strolled slowly through the flower garden, thinking back to yesterday when he'd parted with Jimothy shortly after their arrival in Couvin. He'd felt the pull of him long after he'd gone. Seeing him today, he'd felt as if a weight was lifted from his gut. It was strange how strong the feeling was after knowing him for such a short time.

He thought back further, this time to their first meeting, so unexpected and providential. Ricky smiled, remembering the night they'd spent together and looking forward to more of the same nature. In his mind's eye, he pictured Jimothy as he had appeared that night in the waycabin. Envisioned the way the waves of his hair flopped carelessly into his face as his ardor intensified. Recalled the warm flush of his stubbled cheeks as he drove them both to climax. Ricky's smile broadened. Those were definitely moments he wished to repeat as often as possible. It had been wicked of him to seduce Jimothy in the garden just now, but somehow he couldn't help himself and he certainly couldn't regret it. Jimothy brought out that side in him like none had before.

Not yet ready to go back inside to deal with the daily business of Government, Ricky turned and headed towards the small orchard—remnant of a much larger expanse—that was enclosed within the estate grounds. He nodded pleasantly, if distractedly, at the old man tending the nearest trees. Farther off, he saw a handful of workers harvesting pears from the easternmost row of trees. There would be pear tart tonight, he guessed happily. He wished Jimothy could be there to share it with him.

Blessed Martha, since when am I so sentimental? The thought was more than a bit startling. He'd had several lovers—although not as many as he'd have liked, to be honest—and he'd enjoyed the company of all of them. But each time he'd said a final good-bye, it had been…not comfortable, exactly, but right. Never painful as it was parting with Jimothy. He'd certainly never felt the ache he had yesterday, nor the romantic longing he did today.

His musings were interrupted at that moment by a feminine voice calling, "My lord! My lord!"

Ricky turned to see the housemaid, Jenja, hurrying towards him, her dark curls falling from under her cap and her face flushed. "What is it?" She seemed to be quite flustered and he worried what could be wrong.

"Her highness and your brother are waiting for you, my lord. In the chapel," she added meaningfully.

"Oh bollocks! Thank you, Jenja. I'd completely forgotten what day it was." He rushed away, her reply of "Yes, my lord" all but lost behind him.

He rounded the back of the manor house and the chapel came into view. It was small and built of the same local stone as the wall of the estate. He glanced at the clock in its short, domed bell tower and cursed again. It was nearly a quarter past the hour. He'd been so caught up in his thoughts of Jimothy that he'd missed the bell entirely and now he was late for the mid-week service.

He paused before the side door nearest the chancel end and collected himself before entering. He slid quietly into the pew beside his mother, who simply raised an admonishing eyebrow at him before nodding once to the waiting chaplain. Coran, on the other side of the lanmere, leaned back enough to catch his brother's eye. His expression was disapproving—as Ricky knew it would be. He returned the look impassively, although inside he scowled, and faced the front before their mother could catch either of them. Ricky knew Coran took issue with what he called Ricky's "lack of proper devotion". The lanfis didn't bother trying to explain that a lack of chapel attendance did not constitute a lack of faith. Coran was too much of a dogmatist to listen. Ricky believed his mother understood, but that didn't stop her requiring her sons' presence at twice-weekly services whenever they were staying at home.

At least Ricky liked the chapel itself. It was cool in summer and warm in winter and the stained glass windows caught the light beautifully. He leaned back, enjoying the play of color on the walls and the people within them. There were only a couple of dozen people present. With no diplomats currently visiting, it was just the family and the members of the house and garden staff who chose to attend. Not for the first time, Ricky wished he had the freedom the servants had to skip chapel. It hardly seemed fair. But then, he figured, someone had to keep the grounds and household running while the family was stuck in here.

Ricky lent the chaplain's lesson half an ear as he allowed his eyes and thoughts to continue to wander. As usual, the lesson was about caring for others in some way. Stewardship seemed to be his key word today. Stewardship of the land. Stewardship of its people. Ricky had heard it all before—and better spoken, too, in his opinion. He found the current chaplain less than inspiring. The lanfis missed the old one, the chaplain of his childhood. She had been a great speaker and he'd always left chapel feeling uplifted or inspired by her words. Sadly, she'd passed away while he was off at university and The Heathers had been lumbered with this fellow. He was nice enough. He was competent and knowledgeable. He was just deathly dull. Ricky stifled a yawn behind a hand, hoping no one noticed. He didn't understand why his mother hadn't requested a better replacement from the Rabbinical Diocese.

The chaplain reached the end of his lesson. He began to sing the traditional blessing in the Ecclesiastical Speech. And Ricky remembered why his mother kept the man around. His voice was bell-like in clarity and heartbreaking in purity. His final "amen" hung in the air for a suspended moment. When silence fell, he broke the spell with a nod to Linnie, who began to play the postlude on the chapel's small harpsichord. He began to walk down the aisle towards the front door. Fallon rose and followed the chaplain, and Ricky and Coran followed her. The four stood as a receiving line outside the door, greeting the servants as they exited.

Through all the routine pleasantries, Ricky could feel Coran's stiff, critical presence at his side. Censure seemed to flow from him like water running along a swift moving streambed. The lanbrou had made it clear on many occasions that he found Ricky's general behavior to be inappropriate for a member of the ruling family. He looked askance at Ricky's sexual dalliances, free-thinking faith, and even the relatively informal way in which he interacted with the servants. Ricky did his best to ignore him whenever the opportunity presented itself—like now.

Once the last hands were shaken and the last greetings spoken, the chaplain bid them good afternoon and went on his way to the rectory. Ricky and Coran followed Fallon back towards the main house. Coran put a hand on his brother's arm, holding him back a step and out of their mother's hearing.

"You might be on time if you weren't idling in the gardens," Coran said in a cautionary undertone.

"I was in the orchard, actually," Ricky corrected him. "I was lost in thoughtful contemplation." He deliberately put on the most overtly pious tone he could, knowing it would irritate his sanctimonious sibling. Coran frowned and Ricky silently congratulated himself. He was all the more pleased with himself because what he'd said was absolutely true. Irking Coran with a joke wasn't half as satisfying as irking him with a truth.

"You'd do better to contemplate your position and responsibilities rather than your new plaything."

Ricky stiffened at Coran's pointed words. Before he could make a pithy reply, Fallon called to them from several steps ahead. "Patrick, I expect you in my study in five minutes." She didn't glance back or even slow down as she spoke. She reached the house and strode purposefully inside.

Ricky moved to follow her. Coran was at his elbow, advising sharply, "Whatever she wants, you'd do well to listen and do what she says for once."

"Why don't you go back to your precious university and leave the rest of us in peace?" snapped Ricky angrily.

"I would if I thought—" Coran stopped short, his expression unreadable.

"Thought what?"

"Nothing." He shook his head and went inside.

Ricky glared after him, and then took a calming breath. His mother didn't need to see more evidence of her sons' acrimony; she knew well enough that they didn't get along.

He wondered what it was she wanted to talk to him about, and guessed it had something to do with the letter Jimothy had delivered. He hurried upstairs to his mother's study.

She stood by the windows waiting for him. "Patrick, come in. Sit."

He sat in one of the comfortable, well-stuffed chairs and Fallon sat across from him. Her expression was tight and Ricky felt a foreboding in the pit of his belly. Her words confirmed his fears.

"I need to ask you to do something, and I think you're not going to likc it."

She went on to explain, and Ricky's foreboding became a sick feeling in his gut. No, he didn't like it. Not one bit.

Chapter Four

That evening was much like the one before. Jimothy delivered his two remaining spoken letters—one bringing sorrowful tears to the couple who received it, just as he'd anticipated it would. He'd prepared himself as best he could, but for as long as he worked in the field he doubted he would get used to delivering sad news. He watched the pair comfort each other, arms wrapped around one another's shoulders as they left the pub.

Nita sidled up to him, a pitcher of ale in her hand. "That looked awful," she said.

Jimothy looked up and saw that her eyes were bright with unshed tears. "Some people think that what I do is glamorous," he said. "I travel the world. I perform for people from the courts of monarchs to the market and festival crowds. Most people don't think about the rest of the work."

"What did you say to them?"

"I can't tell you that. Pain should be as private as joy should be public." Then he smiled up at her from where he sat. "And I'd get in big trouble if it got out that I'd revealed someone's private correspondence."

"Oh!" She looked ashamed. "I didn't even think of that! I'm sorry." She moved to go.

"Wait." Jimothy stopped her with a quiet word. "That

woman alone in the corner booth—who is she?" It was the ginger-haired woman he'd seen that afternoon and the previous evening. A stylish cap topped her short-cropped locks and she wore a different dress than earlier, but it was still in a shade of coral that couldn't help but catch the eye.

"She's a guest, Minstrel. Just like you."

"I know that. I saw her earlier upstairs. She has the room next to mine."

"That's right."

"But who is she?"

Nita shook her head. "Imagine the trouble I'd get in if I started giving out our guests' private information."

Jimothy nodded, his expression wry. "Touché."

Nita headed back out into the throng to refill the mugs of a trio of men at a table on the far side of the room. Jimothy watched her thread her way through the crowd at the same time he scanned the audience. He'd learned long ago to keep his eyes on those who also watched him. It was only good sense. One never knew when someone might take offence or issue with a song or story or even a letter they received and decide to take it out on the messenger.

The waitress headed back towards the bar and Jimothy's gaze was caught by a man standing there, leaning against the bar. For a brief moment he thought it was Ricky, disguised in rough clothing and a workman's cap. It didn't take long for him to realize his mistake. The fellow was pale with dark hair, but his eyes were also dark and his expression was brooding. Jimothy lingered only long enough to register the differences and moved on. Watching was one thing, staring was something else entirely. He smiled and nodded as his roving gaze caught Vashti's eye. She smiled back and licked her lips at him. He found the offer tempting, but the timing was inescapably wrong.

Nita appeared at his elbow once more. “Maeve said to tell you your break’s over,” she said softly.

“Maeve is absolutely right.”

“She also said she wants something romantic tonight.” Nita’s voice dropped even lower. “Personally I think her humors are out of balance because of her pregnancy. She’s been trying to get Japheth to take a break since five o’clock, if you know what I mean. And five is when the dinner rush started!”

Jimothy chuckled. “I’ve heard that about pregnant women, but I’ve never had occasion to find out first hand.”

“Just play something tragical and supremely drippy, eh? She’ll love it, and she might give you your dinner for free tomorrow if it gets the result she’s after.”

“I’ll see what I can do.”

She drifted away and Jimothy quickly checked his tuning before beginning an instrumental piece that permeated the room without intruding on the customers’ conversations.

He followed the piece with another, one that struck a romantic note even without lyrics. The tenor of the crowd shifted with the music just as he’d planned, evoking the mood he desired for his next song. As Nita recommended, he chose a sentimental piece in which one of the lovers was dead and the other one died at the end. It was full of romantic images of a stormy ocean and a lonely man wandering the rocky coasts waiting for his lover who would never return.

“For she’d gone far away to a distant shore,” he sang. “And left him there alone.” He glanced over at Maeve during the bridge and found her smiling, a suspicious gleam in her green eyes. He wasn’t sure if he envied or pitied Japheth that night, and in the end decided it was a bit of both. The song went on telling its tale of true love doomed by circumstance and what amounted in Jimothy’s pragmatic opinion to damnably bad luck. He reached the end of the final verse with some relief. "He laid his head on her cold stone bower and died out there alone."

Maeve led the applause with enthusiasm, and much of the audience joined her. Jimothy knew from experience that most who did so did it out of simple politeness. The genuine ones were obvious by the tears in their eyes, and they were in the minority. Still, if it got him a free meal tomorrow, he didn't mind.

Time for something a little peppier, I think. He launched into a sprightly tune and the atmosphere changed immediately. Soon folks were clapping along. Several even got up to dance between the tables.

It was nearing one as the last patrons lingered, finishing up their drinks. Jimothy plucked out a final quiet piece for them, receiving a smattering of applause and a few more coins in response. Then they paid their tab and departed. Japheth locked the door behind them as Maeve wiped down the bar with a damp rag.

"Another good night, I hope," Jimothy said as the host secured the shutters over the windows.

"Another great night, thanks to you. I wish we could keep you around all the time," Japheth answered.

"Ah, but that would contradict the whole 'Wand'ring' part of my title," Jimothy pointed out lightly.

"Yeah. I suppose it would."

"And the novelty would wear off after a while," Nita put in.

Vashti spoke up then. "Not for me." She waggled her eyebrows at him.

As Japheth passed him on the way to the back, he muttered under his breath, "I told you so." Jimothy had no time to respond before he disappeared behind the curtain. Maeve watched him go, a dangerous light in her eyes.

"Nita, finish up for me, will you?" She didn't wait for an answer, leaving her rag behind and untying her apron as she swiftly followed her husband out.

Nita looked mildly annoyed but made no complaint. Vashti shook her head. "My brother is a lucky man."

"You think so?" Nita said. "I think if I were him tonight, I'd be scared witless."

Jimothy laughed. "If you'll excuse me, ladies, it's time I went to bed."

"Call me if you get lonely," Vashti called after his retreating form.

Alone in his room for another night, Jimothy sat down at the table with his guitar. Parchment, ink and quill waited where he'd left them, and he looked over what he'd written so far.

Their meeting was strange under lowering grey skies

He woke from his dream to see a man on horseback looking down at him

The man with the mile-wide smile.

"Well, it doesn't completely suck," he muttered to the empty room. He picked up the quill, dipped it in the pot of ink and picked up where he'd left off.

They rode together through rolling hills of green

That evening they reached a...

"Lonely? Cozy? What?" Jimothy sighed in frustration. "This shouldn't be so difficult. Maybe I'm leaping ahead too much?" He thought back two days to the ride with Ricky. "No, really not," he decided. "Nothing much happened that day. It was the evening that mattered." A hungry, sexy smile curved his lips. "Maybe this should be a bawdy song rather than a love song." But that idea didn't really appeal to him. While he was reluctant to consider the possibility that he was in love with Ricky—that would be foolish for so many reasons—he was honest enough with himself to know there was something more than ordinary animal lust drawing the two of them together.

He shook his head and capped the pot of ink. He would get no further tonight and he had an early morning tomorrow.

He packed up his gear for the morning so it would be ready and waiting for him, and then made himself ready for bed. The night was colder than the last had been—a precursor of the coming autumn—and he shivered as he slipped naked between the sheets. He pulled the blanket up and curled onto his side. Thinking of Ricky and the coming visit to The Heathers, he fell into a pleasant sleep.

✧

Breakfast at The Heathers was a tense and unpleasant affair. Ricky was still angry over his mother's revelation the previous evening, but Coran's presence at the table kept him silent. He could see the lanbrou watching him and their mother, his eyes shifting from one to the other and back. It was obvious he knew something was up, and it was just as obvious that he wanted to know what it was. Ricky wasn't about to let him in on the argument he'd had with the lanmere. And there was a tacit agreement between mother and son to keep the disagreement private, for Fallon too kept quiet on the matter.

"Coran," said the lanmere, breaking the uncomfortable silence. He looked at her with a dutiful and inquisitive expression that made Ricky want to gag. "Luke needs to settle the bill with the farrier who was here the other day. Will you please see to it that he has the funds he needs? And that the farrier's bill is correct?" she added.

"I don't know why you insist on using that farrier when you know he tries to cheat you," commented Ricky, more for the sake of arguing than because he cared.

Fallon ignored him. Coran shot him a pursed-lipped glare and then looked obediently to the lanmere. "Of course, Mother. I wonder," he went on in a thoughtful tone, "will that Wand'ring Minstrel be back today?"

Ricky stiffened. Coran's eyes flicked to him and back to Fallon almost imperceptibly, and the lanfis knew that he'd given himself away. He silently cursed his lack of self-control.

Fallon appeared undisturbed by Coran's inquiry. "I certainly hope so. I asked him back myself to work with Gretta and the others."

"That's good. I'd love to hear him play. The house musicians are all superb, of course, but it's nice to get a bit of new blood in once in a while, eh?"

Ricky almost believed him. He certainly sounded sincere. But Ricky couldn't help wondering if perhaps his earlier assessment was incorrect and Coran in fact knew what had passed between Ricky and Fallon. If he didn't, it was a preternaturally close hit. Or maybe he was just testing the waters, seeing what he could learn from their reactions. Ricky forced himself to relax and smile. "I heard them practicing yesterday," he said as casually as he could manage. "It was lovely."

"Yes?" Coran turned to him with a smile both shrewd and curious. "Good. I assume you've heard him play on his own, too, and that's why you recommended him. Was it in a pub somewhere on your recent travels or a private performance?"

An innocent question on the surface, but with an underlying innuendo that Ricky couldn't fail to grasp. *You want to play that game? I can play that game.* "I have heard him, yes.

We met on the road to Couvin and I was treated to a fantastic private performance." Coran's expression went from calculating to cold. "He's quite an artist. Very skilled fingers, eh?" Ricky smiled at his brother in false innocence.

Coran stood, his barely controlled emotions obvious in spite of his efforts to hide them. Ricky kept his expression even, but inside he was pleased with his spiteful little triumph. It was nice to be able to take some of his bad mood out on his perpetually irritating little brother. He was so easy to read, easy to play. How could he even imagine he could match Ricky at this little game?

"Excuse me," Coran said, nodding deferentially to Fallon and ignoring Ricky completely. "I'll go speak to Luke about the farrier's bill."

"Thank you, dear," smiled Fallon.

Silence descended in the wake of his exit. Only the clinking of silver on china broke it.

"You shouldn't tease him like that," Fallon chided eventually.

"You don't expect me to let it slide when he deliberately baits me like that." He speared a bit of sausage with unnecessary fierceness and popped it into his mouth.

"You're angry with me. It's not fair to take it out on Coran."

"No," agreed Ricky around the mouthful. "But he makes it so damned easy!"

Fallon speared him with a look almost as fierce as the force he'd used on his breakfast. He paused with another bite suspended before him. "I'm not happy about this either, Patrick, but it is for the best at this time. Like it or not, you're responsible to and for more than just yourself."

Ricky knew it, but at the moment he had trouble caring. He

took a deep breath and let it out slowly. "All right. All right." He turned his best puppy-dog look on his mother so she'd know there were no hard feelings. "But you've got to let me have some fun." He blinked wide blue eyes innocently.

Fallon pursed her lips. "You're a wicked boy," she said, but her eyes held a hint of mirth kept very carefully in check.

"I know." He flashed a mischievous grin and the lanmere chuckled and shook her head. Having charmed his way back into her good graces and having forgiven her for her part in the current unpleasantness, Ricky asked, "Do you really think it's as important as all that?"

She grew solemn again in an instant and he knew he wasn't going win this one. "I do and you know I'm right. Behave yourself, Patrick. And stop teasing your brother."

Ricky fought back a sigh of frustration. "All right. I will try." He met her dark gaze squarely and was glad she didn't demand anything further. He wasn't sure he could qualify his answer if she had.

✧

"Good morning, Jimothy!" said Maeve brightly. There was a light in her eyes and a glow about her that suggested a very pleasant night. Her smile shone as warmly as the sun filtering through the front windows. "You're up early this morning."

"I'm expected at The Heathers at nine," he explained as he sat down at the bar.

"You can have eggs or oatmeal, and sausage with either."

"Oatmeal and sausage, please. And tea," he added through a yawn. "The strongest tea you have." She brought him his breakfast, setting a small pitcher of cream and a bowl of dark golden honey next to it. "Thank you."

The tavern's only other guest wasn't up yet and the bar wasn't open to the public before lunch, so the pair had the place to themselves. Maeve pulled over her stool and sat across from him. Resting her elbows on the bar, she leaned forward. "So," she said. "The Heathers, eh?"

"Mm-hmm," answered Jimothy around a mouthful of sweetened oatmeal. It had been cooked with chunks of pear in it, and he could taste a hint of cinnamon, too. "This is delicious."

"What are you going to do there?" She spoke with a tone of casual indifference, but he knew it was feigned. The light in her eyes was too bright and he knew from Ricky that she and Japheth were friends of his. Jimothy decided to play along.

"The lanmere asked me to meet with the house musicians again."

"Uh-huh."

"I brought them three new chamber pieces yesterday. Undoubtedly she asked me back to work on them."

"Yeah? And what else are you going to do while you're there?"

"I don't really know. I hope to have the chance to tour the grounds a bit more today. I was given a short tour of the flower garden yesterday." He thought of what had happened there and knew in an instant he was caught. Maeve's eyes widened in delight and she leaned closer to him.

"You had a garden tryst," she declared. To his shock, Jimothy felt his cheeks heat as he blushed. *I don't blush!* he thought indignantly. But he was blushing now and it only made Maeve grin like a cat. "You did!"

He spoke in a quiet, restrained voice. "If you must know, I

did. But I'd appreciate it if you kept that information to yourself."

"My lips are sealed," she swore, but the sparkle never dimmed in her eyes. "So, it *was* Ricky who sent you to us, wasn't it?" It was obvious from her tone that she'd guessed this early on and had only been waiting for the opportunity to confirm it.

Jimothy had to swallow his tea quickly to keep from choking on it with laughter. "How do you know Ricky, anyway?" he answered with a question of his own. "I mean, there doesn't seem to be a strict class system in Kanbec, but I can't quite imagine it being so free spirited that the lanfis can just stroll about town frequenting the pubs."

Maeve shrugged, sitting back a bit on her stool. "I knew Ricky when we were children," she said. "My parents run a small dairy farm and the Rosslyns are very good customers. I used to go with my mother when she made her deliveries to the estate. I met Ricky there when we were children. He always had to be the first one to try whatever new cheese we brought. Over time we got to be friends. When I married Japheth and we set up this place—" she indicated the room around them, "—he was our first customer. The fact is, despite that huge smile and those stunning blue eyes of his, Ricky is very good at blending into a crowd."

"Really?" Jimothy was surprised. He would have thought it impossible, considering not only his looks but his position.

"Oh yeah. It's a little disturbing sometimes. You look up and suddenly there he is, sitting at the bar and you never even saw him come in."

"Huh." In the distance the clocks chimed half past the hour, disrupting Jimothy's thoughts. "Crap. Is it really eight-thirty?"

"You should be glad," Maeve chided. "You'll get to see Ricky soon."

"Not that soon. Musicians first, remember?" He took a last bite of sausage and washed it down with a gulp of tea. "I've got to run. Thanks for breakfast and the chat." He smiled as he rose and grabbed up his guitar. "I'll see you this evening."

"Have fun!" Maeve called after him as he headed out into the street.

The streets were already busy with workers and shoppers and he garnered a few curious glances and several smiles as he hurried along his way. He'd forgone his cloak this morning; the day promised to be warm despite last night's chill and he didn't want the hassle of carrying it. As a result anyone could see the cased instrument slung across his back. *That should be good for business tonight,* he thought. Anyone who didn't already know there was a Wand'ring Minstrel in town would find out by tonight.

He reached his destination and this time the guards at the gate just nodded in recognition and let him through. He headed quickly along the walk to the south side of the house. He rang the chime just as the city clock struck nine in the distance and an unfamiliar bell rang sweetly nearby.

To his surprise it was Gretta rather than the ancient porter who opened the door for him. "Good morning," she said.

"Good morning," he echoed.

"Your timing is perfect," she went on as she ushered him in and closed the door. She led the way along the same path the porter had taken him on yesterday, and the cook waved a floured hand in hello as they passed through the kitchen. "The others are already in the music room. I got one of the three pieces you brought us transcribed into parts last night. We'll work on that this morning."

It was a long morning full of hard work, and Jimothy enjoyed it thoroughly. It had been months since he'd had others to play with. There was a dynamic to playing in a group that working alone could never match. They broke at one o'clock for lunch, heading into the servants' dining hall. A cold spread was laid out on the sideboard along with chilled tea, cider and beer. They helped themselves and found places at one of the larger tables.

"So, Jimothy," Liam asked, "how did you become a Wand'ring Minstrel? I mean, I know you must have studied with the Sect, but how did you get there?"

"The same way most of us get there—luck, timing, and talent." Before any of them could take offense at a perceived insult, Jimothy added, "Which isn't to say there aren't plenty of talented people who never get there. Every Wand'ring Minstrel has a duty to keep his or her eyes open for children with potential, but that doesn't mean we don't miss some. And sometimes a family won't allow their child to go."

"But what's your story?" Liam persisted.

"You don't really want to hear that, do you? It's pretty ordinary. I think you'll be disappointed."

"I bet you're understating it," put in Gretta. "How old were you? You can tell us that much at least."

"I was twelve, which is about the average for new recruits. A Wand'ring Minstrel named Trevor found me and before you could say go, we were gone."

"And did your parents let you go willingly?" Jenna asked. They were all curious now, leaning in to hear his story.

"It was just my mother, and I think she was glad to let me go. Not that she didn't want me around exactly," Jimothy said quickly. He didn't want them thinking his was some tragic case of an unwanted child shunted off to the first place that would take him. "I have two older sisters, and our father died when I was a baby. I think Mother was just glad to have one less mouth to feed and one less unruly child to keep track of."

Before the musicians could continue their inquiry, the main door opened and a tall, thin man with salt-and-pepper hair and dressed in the lanmere's personal livery peered around the room. Everyone froze in anticipation; it was obvious that he held a high position among the staff. His eyes fell on Jimothy. "Lanmere Fallon requires your presence," he stated formally. "Bring your things."

Jimothy glanced at his tablemates. "I guess we're finished for today."

"I'll have at least one of the other pieces ready if you're back tomorrow," Gretta said as he rose to leave.

"I hope I'll be here. Thanks for a great morning." He smiled and crossed the big room to join the liveried man at the door. The fellow led him through the ground floor to the central wing of the house and then up a long, grand stairway.

As he had the previous morning, Jimothy took the opportunity to observe his surroundings. Paintings hung on the walls along the front hallway and up the stairs. Men and women dressed in richly colored clothes, each wearing a sash of office. He guessed they were portraits of previous lanmeres and lanperes. He stole a moment to lean in and read the small plaque below one painting and learned his guess was correct.

While ornate tapestries covered the walls and tables displaying statues and cut vases lined the upper hallway, he couldn't help but notice that the tapestries were wool rather than silk, the statues granite rather than marble, and the vases leaded glass rather than crystal. He got the feeling that whoever collected them wasn't out to impress anyone with their wealth but rather displayed the pieces because they liked looking at them. It certainly fit with what he knew of Ricky and the brief impression he had of the lanmere.

They stopped at double doors at the far end of the hall. The liveried man knocked twice and then opened them. "The Wand'ring Minstrel, your highness," he announced, bowing Jimothy into the room.

"Thank you, Martin. You're dismissed."

The man bowed again, deeper this time, and pulled the heavy door shut as he departed. The lanmere was dressed more formally than when Jimothy had seen her last, but still her appearance leaned towards the practical and the comfortable rather than the opulence he was accustomed to seeing on members of the ruling classes. Her gown was a mix of linen and lightest weight wool—not even as opulent as the velvet tunic Ricky had worn yesterday. But the exquisite embroidery on her bodice was a clear indication of her wealth and rank. It wasn't everyone who could afford such fine work.

"Come in. Have a seat," she said. She gestured to a comfortable looking chair opposite her own, and Jimothy sat, setting his guitar beside it. "I hope you had a worthwhile time with our musicians this morning."

"Yes, thank you, your highness."

"That's good. I hope you'll return again tomorrow to work with them further."

"I'd be happy to."

"Hm."

She was silent for a moment and Jimothy got the distinct impression that her musicians were not why he'd been called to her presence. His stomach sank. He was certain this was about his relationship with Ricky. The lanfis had undoubtedly been wrong when stating that she liked him. Or perhaps she did, but didn't consider him a suitable lover for her son and heir.

"That letter you brought yesterday," she said, surprising him. "You said you knew generally what it was about. Tell me more."

"The Wand'ring Minstrel who gave it to me is named Darius. He'd been in Korpi for several weeks, assessing the atmosphere."

The lanmere nodded. "Go on."

"He said the university's dons are unhappy with certain current policies—policies instituted by your father, the late lanpere, and supported by you. He didn't say which ones."

"Anything more?"

"Yes." Jimothy shifted, sitting up a little straighter in his chair. "He said there were rumors that the dons were preparing for something, but he didn't say what that was. I got the impression that he wasn't entirely sure."

"I'm not surprised. The dons can be wickedly clever and surprisingly organized when they put their minds to it. Fortunately, the author of the letter you delivered was better informed." She frowned. "I have to ask you to do something you won't like, Master Minstrel. You're not obliged to agree to it, and I won't force you. I respect the autonomy your position gives you and, besides, that's not the way I run things."

"What is it, your highness?" Jimothy felt ready for whatever she requested. He'd been sent on of plenty of royal errands in his time; it was part of his job to carry information to and from the courts.

"I need you to keep away from my son."

It was the one thing Jimothy wasn't ready for. He'd dreaded it, even expected it, but when the moment came, he found himself entirely unprepared. He kept his voice even as he said, "May I ask the reason, your highness?"

She looked at him with anger in her dark eyes, but he knew instinctively that it wasn't directed at him. "Did Patrick tell you he'd been at university?" Jimothy nodded. "Did he tell you he'd been expelled?"

"No. He only said that he and the dons 'disagreed on some fundamentals'. They actually expelled him? But he's your heir!" He was shocked and indignant on Ricky's behalf.

"They didn't call it that, naturally, but that is what it amounted to. Patrick was only there eighteen months, but it was more than enough. Frankly I was glad when he came home. There's only one don worth his salt over there and if I had my way he'd be running the place. Those self-righteous pedants at the university wouldn't know progress if it bit them on their tight arses." Jimothy's eyes widened in surprise and the lanmere laughed outright. "Come now. You can't tell me you've never heard that sort of language before."

"Not from royalty, madam, no."

She laughed again. "Royalty," she echoed. "Hardly. You know our first lanpere was elected, don't you?"

"Yes."

"Even thirteen generations on, this family isn't what traditional royal courts would call royalty. As long as it doesn't stop them respecting our borders and our laws, I'm perfectly happy to keep it that way."

"If I may," Jimothy began again, "what has this to do with Ricky and me?"

"Surely you've guessed what policies the dons object to." She eyed him intently until understanding dawned. "Now you've got it. Understand that I have no intention of pandering to their demands, but their power is second only to my own in Kanbec, and I do need to play the politics until I have this situation under control. That means, unfortunately, that you and Patrick need to stay away from each other for the time being."

"I understand." Jimothy hated it and guessed that Ricky did too, although he had yet to see him since he'd arrived. He wondered if he could catch a word with him before leaving the estate.

As if she'd read his thoughts, the lanmere said, "Ricky can't see you. I made that very clear to him last night. He fought me on it, of course, but he's smart. He understands politics as well as I do even if he likes to pretend otherwise."

"Did you hear that in my mind, or are you only following the logical path of our conversation?" Jimothy asked brazenly. The lanmere smiled at him and he knew the answer.

"He said you were sharp and he said you were trustworthy. Do you have any *cheel* talents of your own?"

"No."

"You're lucky...and unlucky all at once."

"Yes, your highness."

Her expression grew soft. "I am sorry, Jimothy. Sorrier than you probably realize. You've made Ricky happy in a way that I've never seen him before, and it's the sort of happiness every mother wishes for her children. I know that's of little comfort."

"Actually, your highness, I'm glad to know it. Thank you."

There was a knock on the door but rather than Martin as Jimothy expected, it was another man. This fellow resembled Ricky to a degree, but his surly expression was one he could never imagine on the lanfis.

"Yes, Coran? What is it?" the lanmere asked the new arrival.

"It's Cook again. She's arguing with Martin over tonight's menu." His tone was dutiful but with an edge to it. Jimothy thought it was annoyance, but at what or whom was unclear.

"All right. I'll be right there."

"Yes, Mother." He nodded respectfully and left.

"I didn't know you had any other children," Jimothy said. *But that explains the family resemblance.*

"Your intelligence was incomplete. I'm surprised. Usually I've found that the Sect keeps its people well informed."

"My map was out of date, too," he added dryly.

"Coran's a good boy. A bit too earnest at times, but good at heart." There was something in her tone that made Jimothy wonder if she was trying to convince herself of her own statement. "I have to go." She rose and he followed her, grabbing his guitar as he stood. "You're welcome to return tomorrow, but I ask again that you abide by my request."

"Yes, your highness. I will," he agreed, although it made his stomach sick to do so.

They left the room and descended the stairs together. "Use the front door," the lanmere instructed. "It's ridiculous to follow me to the south wing when there's a door right there."

"Yes, your highness," he said again. She turned and headed towards the kitchen, soon disappearing around a corner. Jimothy paused in the grand entry hall and took a few moments to look closer at the paintings. In part it was a stalling technique; he hoped Ricky might find him there. It was also a chance to look around unobserved. He found Lanmere Fallon's portrait easily. Smaller paintings hung to either side of it. On the left was one of her with a tall, fair-haired man. *It must be their wedding portrait,* he thought, looking at their particularly formal garb. *Or her coronation.* He'd not heard a word about the lanmere's husband. He wondered if he were simply away being diplomatic somewhere or if he'd passed on. His gaze moved to the painting on the right, obviously done within the past few years. It was a family portrait of the lanmere and both her sons.

Ricky's wide grin had been perfectly replicated by the artist. His brother, Coran, also looked surprisingly cheerful and handsome. His sharp features were softened by his painted smile, but that softness could be due as much to artistic license as to reality. It was certainly a stark contrast to Jimothy's impression of Ricky's brother a few minutes ago. He considered the painting intently and realized that Coran's smile wasn't echoed in his eyes. Instead the brown depths held thinly veiled pain or sorrow. The portrait painter was a master, and probably had more than a touch of *cheel* behind his art to have captured so much detail. It was like a moment of time suspended and perfectly recreated.

He guessed from his absence in the painting that the lanmere's husband was dead. Then he remembered Ricky's early comment, "My father used to call me nosy." *Definitely passed on, then.* He decided that Ricky took after his mother—short, slight, and dark haired. The only way in which he didn't favor her was his eyes. Coran had gotten their mother's brown eyes, but Ricky's were a startling bright blue. *He must have gotten those blue eyes from his father.* He looked back at the wedding portrait to confirm his suspicion, but at that moment he heard footsteps and turned to see Martin approaching.

"May I help you?" the liveried man asked, his tone one of mild reproach at finding him in the front of the house unescorted. Martin looked down his nose at Jimothy, who had the rare experience of having to look up to meet someone's gaze. "No, thank you. I was just on my way out." Jimothy smiled with professional pleasantness and slipped out the door before the liveried man could expel him.

He walked back into town with a heavy heart. It wasn't the first time that politics had spoiled his pleasure. *I should have expected it,* he thought dourly.

Finding himself with some unexpected free time, he decided

to put it to practical use. He still had two letters he needed to deliver. When people didn't seek him out, he found the best way to find them was to find the local magistrate or clerk's office. With a bit of luck, he could find out where the recipients lived or worked and deliver the letters that afternoon. *Assuming the city keeps those sorts of records, and assuming I can find the office.*

Deciding the direct course was usually best, he stopped at the first shop he came across. It was a fruit seller's. He bought a pear and a bunch of grapes, and, flashing his most winning and flirtatious smile, he asked the middle-aged woman behind the counter for directions.

Twenty minutes later, he was lost.

I should have known better, he chided himself, looking around the completely unfamiliar streets. *I should have asked for a map.* He'd foolishly left the one Maeve had given him at the tavern, figuring he wouldn't be going anywhere he didn't already know. He turned around, determined to retrace his steps, only to find himself facing three men with distinctly unfriendly looks on their faces. He nodded politely and tried to step around them, but they moved with him, blocking his way. "Excuse me," he said firmly and tried to move around them again. Again they blocked his path. "All right. Tell me what it is you want and perhaps we can make this quick and easy for all of us." Jimothy waited, expecting a demand for his purse and glad that he'd brought only a little cash with him that morning.

"We have a message for you," the burliest of the trio said in a low, rough voice. In another situation, Jimothy would have laughed; it was such a stereotypically "bad guy" voice. As it was, his gut went cold and he wondered how to keep his guitar safe when he was outnumbered three to one.

I didn't wear my knife today why? He was just as glad he

hadn't, though. It would be too easy for someone skilled to turn his own weapon against him. He braced himself internally, ready to run. "Your message?" he asked coolly.

"Just this." The man was quick despite his bulk. Jimothy had no time to dodge the ham-sized fist that slammed into his gut, knocking the wind from him. He doubled over, gasping, and another blow sent him to his knees. Before he could put two thoughts together, the man struck upwards, catching him under the chin and snapping his head back painfully. Another blow connected with his jaw and he tasted blood. Then he was pulled to his feet, the tight grip on his collar choking him. "Our boss says it's time you left town. Got it?"

Jimothy managed a stiff nod and the thug dropped him, apparently satisfied. He slammed to the ground, knees hitting cobblestones and hands scraping as he caught himself from face-planting. Heavy footsteps receded and he knelt there for several minutes, regaining breath and sense slowly. He heard wary footsteps behind him and swung around to meet them defensively. His head screamed in protest and he fought down a wave of nausea.

A small girl stepped back, startled, a frightened look on her face. He guessed she was about eight years old, and she was already outgrowing the obviously hand-me-down clothes she wore.

"I'm sorry," Jimothy said roughly, wincing as he felt and heard his jaw click. He coughed, clearing his battered throat. "I didn't mean to scare you."

"You don't scare me," the girl stated staunchly, but her eyes belied her brave front.

"I wonder if you could help me." He rose painfully to his feet and beat down another wave of nausea. "Do you know Five Corners?" She looked at him like he was an idiot. "Right. Can you tell me the easiest way to get there?"

"Gimme a copper and I'll show you, eh?"

"I'll give you two if you can take me to the door of the Cat and Turtle. One copper now, one when we get there."

"Deal!" She held out her hand. He fished in his purse and placed a small copper coin in her palm. "Come on." She didn't wait, striding boldly down the narrow street back the way he'd come. He hurried to follow her, his bruised knees protesting the quick pace.

They reached the tavern sooner than he expected, and Jimothy gratefully gave her the other half of her pay. "Thank you."

"Bye!" she said with a grin, and raced off.

Jimothy could see patrons inside the bar and wished he'd had the forethought to come in around the back. There was no help for it now, though. It was a long way around the block to the back of the building. He pushed open the door and practically fell into the room.

Startled exclamations greeted his unorthodox entrance. He heard Maeve shout for her husband, and suddenly she, Nita and Japheth surrounded him. He heard an unfamiliar voice, one full of open distress. "Please, let me help."

Who's that? he thought, dazed.

"We have him, thank you," Maeve said, her tone kind but firm.

"I'm sorry," Jimothy started, and was promptly shushed.

"Not a word from you until you're settled," stated Maeve in a tone that brooked no argument. She looked at Nita. "Send Aren to the Sisters, then cover the front of the house."

"Yes, ma'am," the young woman said quickly. She ran ahead of them to the back and before they could meet her there,

Aren sprinted past them out the front door. Nita promptly took the post behind the bar as Japheth and Maeve half-ushered, half-carried the injured man past the curtain. Nita's voice followed them out. "All right. Excitement's over," she stated with authority. "Who needs another drink?"

Jimothy gave a small chuckle and then winced as the movement made his ribs protest painfully. He tried to turn up the stairs towards his room, but Maeve stopped him. "No you don't. This way." They led him past the kitchen and into a room that he was sure must be their own.

"I can't—" he protested.

"You can and you will. Do you think I'm climbing those stairs if I don't have to?" She'd maneuvered him perfectly. He would protest for his own sake, but he wouldn't make the pregnant woman climb the stairs if she didn't want to.

"Thank you."

Japheth took his guitar from him carefully, not wishing to damage either it or Jimothy. He placed it in a corner, safely out of harm's way.

"Sit," Maeve ordered, pointing to the chair nearest a black, pot-bellied stove. Jimothy sat.

"I'll get hot water," said Japheth. He rushed out and was back in moments with a bucket of hot water in one hand and towels in the other. He set the water next to Maeve and handed her the towels. She knelt down in front of Jimothy. Then she dipped a cloth into the water, rung it out and began cleaning his battered face. He felt like a child but he made no protest. He didn't really feel like speaking at all, not even to complain about the pain.

"What happened?" she asked, dabbing at blood that trickled from the corner of his mouth. It occurred to him that he must have bitten his tongue at some point, but he didn't remember doing so.

"I got jumped," he answered stiffly, trying not to move his face any more than necessary.

"How much did they take from you?" Japheth asked.

"Nothing."

"Is that why they beat you? Because you didn't have any money on you?" queried Maeve.

Jimothy shook his head and discovered instantly that it was a bad idea. His stomach lurched and he felt bile rise in his throat. He swallowed it back down. "No. They didn't want money."

Maeve and Japheth exchanged a look. "Well that's odd," the host said at last. Jimothy would have agreed, but he had an idea who the thugs were working for, at least peripherally. They'd mentioned a boss, so this wasn't just a random attack against a foreigner. Someone had sent them to do this to him. Based on what he and the lanmere had discussed, he suspected that someone had connections to the university. He was, after all, the sort of person to whom the dons objected.

There was a knock on the open door and they looked up to see Aren and a tall woman dressed in a simple light blue gown. Her cuffs were neatly buttoned at her wrists and the hem of her skirt brushed the ground. Her head was covered with a scarf of the same color as her dress and pinned under her chin, and there was a red leather satchel in her right hand.

"It's the Sister you asked for," Aren announced proudly.

"Thank you, Aren," said Japheth, and Maeve added, "Tell Chef I said you could have a sweet." The boy's eyes sparkled and he disappeared towards the kitchen. "Then stay out of his way!" the hostess called after him. She rose heavily, and Japheth reached out to help her up. She smiled her thanks at him, and then turned to the woman. "Thank you for coming so quickly, Sister."

"It's why we're here, Daughter," the woman said. She stepped into the room and took Maeve's place in front of the patient. "Now, what can you tell me?"

Jimothy looked hopefully up at the host and hostess. "He was attacked," Japheth said.

She leaned down and looked intently into Jimothy's eyes. He was surprised to see that she was much younger than he'd first thought, younger than himself. Fair brows arched almost severely over dark brown eyes. "You weren't by chance looking for trouble, were you?" He shook his head once, very carefully. "All right." She stood and turned to the anxiously waiting couple. "I'll take it from here. You two have a business to run."

"Thank you, Sister," said Japheth, and the pair left the room.

"I'm Sister Martha Joan," the woman said as she unbuttoned her cuffs and rolled her sleeves up above her elbows. "I take it you're the Wand'ring Minstrel we've all heard about over at the hospital." This time he nodded once, very carefully. "They clocked you a good one, I see," she went on, carrying the conversation for them both. She examined him with strong but gentle hands, checking the swelling along his jaw and the bruising at his throat. "Can you open your mouth?" He did so reluctantly and again there was that sickening clicking sound. "Thank the Blessed Martha it's not broken. Here, rinse your mouth with this." She pulled a bottle from her bag and poured a small measure of something pale pink into a mug. "All of it at once," she instructed, handing it to him. "But don't swallow it."

Jimothy took the mug and eyed its contents dubiously. He tipped it back and fought not to gag as the vile stuff touched his tongue. Then the stinging began. His mouth burned and he looked at her with wide, pained eyes.

"Swish it about," ordered the Sister. He did, despite the taste and painful tingling. "Now spit." She lifted his hand that held the mug and he spat into it willingly. "Good." She opened the stove and emptied the mug into the fire, which flared bright blue for a split second and then returned to normal.

"That was awful," complained Jimothy tightly.

"You'll be glad of it when that bite on the inside of your right cheek heals up clean and quick. Put this on your face." She pressed a hot, moist cloth stinking of strong herbs into his hands and he held it against his bruised jaw. The smell made his eyes water, but this time he didn't complain. The Sister smirked. "You learn quickly," she said, pleased. "Where else did they get you?"

"My stomach," he answered.

She reached for the neck of his tunic, loosening the laces. "Off you come." Carefully, one arm at a time, together they got his tunic and shirt off over his head without unduly disrupting the poultice he held. She clucked her tongue. Jimothy looked down and saw the flesh already purpling over his lower left ribs. "Did they use a club?" She examined the area, and Jimothy couldn't help but suck in a sharp breath.

"No. Big, big fist. Twice."

Jimothy was relieved when she completed her examination. "Nothing out of place that I can find, nor broken. How many were there?" she asked, preparing another poultice with a completely different set of stinky herbs.

"Three, but just one did the pounding."

She clucked her tongue again and carefully pressed the second cloth against his ribs. He felt the pain ebb almost immediately followed by a disturbing numbing sensation. He looked at her quizzically.

"That's supposed to happen," she assured him. "Hold it there." He obediently put his free hand on it, keeping it in place. She took a long strip of cloth bandage from her satchel and used it to bind the poultice to his body, releasing his hand from the task. "Did they get you anywhere else?" Again she captured him with her intense stare. "No need to be shy or proud."

"That's all," he assured her.

"All right. I don't believe your spleen has been ruptured, but if that bruise gets any bigger or starts swelling strangely, send to the hospital for a Healer immediately. I'll leave some medicine with you. It will help with the pain and it will make you sleep." She took a bottle from her bag and carefully shook an ample measure of greyish powder into a paper cone. Then she twisted the cone shut and put the bottle down. "Don't move." She left the room abruptly and returned a minute later with Maeve and a green glass bottle. "You both get instructions on the medication. There has to be someone clear headed who knows what to do with it."

"Of course," the hostess agreed.

"Half a teaspoon of powder dissolved in an ounce of liquid—preferably wine but tea will do," she explained, demonstrating as she spoke. She swirled liquid and powder together in a mug before trading the mug to Jimothy for the cloth he held against his cheek. At her nod, he drank it down, relieved that it tasted only like the wine. He handed back the empty vessel. "Very good. Here's the important part. Do not take more than eight doses in a single day. That's one every three hours, tops. Understand?" She looked from Jimothy to Maeve and back. Both nodded. "Good. Now you'd best get him up to his bed," she told the hostess, "unless you want to give over your own for the night."

"I'll get Japheth and Vashti." She ducked out.

Sister Martha Joan rolled her sleeves back down and buttoned the cuffs. “Do you have any idea why they targeted you, Master Minstrel?” she asked as she packed up her things.

Jimothy couldn’t decide the motive behind her question, but chose to err on the side of caution. “No.”

She eyed him again and he got the distinct feeling she knew he was lying. “All right. Remember what I said about those ribs. Send a runner immediately if it worsens.”

“I will.”

“I’ll be back in the morning to check on you.”

“Thank you, Sister.”

It was a production number getting him up the stairs. The medicine made him fuzzy-headed and it took both Japheth and his sister to get him safely to his room. Aren followed behind the awkward trio with Jimothy’s tunic and shirt, guitar and medicine all held with exaggerated care in his hands.

At last Jimothy was settled on his bed. His head was heavy and he was only vaguely aware of someone removing his boots and helping him to lie down. Someone pulled a blanket over him and in moments he was fast asleep.

✧

Ricky was alone in his rooms, yawning over trade agreement documents. Normally he found domestic and international trade interesting, but his mind was not on his subject today. It was instead focused on a certain Wand’ring Minstrel. He leaned back in his chair, a thoughtful expression on his face. Warm sunlight poured through the window, cutting a bright swath across the bed. He eyed the bed wistfully, wishing he had company to share it. But he and Jimothy hadn’t gotten that far yesterday and he'd never even gotten to see him today. Politics had seen to that. He frowned and then stood abruptly, pacing the carpeted floor in the hopes of burning off a bit of his anger and frustration. When that didn't work, he flopped heavily onto the bed and stared up at the canopy. The late afternoon sunshine warmed him and he closed his eyes, a small smile turning up the corner of his lips. Jimothy. He pictured the handsome Wand'ring Minstrel in his mind and eased a hand into his breeches. He recalled the dark eyes and strong jaw, the wavy brown hair that turned a dark honey color in the right light. Between imagination and manipulation, Ricky was soon hard. He massaged his cock with his hand while he simultaneously stripped the mental image of his lover, revealing Jimothy's broad shoulders, smooth chest, narrow hips and nicely muscled legs. Ricky smiled at the mental image. Despite his itinerant lifestyle and its consequential uncertainties, Jimothy was lean and fit, but not skinny. The perfect shape and size in all ways, in Ricky's opinion.

Out of nowhere he felt as if the wind was knocked out of him. His ears rang with the force of an illusory blow. Arousal lost in the surprise onslaught, he released his cock and looked around. The room was empty. He sat up and took several deep breaths, trying to determine what was going on. He closed his eyes again and rubbed a hand against his temple. He knew it was all a chimera—at least for him. What he felt was distant but very real. The ringing faded to a silent ache and he was able to focus his mind. His eyes flew open in sudden realization. "Magdalene's tits!"

He rose so quickly that he nearly collapsed and had to grab the bedpost to stay upright. His head swam and he waited impatiently for it to clear.

Against his instincts he took a moment to tidy the papers on his desk and cap the small inkwell. It had to look as if he'd just stepped away for a moment. He didn't want anyone who might come looking for him to find anything out of the ordinary or amiss. Otherwise they were sure to sound the alarm—or at least tell the lanmere. In either case, it would be a bad situation. He took a small purse of coins from his dresser and slipped his boot knife into its sheath. Hastily throwing on his cloak, he hurried from his rooms.

Heart racing, he forced himself to walk leisurely, making his way through the manor house and outside. He saw only two servants on his way and was careful to move as unobtrusively as only he could. Neither servant looked up at his passing, nor did the guards at the side gate. Still, he couldn't be too careful. He was going against his mother's directive and the last thing he wanted was witnesses to his departure. He picked up his pace as soon as he was around the first corner, but it wasn't until he was well on his way to his destination that he relaxed his guard. He could move faster when he wasn't concentrating. He began to run.

Chapter Five

The tiny knock at the door insinuated itself into his dream. It continued, soft but insistent, and he woke reluctantly. It was dark. Jimothy didn't remember it growing dark. It was still light out when he'd gotten back. Then the door opened a crack to let in a shaft of shuttered light from the lantern in the hallway. A figure loomed in the opening, back lit and unfamiliar. "Who—?" he started, and was promptly shushed.

"It's me," the figure whispered, and even in his drugged state Jimothy recognized the voice.

"Ricky? What are you doing here?" He tried to sit up and failed. Ricky stepped into the room, softly closing and locking the door behind him.

"I heard what happened and I had to see you. Maeve gave me a key and let me up." Ricky sat down on the edge of the bed. Jimothy tried again to sit up and this time had better success. He rose up on an elbow and Ricky helped him the rest of the way. The lanfis edged around behind him and supported him against his chest. "What happened?"

"You said you'd heard."

"Only that you were attacked."

"That about sums it up."

"Do you know who did it? Do you know why?"

"No and no." He was tired and he hurt. He wasn't up to explaining his suspicions and theories.

There was uneasiness in the silence that followed. Then Ricky spoke cautiously. "I wonder," he began, and then stopped.

"What?"

"That letter you gave my mother..."

"The one for which I was so generously compensated?" Jimothy's belly felt warm at the memory and a slightly goofy smile curved his lips.

Ricky chuckled at that. "Yeah. That's the one."

"I remember. What about it?" There was silence as Jimothy waited for him to answer. It went on so long that he nearly dozed off.

"You said you knew what it was about," Ricky said at last.

"Mm-hmm," Jimothy murmured sleepily, leaning comfortably against the other man.

"You talked to my mother about it today, too, didn't you?"

"Mm-hmm."

"I wonder if this was something to do with that."

"Do we really have to spend the night discussing politics?"

There was another, shorter pause. "No," Ricky said gently. "You're in no shape for it, and frankly neither am I. Do you need any medicine?"

"Mm-mm," Jimothy replied in the negative. He tried to shake his head, but wasn't sure if he actually managed it.

"All right." He helped Jimothy to lie back down. Ricky took off his boots, tunic and breeches and climbed into the bed dressed in only his long shirt. He wrapped his arms around his lover and Jimothy snuggled into his embrace. They drifted off to sleep.

Jimothy knew he was dreaming. The light was too diffuse, the colors too true for it to be real. He was seated at the hearth in the bar room of the Cat and Turtle, and he was taking a break between sets. Nita sidled up to him and refilled his wine goblet.

"By the way, Minstrel," she said softly before heading out into the crowd, "there's a fellow at the bar looking for you."

She wafted away and Jimothy glanced over towards the bar. He smiled to see Ricky there, dressed like any other common citizen, from rough boots to workman's cap. He nursed a pint of ale, which he raised in greeting when he saw Jimothy looking at him. Jimothy nodded back, but his break was over and it was time for another set.

He began with a love song that was tender and sweet, one of the few epic love songs he knew in which both people lived and loved happily ever after. He was enough of an optimist to believe that sort of thing was possible, but he was enough of a realist to know it was rare. He let his own feelings infuse the music more than he normally would for just that reason. The silent observer in him wondered if Ricky would understand the message he was trying to send.

The song reached its blissful conclusion and people applauded, although they were blurred and at a distance. He heard one or two sentimental sniffs from the crowd, but the only person that mattered was Ricky. Jimothy glanced towards the bar but Ricky had his back turned at that moment. *What does that mean?* he wondered. Then he forced himself to stop wondering and do his job.

Time folded in his dream and the night was at an end. The only one left in the bar was Ricky. Even Maeve and Vashti had vanished. Ricky still sat on the barstool where he'd spent most of the evening. His cap rested on the bar beside him and he held his mug of ale in one strong hand.

"Are you staying the night?" Jimothy asked him.

"If I'm invited to," he replied easily, and then looked at Jimothy with a tiny lascivious smile. "Am I invited?"

"Please, will you stay the night?"

"I'd love to."

The dream image Jimothy and Ricky transported to his room on the second floor. They floated naked into the bed, arms and legs intertwined, sharing kisses both passionate and sweet…

Jimothy woke slowly with a smile on his face and strong arms around him. He sighed happily and rolled over—and instantly regretted it. He groaned as every bruise in his battered body made itself felt. Ricky stirred at the sound and opened his eyes. "Heya," he said in a quiet voice. He used one hand to brush a lock of wavy brown hair from Jimothy's forehead. "How are you?"

"Sore. Very, very sore." He opened his eyes, squinting in the morning sunlight that poured in through the window. He tried to sit up and groaned again.

"Stay put," ordered Ricky. "I'll get whatever you need." He sat up and swung his bare legs over the edge of the bed.

"Thanks, but you can't help with this."

"Why not?" he asked earnestly. "Tell me what you need."

Jimothy gave him a wry half-smile. "I need to pee."

Ricky chuckled. "You're right. I can't do that for you. But I can help you." He put an arm around him and helped him carefully to his feet. "Can you stand on your own?"

"Thanks. I'm not broken, I'm just sore." Jimothy looked down at himself and then looked at the man next to him. "I'm sure I had pants on when I got into that bed." He was now fully naked, the purple-red bruises that peeked out from the edge of his bandage standing out in sharp relief on his pale torso.

Ricky shrugged one shoulder. "Not when I got here. You must have passed out before you were fully in bed. Who got you up here, anyway?" He helped Jimothy move gingerly across the room to the chamber pot.

"Japheth and Vashti."

"Must have been one of them. Should I ask them which?" There was a hint of amusement in his voice.

"No," said Jimothy firmly. "I don't want to know."

They reached the corner, and Ricky said, "Do you need any more help?"

"I can manage on my own, thanks," Jimothy said wryly. "Just let me lean against you. I'm feeling off balance this morning."

"I'm not surprised. You took a nasty beating." Tenderness turned to sly suggestiveness. "Sure you can aim?"

Jimothy looked at him, their faces close together. "I'll manage," he repeated. "You touch me and I'll be too hard to pee."

Ricky grinned. "I'll take that as a huge compliment." He provided support while Jimothy relieved himself, and then helped him back to the bed.

"I've never been this sore in my life," he complained wearily. "I feel like I hit a brick wall at a full run."

"What can I get for you?" Ricky asked again. "Do you want tea? Breakfast? Medicine? Maeve said you had medicine from one of the Sisters of Martha." He looked around. "Where is it? Is that it?" He went to the table and picked up the twisted paper cone.

"Yes, but I don't want it."

Ricky looked at him as if he'd gone mad. "Why not? It'll help with the pain, won't it?"

"Yes. It'll also make me sleep more. I just woke up. I don't want to sleep again just yet." He shook his head to emphasize his point. He winced and put a hand over his bruised cheek. "Ow."

Ricky looked pained and came to sit beside him. "Please let me do something to help you. Take some medicine."

"No," argued Jimothy firmly. At Ricky's disappointed expression, he relented. "There is one thing you could do for me."

"Anything." The single word was spoken with such ardency that it made Jimothy's heart jump.

"Bring me breakfast and tea. Please."

"Absolutely!" Ricky rose quickly.

"Hang on," said Jimothy. Ricky froze at the door. "Get me a shirt first, would you? In the trunk there." He gestured vaguely to the trunk that stood against the opposite wall.

"Sure." Ricky opened it and found a clean shirt. "This all right?" He held it up.

"It's great. Thanks."

Ricky helped him into it. "I'll be back in a few minutes with food."

"Thanks," Jimothy said again, and then added, "You might want to put on some pants first."

"Huh? Oh!" Ricky laughed and pulled on the breeches he'd shed the night before, foregoing his boots in favor of bare feet. "I'll be right back."

Jimothy waited until the door was shut behind the other man and then let out a long, pained sigh. "I hurt." The small activities that he normally didn't think twice about were presently arduous tasks not to be undertaken lightly. He'd thought to send Ricky off and then finish dressing while he was getting breakfast, but just the short trip to the pot and back had taken more out of him than he cared to admit. He'd had to swallow his pride and ask for even more help just to get a shirt. "I feel like a bloody invalid," he groused to the empty room.

He hadn't moved by the time Ricky came back with the food. There was a tiny knock before the door opened a crack and the lanfis stuck his head in. "Heya. Ready for breakfast?"

"I think so."

"I have someone with me." Ricky came in bearing a tray with bowls and a teapot on it. He was followed by Sister Martha Joan. She set her red bag on the table and Ricky had to be content to set the tray he carried on the trunk.

"How are you feeling this morning, Master Minstrel?" the Sister asked, eyeing him critically. Her eyes flashed to his bruised knees, and she gave him a scolding look. "You didn't tell me about those last night." Jimothy fought the urge to squirm and wished he'd had the sense to ask Ricky to find him some pants to go with his shirt.

"I didn't think of them. They're not that bad—relatively speaking."

"Hm." She took astringent and soft cloth from her satchel and knelt to clean the traces of dried blood from his scraped and bruised knees. "You didn't answer my question. How are you this morning?" she repeated as she finished and stood again.

"Much better, thank you," Jimothy answered. She pursed her lips and raised a pale eyebrow. "Not well, of course, but better."

"All right. Let's have a look." She examined his jaw first,

nodding in gratification when it moved smoothly under her fingers as he opened and closed it. "You've had no trouble with your vision?"

"None."

"Good, good. Take your shirt off and let me see to your bruises."

"I—" Jimothy tried to protest. Physician or not, Sister or not, she was an attractive young woman and he wasn't wearing pants. He looked to Ricky, hoping for support, and Ricky looked back at him in concern.

"Do you need help?" the lanfis asked, coming to his side. He looked at the Sister. "He's pretty sore. I had to help him get into the shirt," he explained.

You're not helping, Jimothy thought at his lover.

Ricky looked momentarily startled but recovered quickly. *Why? What's wrong?*

Jimothy shook his head. *Never mind.* "I could use your help again, yes. Thank you." He leaned forward and Ricky gently pulled the shirt over his head and off. The lanfis dropped the garment into Jimothy's lap, covering what Jimothy didn't want the Sister to see.

While she unwrapped the bandage, examined him and asked him a few simple questions, he could hear Ricky in his mind. The lanfis's mental tone was teasing. *Since when are you body shy? Or are you just being modest?*

You're not funny, replied Jimothy.

Ricky's tone grew kinder. *It's all right, Jimothy. She's a physician. Neither of us has anything she hasn't seen before. And I'm here for you.*

Her inspection complete, Sister Martha Joan stepped back. "Do you need any more medicine?" she asked as she reached for her case.

"No," said Jimothy

"No?" the Sister echoed. Her tone was chiding and she once again raised an arched eyebrow at him. "You're meant to take if it you need it."

"I will," he lied easily. He did need it, but wouldn't say so and he wouldn't take it willingly. It put him to sleep and right now he wanted to be awake for a while in spite of his aches and pain.

"Very well. You appear to be mending, but you need to take it easy for another day or two. Send to the Sisters if you need anything else."

"Thank you, Sister."

"You're welcome." She cleaned up, packed her case and departed.

Ricky shut the door behind her and retrieved the breakfast tray. He placed it on the table. "I went with oatmeal and some sliced pears," he said. "I thought they'd be easier for you to chew than the sausage. Do you need help with your shirt again?"

"I think I can manage this time." Jimothy worked his way back into the garment while Ricky stoked up the fire in the brazier and added a few small wood chunks to it.

Jimothy raised himself to his feet and moved the short distance to sit at the table. His shirt was just long enough to cover his bum as he sat on the hard wooden chair.

"Here," Ricky moved quickly to help him shift the chair closer to the table.

Jimothy looked up at him. "Tell me something," he said. "How did the lanfis of Kanbec learn to be such a good nurse?"

The younger man shrugged and poured mugs of tea for the

two of them. "I looked after my grandfather when he was dying," he said softly, not meeting Jimothy's gaze. "There were four Sisters of Martha who were the real physicians, of course, and two of them were Healers, but I used to help him out. Get him his tea or help him dress when he wanted to go out to the gardens. We used to sneak out through a hidden passage in his room so the Sisters didn't catch him." A small, sad smile turned up the corner of his mouth, and he sipped his tea. "Grandfather was the best," he went on. "We'd get into all sorts of trouble with the Sisters and he'd just talk them down again. Even on his deathbed he never lost the power in that voice of his."

Jimothy listened thoughtfully, grateful to have been given this moment of vision into Ricky's life. "He sounds like quite a character."

"Yeah." Ricky gave a fond smile and followed it with an exaggerated frown. "Why aren't you eating? Can't you manage it on your own?"

"I'm fine." Jimothy took a small bite of oatmeal, thick with honey and fresh cream, and chewed it carefully to prove his point.

"Good."

"I'm sorry there's not another chair."

"I'm all right." Ricky set down his tea and picked up his own bowl and took a big bite. "Mmm! I love Chef's oatmeal."

Jimothy shook his head a little, bemused. "Your family is quite unique."

"I know we are," agreed Ricky lightly. "But how do *you* mean?"

"You're not typical nobility, for starters."

"My family has worked deliberately to keep it that way. I'm just a product of my breeding." He flashed a wide, white-toothed grin, and Jimothy couldn't help but laugh—and then flinch as his bruised ribs protested. Immediately Ricky frowned in concern. "Sorry. I guess I shouldn't make you laugh."

"I forgive you," joked Jimothy.

Ricky leaned against the wall and the two continued to eat breakfast in silence, each caught up in his own thoughts. Ricky finished first and set the empty bowl on the tray. He refilled his mug and Jimothy's with more tea before returning to lean against the wall again. "I wonder."

"About what?"

"That letter you gave my mother."

"I might have been dreaming," said Jimothy between bites, "but didn't we have this conversation already?"

"We did, but someone wanted to cut it short." Ricky gave him a mock-stern glare, but he couldn't hold it for more than a moment before his expression softened. He grew pensive once more. "I know you weren't robbed, so why else would they target you?" He looked at Jimothy intently and Jimothy felt it was like the look the Sister had given him. "Did they say anything? The men who attacked you?"

"They told me to leave town."

There was a pause, and then, "That's all?"

"They said it was a message from their boss."

"That answers that question. There's no way it was a random attack. They were looking for you, maybe even following you. Where were you?"

"I don't know exactly. I was looking for the city clerk's office. A woman at a produce shop gave me directions but..." He shrugged and Ricky nodded. The town wasn't designed for easy navigation; even natives could get lost if they weren't paying attention.

"Any chance one of the other letters you delivered would have angered someone enough to do this?"

"I doubt it. I mean, there are people who will take their anger out on the messenger, but not like this. I've never heard of something like this. Random attacks because we're in the wrong place at the wrong time, yes. That can happen. Attacks directed at us because a Wand'ring Minstrel alone is presumed to be an easy target, yes. That happens, too."

Ricky looked at him intently once again. "You don't think this was coincidence any more than I do, do you?"

He couldn't deny it without lying outright and there was something in him that would not let him lie to Ricky. "No. I don't. I think it has something to do with that letter that's on your mind." He stifled a yawn and took a sip of tea.

"Who was it from?"

"Your mother didn't tell you that?" Jimothy asked, surprised.

"She's told me precisely nothing," complained Ricky bitterly. "She read it. She told me to stay away from you. That's it."

"And yet here you are."

"I had to come, didn't I?" He was almost defensive, although Jimothy had intended no attack. "I couldn't *not* come. I only wish I'd gotten here sooner," he added in annoyance.

"I'm sorry," Jimothy said.

"Huh?" His words snapped the other man from his small tirade. "It's not your fault. Blessed Martha, it is *not* your fault," he stated in no uncertain terms. He began to pace the room, mug of tea forgotten in one hand. "You can't tell me who sent that letter or what's in it," he said thinking aloud. "Can you tell me if I figure it out on my own?"

"I suppose so. You're the heir, after all. If something happened to the lanmere, you'd need to know about this." The two shared a look. Both knew there was little likelihood of anything unexpected and untoward happening to Ricky's mother. Sharing privileged information—even with the lanfis—was a serious bending of the rules, and they tacitly agreed to ignore the fact.

"Let me think." Ricky continued to pace the small room while Jimothy ate his oatmeal and nibbled on a soft, ripe slice of pear. "It came from Tesna."

"I got it in Tesna," corrected Jimothy. "It came from Korpi."

Ricky stopped and turned to face him, his expression inscrutable.

"You were there when I told the lanmere where it came from," Jimothy reminded him. "I was just refreshing your memory."

"Right," nodded Ricky. "All right. It came from Korpi. The only thing of any note in Korpi is the university. Well, that and the beer at Lena's Pub, and that blond kid that works for her..." His eyes grew a little dreamy, and then he pulled himself back to the present. "But that's beside the point."

"I think I'm a little jealous," Jimothy quipped, his humor returning as his belly filled with good food and hot tea. He yawned and was pleased to find that his jaw had ceased the awful clicking it had made last night.

"Oh, he was a cutie," admitted Ricky, "but he wasn't inclined the right way. Silly boy." He shook his head at the lost opportunity and Jimothy chuckled. "Back to business." He began pacing yet again. "If the letter came from the university at Korpi—" he shot Jimothy an inquiring look, which was answered with a nod, "—then that narrows the possibilities. It was addressed to the lanmere. There was a wax seal on it, wasn't there?" Again, Jimothy nodded. "What color was it?"

"Red."

"Hmm... Could be from the university president or the Council of Dons or from any one of the department heads. Mother is friends with Don Savion, the head comparative religions professor over there. But if the letter was from him, why wouldn't she say so? And why would she tell me to keep away from you?"

"Did she tell you why you should stay away?" asked Jimothy, partly from curiosity and partly to lead Ricky towards the answers he sought.

"Politics," he said with disgust.

"She told me you argued with her. Surely she must have said more than just 'politics'."

"She said there was a potential threat against current laws—laws affecting employment, privacy, property, personal freedom...Magdalene's tits!" he exclaimed. He spun around, splashing tea on the floor. "How thick am I? This is the same damned disagreement I had with the dons when I was at university! Those tight-assed prigs!"

"Your mother said almost the exact same thing."

"I love my mother," Ricky stated firmly. He frowned and sat heavily on the bed, setting his nearly empty mug on the floor beside him. "But that doesn't explain who jumped you or who their boss is."

"Logic would suggest they're working for someone at the university."

"But that's leagues away. Eight days hard ride. Twelve if you want your horse to survive it. You only got here a couple of days ago. They wouldn't have any way of knowing you were here, let alone that you and I are trysting." He frowned in thought. "You said they said their boss sent them."

"That's right."

"That implies that they're working for someone here in the city. Someone with connections to the university but who has the authority to act without having to consult superiors." Ricky paused, frustration written on his handsome face. "I have no clue." He looked hopefully at Jimothy. "You can't possibly shed any light on it, can you?"

"I'd be happy to if only I had a lantern. I don't even know if that letter came from this Don Savion you mentioned or someone else."

"I don't suppose it makes much difference if it was from a friend or an enemy, really," Ricky said analytically. "Either way the news isn't good." He sat thinking, a small frown furrowing his brow.

Jimothy finished eating and downed the last of his tea. "I wish I knew what to tell you." He yawned again and blinked his eyes several times. He was unaccountably sleepy. *Must be the good food,* he reasoned.

"I wish you did too," joked Ricky mirthlessly. He looked at Jimothy and his eyes softened. "I'm so sorry this happened to you."

"It's not your fault any more than it is mine," Jimothy assured him. "I don't blame you."

"But I blame me." Jimothy was about to protest, but Ricky held up a hand to stop him. "I understand, but even if you weren't my lover, you'd be my responsibility because this happened to you in my city."

"You're not in charge yet. And even if you were, you can't take the burden for everything bad that happens."

"I know that, but it's still my responsibility. I have to see it that way if I hope to rule Kanbec even half as well as my mother and my grandfather before her."

Jimothy nodded thoughtfully. "All right. I think I understand that as much as anyone not of the ruling class can. Wand'ring Minstrels have responsibilities, too. Things that have nothing to do with singing songs and delivering the mail. The mail!" he exclaimed, eyes widening. "Blast! I still haven't dealt with those last two letters. I have to do that today."

"Let me," offered Ricky.

"I can't. That's entirely against all the rules."

"Who are they for, then? If I can find the people, I can send them to you here. You won't have to go out."

"I don't mind going out," Jimothy said, frowning just a little. He sensed there was more to this than what was on the surface. "What are you doing?"

"Nothing," said Ricky, and Jimothy knew he was lying.

"Bullshit. What are you doing?" he repeated.

"Look," the lanfis tried another tactic. "Do you really want to go wandering around the city looking for these people? I mean, physically do you really feel up to it?"

"I'll manage," he insisted. Then he yawned again and tried to focus on Ricky, but the lanfis was looking distinctly fuzzy.

"No, you won't. The Sisters would tell you the same. You need a day to heal before you start Wand'ring again, even just around the block." Ricky's expression grew guilty and apologetic at once. "That's why I put some medicine in your tea."

"You—?" But he was interrupted by another huge yawn.

"I'm awful, I know. And I'm sorry. I had to."

The lanfis rose and moved to Jimothy, who swayed a little in his seat despite all his attempts to stay upright. "You...prick," he muttered as Ricky caught him before he could fall.

“I am,” he agreed, half carrying Jimothy to the bed. He used one hand to push the blankets out the way. “I’m an utter prick and I tricked you.” He helped Jimothy into the bed and pulled the covers up over him.

“Damn you.” But the curse lacked conviction. Unable to stay awake any longer, Jimothy fell into a deep, heavy sleep.

✧

It was twilight when Jimothy woke again. He was alone in the room, but someone had cleared the breakfast dishes and left a covered pot and a kettle on the brazier. There was something new on the table, too, which he couldn’t immediately identify. He pushed back the covers and sat up, relieved and pleased to find the movements so much easier than they’d been that morning. He stood and waited until he was certain he had his balance, and then cautiously crossed the room to the chamber pot. It had been emptied while he slept and someone had brought a bucket of hot water and placed it next to the brazier. He was grateful the amenities were taken care of, but there was a part of him that felt strange at the thought that someone—more likely several someones—had been in and out of the room while he slept.

He used the facilities and then checked the small containers on the table. One held tea leaves, the other honey, and there was a small pitcher of milk that he hadn’t noticed before. A cautious peek under the lid of the covered pot on the brazier released a steam rich with the scent of vegetables, meat and herbs. He let the lid back down, keeping the warmth inside until he was ready to eat. He spooned tea leaves into the simmering kettle and then went to clean himself up. He moved slowly and cautiously, not wishing to cause himself any unnecessary pain. Eventually, he managed to sponge himself off with soap and hot water and dress himself. He opted not to try shaving; it simply wasn't worth it under the circumstances.

His tea was well steeped by the time he was dressed and ready to eat. He poured some into his mug and used a splash of water to weaken it. Then, using a towel to protect his hands from the heat, he took the pot from the brazier and set it on the table.

He ate slowly, enjoying the flavor and the rare opportunity to dine alone in a quiet place. Eating alone was commonplace when he was traveling, but it was a rare chance to have a roof over him and hot meal that he hadn't cooked himself over an open fire. It gave him a chance to think. His first desire was to think about what had transpired between Ricky and him—not the illicit drugging of his tea, but the unexpected look into the lanfis's past and the cozy way they had fit together in sleep. The comfort of the other man's presence had gone beyond the merely physical. The sensible part of Jimothy's mind knew that the complications implicit in the situation were tremendous. For the moment, he had the luxury of ignoring that truth.

He reluctantly left that line of thought and concentrated instead on something else entirely. Something far less pleasant. *Why attack me?* He knew part of the answer: he was the lover—the male lover—of the lanfis and apparently the university took issue with that sort of relationship. Lanmere Fallon had told him that the dons were second only to her in power. Was it possible they had enough power to overthrow her and her heirs? Did they really have the support for that? He found it doubtful, considering what he knew of Kanbec and what he'd seen of the citizens of the capital city, but nothing was impossible if one knew the right moves to make and the right political points to press. It was possible the dons had already won over the rest of the city of Korpi to their way of thinking and were planning a coup. In which case, Jimothy was little more than a convenient political pawn.

Someone in Couvin had to be working for the dons, and that someone must have a great deal of power to act autonomously. Then another possibility occurred to him. *Unless they have* cheel *talents that allow them to contact the dons.* The idea was unexpected and more than a bit disturbing. Among the many ways *cheel* abilities manifested themselves, mindspeaking over short distances was probably the most common. He knew it existed in the Rosslyn family. But to have the power to communicate over such a distance as would be required in this case was impossible. Wasn't it?

He shook his head and put the whole idea aside. "Worry about it later," he told himself. "Right now you need to go to work." He rose, finding each movement easier than the last, and rinsed out his mug, drying it so it was ready to receive any coins he might earn that evening. Then he took his guitar from its case and left his room, careful to lock the door behind him.

The door to room eight closed a moment later, and the tavern's only other overnight guest emerged. As always, she was dressed in what Jimothy thought of as her signature color. "Good evening," he said. He allowed her to pass him and precede him down the narrow stairs.

"Good evening," she replied in a brassy voice that only avoided unpleasantness due to its low pitch. As it was her tone was a deep alto, low enough to mitigate the sharpness. "Are you feeling better tonight?" she asked solicitously as they descended.

It was then that he remembered hearing that distinctive voice in yesterday's chaos, the offer of help when he'd entered in such dramatic fashion. *So that was her.* "I am, thank you," he replied. "I hope the commotion wasn't too upsetting for you and the other patrons."

"Not as long as you're well. There are few things of more value to me than a talented musician."

Jimothy wasn't quite sure what to make of her reply. It carried the weight of truth, but he felt there was something he was missing. He said again simply, "Thank you."

She smiled at him and, without another word, passed through the curtain into the bar. He waited a moment, contemplating the brief encounter.

"Jimothy!" Maeve exclaimed as she came up behind him. He turned to face her and saw the worried frown that furrowed her brow. "Should you be up? How are you feeling?"

"I'm sore but living," he replied. He gave her a lopsided but reassuring smile. "I'll be fine, thank you."

"You're not planning on performing tonight, are you? You should take the night off."

"I've already missed one night of work. I can't afford to miss another, and I dare say your own coffers would appreciate a bit more padding." She didn't deny it and he went on. "I'll take it easy, I promise. I'm not up to singing anything tonight, but my hands are fine for playing."

"Hm." She looked doubtful, but she didn't argue further. "All right. But if you need a break, you take a break. Don't let Japheth or me or the crowd bully you into more than you can handle tonight."

He smiled again with the undamaged side of his face. "You'll make a great mom," he said sincerely. "Your child is very lucky."

The hostess flushed, surprised. "Thank you."

He held the curtain aside and followed her into the bar. He

scanned the room swiftly. Roughly a score of customers peopled the booths and tables. *Barely half full,* he frowned internally, and then relaxed. *But it's early yet.* His eyes continued their assessment. The Coral Woman, as Jimothy thought of his next-door neighbor, sat in the corner booth as seemed to be her wont. It was the same spot she'd occupied each time he'd seen her in the bar. A goblet of wine stood on the table before her and one pale hand was wrapped loosely around its stem. He allowed his gaze to move on. He looked to the bar itself and the three people seated at it—Vashti and the old regular, seated on their usual stools, and a man in rough clothes and a workman's cap nursing a pint of ale. Jimothy thought him familiar, but he couldn't see the man's face from where he was. Not wanting to be caught staring, he moved to his post by the hearth, but the angle was worse from there. *I know I've seen him before.* Then suddenly he remembered—it was the man he'd briefly mistaken for Ricky. He'd stood at the bar just the other night wearing that same cap and coat.

Something's not right about that man, he thought. Was it something about his clothing? The way he moved? Jimothy couldn't put his finger on it. He shook his head in frustration and gave up trying for the time being. There would be time later to ponder the oddities. As his gaze traveled back over the crowd, he inadvertently caught the eye of the Coral Woman. She took a sip of her wine and looked at him with an inscrutable expression in her large, hazel eyes. He nodded, acknowledging that she had indeed caught him looking, before he broke the connection and leaned over his guitar. He checked the tuning, adjusted two of the strings and began to play quietly. He would supply only background music tonight or maybe one or two dances if the crowd seemed inclined.

He continued to allow his gaze to rove over the crowd as he played, as ever watching those who watched him. There was a chance that someone here was connected with the men who had attacked him. *Not that I have any way of knowing who that might be.* He watched fruitlessly for something that might give that someone away.

Inevitably, his eyes were again drawn to the Coral Woman. Even if she weren't so puzzling, her bright attire would have attracted his eye. This time, though, she seemed unaware of his attention. In fact, she seemed unaware of anything as she stared blankly out the front window. Something in the woman's unfocused gaze made Jimothy shiver. It was so unlike the keen look she'd displayed only minutes ago. He forced himself to look away, across the room...to the strange and suspicious fellow at the bar. What was it about the man that bothered him so much? Before he could ponder the question further, the fellow tossed some coins onto the bar and rose. He looked about the room. Jimothy observed him as he moved quickly to the door, his eyes flicking to the Coral Woman as he passed her booth. Jimothy followed the brief glance and saw that she was once more clear-eyed. Rather than be caught again, he immediately shifted his focus to Vashti at the bar. She smiled at him and he nodded back at her pleasantly.

The rest of the evening passed calmly and quietly. The tips he received were fewer than on previous nights, but when he counted them up later they were more generous. *Maybe there's something to be said for the battered look,* he thought wryly. *Not that I plan to sport it often.* He knew he was a bit vain, perhaps more than just a bit. He didn't mind. There was nothing wrong in taking pride in one's looks—especially when that little extra care of his appearance won him so many amicable encounters. Jimothy smiled over his guitar at the memories.

"You look pleased with yourself," a quiet voice said from nearby. Jimothy looked up and his smile widened.

"Don't take this the wrong way because I'm really glad to

see you, but you shouldn't be here."

Ricky shrugged. "I've been here for nearly an hour and this is the first time you've noticed me. I know how to be unobtrusive. Besides," he went on, glancing around the essentially empty room, "everyone's gone home, and Japheth is locking up."

Jimothy looked around, surprised to find it was true. *I must have been lost in the music,* he thought.

"No one here will say anything," Ricky continued. "They certainly won't give us away to Mother."

"Do you really believe that she doesn't know you're here?"

He shrugged again. "I know that she didn't like telling us to keep away from each other."

"What does that mean?"

"It means that even if she does know—which I admit isn't unlikely—she won't say anything about it as long as neither of us gets into any more trouble."

Jimothy shook his head pensively. "I still think it's pretty risky."

"Do you want me to go?"

Jimothy considered the question before answering. Did he want him to go? *No,* he knew instantly. Did he think that he should? This time the answer was a more reluctant *Yes.* He looked up from his guitar, about to tell Ricky to leave, and caught the expression of barely concealed disappointment on his face, as if he anticipated dismissal. "No," he found himself saying without hesitation. Then his professional mind forced him to add, "I think you should leave, but I really want you to stay." Ricky smiled delightedly and a little salaciously. Jimothy forestalled what he might have said with a raised hand and a lowered voice. "Save it for upstairs."

"Right."

Jimothy stood up from his seat and groaned involuntarily, garnering him looks from Nita who swept the floor and Maeve counting bottles behind the bar. The hostess frowned. "I told you not to overwork yourself tonight, Jimothy," she scolded.

"I've just been sitting too long, Maeve," he said tiredly. "Sore muscles tighten up if you don't keep moving."

"I can help with that," piped up Vashti from her usual spot at the far end of the bar. "But I see you already have a helper." Her expression was a mix of ribald jealousy and wry amusement.

"It's all in the timing, Vashti," Ricky said. "I met him first."

"Fair's fair," the night keeper agreed good-naturedly, "but the next Wand'ring Minstrel who comes through town is off limits to you. Got it?" She looked fierce and stern before bursting out laughing. "I never can take myself seriously at these moments. You gentlemen have a nice night. Some of us have work to do," she added, scowling severely, and then ruined the effect by laughing again.

Maeve held open the curtain to the back and waved the men through it. Her own stern expression was more serious than her sister's-in-law. She pointed a finger at Ricky. "You let him sleep, do you hear me?"

"You just want him healthy so he can bring you more coin," teased Ricky.

"Darn right I do and you want him healthy for your own reasons, so don't go arguing with me. Scoot!" She shooed them off up the narrow stairway.

"She's going to be a terror as a mother, isn't she?" whispered Ricky when they were out of hearing range of the hostess.

“Yes,” agreed Jimothy, “but in a good way.”

Ricky chuckled at that. “I’m not entirely sure what that means, but somehow I think you’re right.”

Reaching the second floor, Jimothy unlocked the door to his room and they went inside. “Wait,” he said, stopping abruptly in the center of the room. “Something’s not right.” Placing the guitar and mug of coins on the bed, he moved carefully around the room. Light from the hallway spilled through the open door, allowing him to reach his own lantern and light it.

“What is it?” Ricky asked. He stepped to one side of the door to let in more light from the hall.

“I’m not sure.” Jimothy spoke softly. Holding up the lantern in one hand, he turned in place and assessed what he saw. The unmade bed was as he’d left it plus the things he’d just put there, as was the detritus of his dinner. The thin skin over the top of the small pitcher of milk insisted nothing on the table, at least, had been disturbed in his absence. His eyes landed on the clothes chest. “I left that open.”

“It could have fallen shut,” offered Ricky in a quiet voice.

“It could have, but I don’t think so.” He looked at the other man. “Look at the door lock. Does it look all right?”

“Give me the light.” Jimothy brought it to him, held it up. Ricky knelt and examined the lock and handle carefully. Several moments ticked past in silence. Eventually Ricky shook his head and rose. “I can’t see anything odd, but with old locks like these, who knows? It could’ve been picked and relocked for all I can tell.”

“Close the door and lock it,” ordered Jimothy softly. Ricky did as he was told. Jimothy crossed to the chest and knelt awkwardly before it, bruised knees protesting. He hissed a breath and Ricky stepped quickly to his side. “I forgot I’d slammed my knees into the cobblestones yesterday," he explained to assuage Ricky's concern. "Take this, will you?" He handed over the lantern. "I'm going to open the chest."

"Don't." Ricky's sharp tone made Jimothy pause. "Whoever broke in might have booby-trapped it."

"After what you just said, you're that sure someone broke in?"

"All right. Call it paranoia if you like, but it's healthy paranoia so just be careful."

Jimothy nodded and looked around the edges of the lid. Then he pulled his sleeve over his hand and ran a feather-light touch around it. The fabric caught on neither ordinary wooden splinter nor more sinister hidden trigger. He shook his head. "I can't find anything."

"All right. Be careful."

"Stand away." Their eyes met in a challenge. "You called it healthy paranoia, didn't you, my lord?" Jimothy used the honorific as a deliberate reminder. Ricky nodded and backed away as far as the small room allowed, an unhappy expression on his face. Jimothy opened the lid cautiously, but to both men's relief nothing untoward occurred. "Hold up the light." Jimothy methodically searched the chest for a sign that anything was missing. His heart beat quickly in worry. He had so little, there really was nothing worth stealing. His only possessions of any monetary value were his guitar and its case. The former he'd had with him downstairs. The latter was where he'd left it on the floor by the bed. What could anyone have wanted? What could they have been looking for?

"Could they have been after the letter you gave to Mother?" asked Ricky, his quiet question breaking the rhythm of Jimothy's increasingly frantic thoughts.

"Possibly," he answered, glad for the interruption. "Or

perhaps they were after her reply."

"She hasn't replied yet. ... Has she?"

"No. But they wouldn't know that."

Eventually, with everything piled neatly around him on the floor, Jimothy shook his head. "It's all here—not that there's much." He looked around at his meager belongings. "It would be easy to tell if something were gone." Even his folded bit of parchment containing his abortive attempt at a new love song was there. He began putting it all back, starting with the pages. He didn't want Ricky to see them yet.

With everything put away, he closed the chest and leaned heavily on it to rise. Ricky reached out his free hand to help him up. "Thanks. I feel like an old man."

"You know," Ricky said, placing the lantern on the table, "I still owe you that backrub. You could collect now if you like."

Jimothy was strongly tempted, but shook his head. "My ribs are so sore I don't think I can hold myself upright much longer tonight, and lying on my stomach just sounds like a bad idea right now."

"I suppose you're right." Ricky sat on the edge of the bed and looked around, frowning. "Why would someone break in and not take anything?"

"Why would someone mug me without stealing my money?" Jimothy sat next to him. "Who could have gotten up here this evening?" he wondered aloud.

"Anyone going to the privy would have had the opportunity."

"But would that give someone enough time to come all the way up here, pick a lock, search a room, relock the door, and come back down without anyone wondering?" Jimothy shook his head.

"It is unlikely," agreed Ricky.

"Besides, there are people coming and going from the kitchen constantly. Surely someone would have spoken up if anyone headed upstairs without permission."

"They could have slipped in between the staff. Or it could have been another guest," mused Ricky as the idea struck him.

"Could be. Seems more likely, too, doesn't it? And there's only one other guest." Jimothy fought back a yawn. His mind was spinning, but his body was about worn out. "At least, as far as I know," he added wearily.

"We'll ask Maeve or Japheth in the morning. You should get some sleep," advised Ricky, concern in his voice. He wrapped a warm arm around his lover who happily leaned into the embrace.

"When there's the chance someone could break in while I'm asleep?" he argued half-heartedly. "I'm not sure that's such a good idea."

"You can't stay awake all night, and there's no real evidence that anyone was in here."

"What about that healthy paranoia you invoked earlier?"

Ricky shrugged, admitting stalemate. "All right," he admitted. "Still, I'd rather you not be alone tonight. I'll stay. I'll have Nita bring some strong tea to keep me awake."

"No." Jimothy shook his head and sat up. "I'm not the only one who needs some rest. I see those dark circles under your eyes," he said, his tone almost scolding. "You should go home. Get some sleep. If the woman in the next room really did break in here, she didn't find anything. There's no reason for her to try again."

"Except maybe to finish what those thugs started," said Ricky darkly.

Jimothy shook his head again. "They did their job, and she won't hurt me. But you–" He hated it, but it had to be said. "There's no guarantee you'll be safe if you stay here tonight." He stood up slowly and, as they talked, he carefully put away his guitar and transferred his night's earnings from his mug to his purse.

"What makes you think you're safe from her?"

"Something she said earlier tonight. She said that a talented musician was valuable to her."

"And you believed her?" Ricky challenged.

Jimothy met his lover's doubtful, worried gaze. "I couldn't tell you why, but I do believe her, yes."

They stared at one another for several moments. Ricky was the first to relent. "All right. But I'm not leaving you here alone." Before Jimothy could argue, he went on. "I have an idea." He rose and took the chair from the table, lodging it carefully under the door handle. Next, he took the bucket of water from beside the brazier and placed it about a foot to one side of the chair, in the path of anyone who might be hoping to sneak into the room. "Satisfied?"

Jimothy nodded, yawning. It was a stop-gap solution at best, but he was too tired to argue any more. "I suppose it'll have to do."

"Good. Do you need anything before we turn in?"

"No." He wearily pulled off his tunic and shirt and couldn't hide the wince that flashed across his face as he did. "Do not offer me any medicine," he commanded before Ricky could even open his mouth.

"I wasn't going to," he protested, but it was clear from his expression that he was lying. "Sit down. Let me help you." He crossed to the bed and knelt, pulling off each of Jimothy's boots and setting them to one side.

Jimothy wasn't such a fool that he didn't appreciate the help. "Thank you. This is familiar." A little smile tugged the corner of his mouth.

"Yeah. Isn't it, though?" Ricky looked up at him with a warmth in his pale eyes that was completely unlike the fiery flashes Jimothy had seen there before.

Jimothy stood once more, leaning against the bed to keep his balance. He really was exhausted and the fact annoyed him.

"You're frowning," said Ricky, removing his tunic and shirt and tossing them aside.

"I'm annoyed."

"About what?" He pulled off his boots and set them next to Jimothy's.

"It doesn't matter." Jimothy hated being helpless. *And helpless is exactly how I feel.* He undid the lacing of his pants, but strong hands reached out and stopped him. He met Ricky's blue gaze, and the lanfis smiled.

"Let me." He undid the laces the rest of the way and slipped his hands inside the waistband. He pushed the breeches down, running his hands warmly over Jimothy's hips and down his legs as he did so. "Lean on me." Jimothy put a hand on Ricky's shoulder, lifting his feet one at a time so Ricky could slide his pants off over them.

Then he was naked before his kneeling lover. His memory of the last time Ricky had knelt before him rushed to his mind as blood rushed to his penis, making him hard and hot. He was suddenly very alert.

"You're not so terribly tired, then, I see," said Ricky softly, smiling up at him.

"I am," contradicted Jimothy, "but you seem to have this effect on me." Ricky's smile widened and he took his lover's erection in one hand, causing it to jump with anticipation. He chuckled and licked the tip playfully.

"Do you want me to?" Ricky asked. "Because I'd be more than happy to."

Jimothy wasn't about to lie. "I do, but I think if I came on my feet right now, I'd collapse."

"Better to just sit down in that case." Ricky stood as Jimothy sat on the bed, pushing the blankets back. Ricky took a moment to remove his pants, releasing his own throbbing cock from its fabric prison. Already the end was slick.

"You are beyond sexy," Jimothy stated fervently. "I want to taste you."

"Are you sure?"

Jimothy nodded once.

"Move back." Jimothy shifted back from the edge a little and Ricky knelt on the mattress, knees straddling the seated man's thighs. Ricky frowned slightly. "How's your jaw? Don't hurt yourself."

Jimothy couldn't help but chuckle. "You're about to trust me enough to put your cock in my mouth, and you're worried about me getting hurt. That's so incredibly sweet that I think you're actually even sexier than you were a second ago." Ricky looked down at him, and even backlit by a single lantern, Jimothy could see he was blushing. The blush ran down his neck all the way to his chest.

"I don't know what to say."

Don't say anything. Just trust me, Jimothy answered silently, wondering if he would be heard. Then Ricky smiled and he knew his message was received. Ricky placed his hands on Jimothy's shoulders for balance, and Jimothy put one hand on Ricky's hip, taking his hard penis in the other. He massaged gently, eliciting both a moan of pleasure and a dribble of pre-ejaculate from the other man. He licked at the slickness, tasted salt and sweet, and then ran his tongue in a circle around the silky tip.

"Mmm," moaned Ricky again. He looked down and they locked eyes. "You know I like to be able to see everything," he whispered.

"I know." Jimothy opened his mouth and took just the tip of Ricky's cock inside. Little by little he worked his way up the shaft, lips curled over his teeth to protect the silken skin. Too soon he was forced to pull back. The ache in his jaw was stronger than his drive to continue. He looked up at Ricky apologetically and shook his head. "I'm sorry. I thought I could, but... It hurts."

Ricky held his shoulders in both hands, sat down so he was on Jimothy's lap, and kissed him tenderly. "It's all right. I'd have been surprised if you could manage it, really. Delighted," he added with a smile, "but surprised. Here. Lay down." He shifted off of the bed so Jimothy could turn and stretch out on his back with his head cushioned by pillows. Ricky laid down beside him. Careful of Jimothy's bruises, he ran gentle hands over the supine man's lean, naked body. He leaned over and kissed him again.

This was something Jimothy could still manage—at least in short spurts. He opened his mouth and Ricky took the cue seamlessly, running his tongue along Jimothy's teeth and then using it to tickle the roof of his mouth. His already sensitized groin tingled and tightened, his hardness leaping at the surprising sensation. When Ricky released him, both men were smiling and Jimothy's eyes were wide.

"That was...unusual."

"Good unusual?" asked Ricky, a hint of concern in his

voice.

"Very good," Jimothy reassured him. "I've never had anyone do that before. It tingled."

"Right down to your cock, I hope." Ricky reached a hand down and took hold of him, rubbing his thumb over the wet, slippery tip. "It does that to me."

"Yes," agreed Jimothy, suddenly at a loss for words as the other man's hand worked slowly, toyingly up and down his prick.

Ricky leaned in again, this time to whisper in his ear. "Come inside?"

"Uh-huh. I..." He caught his breath as fingers snaked down and fondled his scrotum. "I have some of that...stuff...you had before."

"Do you?" An excited smile was evident in Ricky's voice.

"Yes. I...went shopping the other...morning."

"Where will I find it?" The words were a bare murmur that vibrated against Jimothy's ear.

"In the chest. On top. I...left it there when I repacked it. Just in case."

Ricky leaned back enough so that they could look each other in the eye. "I like the way you think, Minstrel-mine." He released Jimothy's erection and slipped off the bed, padding across the room to the trunk. He bent over and Jimothy was sure it was intentional as it gave him a fantastic view of Ricky's round, firm ass and his family jewels dangling beyond it. His cock bounced impatiently and he took hold of it, inhaling deeply. *Hang in there,* he told himself. *It's so worth the wait.* Then Ricky turned and flashed a grin.

"Found it." He opened it as he crossed the room. "Are you comfortable? Pillows all right?"

"Yes. Everything is lovely, thank you," replied Jimothy in a mix of amusement and impatience. He released his hold on himself and beckoned Ricky over. "Now come here so I can fuck you."

"Oo!" Ricky said coyly. "Tough talk considering the position you're in."

"I may be bruised, but I'm hardly an invalid." Quick as a flash, he reached out a hand and pulled Ricky to the side of the bed. He pushed himself up on an elbow. It hurt, but he fought to hide it. He wasn't going to let this opportunity slip away. He met Ricky's gaze and said in a husky tone, "I can still give you a ride you won't forget."

"I bet you can." Eyes alight with desire, Ricky knelt on the bed and straddled Jimothy's thighs once more. He took some of the salve on his fingers and then set the jar aside with the lid. Moving with deliberate slowness, he rubbed fingers and thumb together, warming and softening the stuff. He spread it first on Jimothy's waiting cock, rubbing the slick from the tip into the ointment. Certain the job was well done, he reached between his own legs and slipped two fingers into his anus. Jimothy saw pleasure spread across Ricky's face and more ejaculate leaked from his aching cock. Ricky lowered himself enough to brush his erection against his lover's. Both men shuddered with delight.

Ricky's keen blue eyes seemed to stab into Jimothy's dark ones. "I'm ready. Are you?"

"More than ready," affirmed Jimothy.

Ricky removed his hand, used it to grasp Jimothy's prick and guide him in. Jimothy almost whimpered at the intensity of the sensations—hot, cold, slick, tight. After the pain of the day before, this pleasure was what he needed. Physically and emotionally, he craved this sensation of life pulsing through and around him. He put his hands on Ricky's hips to help steady him as the lanfis rose languidly up and plunged down again. They repeated the motion again and again and each time Jimothy thought he would lose control, but Ricky was careful and clever, pulling up just far enough to keep his orgasm at bay before descending on him once more.

"Enough is enough," growled Jimothy hungrily. He grasped Ricky's cock in one strong hand and looked up at him, his expression intense. Ricky grinned back lasciviously, blue eyes alight with ardor. Arching his hips up as his lover came down, Jimothy delved balls-deep into Ricky. Jimothy's whole body shook and his gut clenched and unclenched spasmodically. Ricky rode him hard, driving Jimothy to climax just as he reached his own heights in Jimothy's hand.

Jimothy came with explosive force, so powerfully that it made his head swim. Lights flashed behind his closed eyes and his blood rushed in his ears. He thought he cried out deep in his throat.

He didn't know how much time passed before he opened his eyes again. When he did, it was to find Ricky lounging languidly beside him on the bed wearing nothing but a thoroughly satisfied smile.

"You—" Jimothy began, and stopped. He tried again. "That was—" Words failed him.

"Mind-blowing?" suggested Ricky, pulling up the term Jimothy had used the first time they'd had sex.

"Truly and literally." Jimothy laughed, practically giggled, with glee. He knew he wore a goofy smile and he didn't care.

"I'll be right back." Ricky climbed over him, his soft penis looking innocent as it dangled between his thighs. Jimothy knew better.

"Where are you going?"

"Unless you want to sleep sticky, I'm going to clean us both up. Then I'm going to use that liniment for its advertised purpose."

Jimothy looked down at himself, saw the splatter of white liquid, further evidence of Ricky's satisfaction, on his belly and chest. "Good idea."

Ricky scooped warm water from the bucket and poured it into the washbasin. He dipped a towel into the basin and then wrung it out, rubbing the dampened cloth with the soap he found on the wash table. He returned to the bed and began to wash Jimothy's torso despite the man's half-hearted protest.

"I can do it myself," he said, although he was glad not to have to. With the heat of passion spent, so was any energy he'd had left.

"But it's fun for me." Ricky turned on a pout as effective as any smile and Jimothy willingly relented. Ricky rinsed out the cloth and turned his ministrations to Jimothy's penis, cleansing it with tender care, cleaning gently around the foreskin and all the way down to his testicles.

Jimothy enjoyed it immensely, but was too tired to react. The motions elicited nothing from his cock but a tiny, tired throb. He knew he wasn't up to any more passion tonight.

"There," said Ricky when he'd finished. "Gorgeous."

Jimothy laughed. "I can't imagine anyone's ever said that before."

"Oh, but it is," insisted Ricky. "Fucking gorgeous." He grinned and Jimothy smiled back.

"Well, now I almost believe you," he wisecracked.

"Let me wash up and I'll take care of those bruises for you." Ricky cleaned himself with more speed and less care than he'd shown his lover, but with equal thoroughness. His task complete, he looked over at Jimothy again. "Ready?"

Jimothy sighed wearily. "Yes, please." Now that their ardor had passed, his aching body began to protest the recent activity.

"Here." Ricky sat next to him and with a feather-light touch, rubbed a small amount of the spicy salve on Jimothy's jaw.

"I wish I could've done a bit more tonight."

"It's all right. Plenty of time for that some other time."

"When I'm not damaged, you mean," Jimothy commented a little bitterly.

"When you're hale and hearty." Ricky dipped up a bit more liniment and moved down to the larger bruises on Jimothy's midriff. "Tell me if it hurts." He began to rub it into the contusions.

Jimothy sucked in a breath. "It hurts," he said through clenched teeth.

"Sorry." Ricky's expression was pained and apologetic. "Do you want me to stop?"

Already the heat and cold were working, and Jimothy shook his head. "Just be as quick as you can."

Ricky followed his instructions to the letter. He finished up and rose from the bed. Finding the lid where he'd left it, he recapped the small jar and went to put it away in the trunk. "You should put a shirt on over that. It will help keep the heat against your skin."

"The one I took off earlier is fine."

Ricky found it and helped Jimothy sit up enough to get into it. "Don't you have any proper nightwear?"

"I don't usually need it," Jimothy answered as he lay down again. "On the road, I sleep in whatever I'm wearing."

"And when you're somewhere like this?"

"It's not usually an issue—with or without company. And a nightshirt is just one more thing to carry around."

"Hmm. I do see your point." Ricky blew out the lantern and climbed into the bed beside him, pulling the blankets up over them both. He draped an arm across Jimothy's chest, above the bruised area, and snuggled in close. He kissed him gently on the cheek.

Jimothy sighed contentedly. *I could get used to this,* he thought. He was unsurprised to hear Ricky reply silently.

Me too.

The hospital and city clocks chimed in pleasant concord and they drifted into peaceful, sated sleep.

✧

Jimothy and Ricky sat at a table in the bar room, eating scrambled eggs and toast and drinking hot, black tea.

"Tell me again about the man you saw last night," Ricky said between mouthfuls.

"Tell you what? I've told you everything I can think of," Jimothy replied a little impatiently.

"You said there was something odd about him."

"Yes, and I said I couldn't put my finger on what it was." He was frustrated with himself and it was coming out as anger with his lover. "Sorry."

"It's all right." Ricky thought for a moment. "Describe him to me again."

"He was average height, probably a little taller than you and a little shorter than me. He was unshaven, but both times I saw him it was only one day's growth of beard at most."

Ricky rubbed his chin, which he'd shaved that morning before coming down to breakfast. He'd offered to help Jimothy do the same, but Jimothy had declined saying he'd rather just let it grow for now. It hid his bruises a bit, and his vanity told him that was a good thing.

"What else?"

"Dark hair, fair skin—like you. Like half the people in town," he added in mild exasperation. "He was wearing a cap—again like half the men in town. Boots, a heavy coat—" He broke off, frowning.

"What is it?" asked Ricky, immediately alert.

"That coat."

"What about it?"

"I'm not sure." His frown deepened in concentration. He pictured the man in his mind's eye, recreating him in detail. His Wand'ring Minstrel training had included pinpoint accurate observation and recall skills and he put them to use now. "It was charcoal grey wool, well spun, good quality. There was a mended tear on the upper left sleeve, but..." Finally it clicked. "It was faked."

"Huh? What was faked?"

"The whole outfit. That tear wasn't a tear. It was too neat." Jimothy spoke quickly as realization came to him. "The cuffs were worn, but there wasn't any other sign of wear on it. It's likely he deliberately roughened the cuffs with a metal file or something, and used a knife to cut the fabric of the sleeve. And that fabric! That was far too finely woven to belong to your average worker."

"It could have been his best coat once, consigned to daily use after it became too worn out," suggested Ricky logically.

Jimothy shook his head. "I don't think so. It wasn't evenly worn enough. If it were, the edges of the collar and the hem would have shown some wear, too, not just the cuffs." He referred to the picture in his mind. "The boots!" he exclaimed, startling his companion. "Why didn't I notice before? His boots were very clean, almost shining. Tell me that's normal."

"I can't. Either the streets are muddy from rain or they're dusty from the lack of it, and anyone coming in from the farms would certainly be carrying dirt with them. You may be onto something."

"It's not much."

"It's better than nothing," Ricky reassured him. "It's more than we had before, and it's given me an idea."

"What idea?"

"Not yet." The lanfis shook his head. "I don't like where my mind is taking this. I'm not saying anything until I'm sure."

"All right."

Maeve emerged from the back, wiping her hands on her apron as she approached her only customers. "Do you boys need anything else?"

"No, thank you," Jimothy answered for them both.

"Wait, yes," said Ricky suddenly. "Are there any other guests here besides Jimothy and the woman in room eight?"

"As of yesterday, yes. A couple checked in early in the day. Why?"

"Just putting pieces together and hoping they all fit in the same puzzle."

"Hm." The hostess seemed unconvinced or unsatisfied by his vague answer, but she didn't pursue the matter. "All right." She nudged Ricky's shoulder in a familiar and friendly way. "Your breakfast isn't free, you know."

"I know," he replied, a small smile on his lips. He brought out his purse and opened it.

"And if you want your sheets cleaned before the usual washing day, it'll cost extra," Maeve added to Jimothy, a wicked gleam in her eyes. The men looked at each other guiltily and Maeve smirked at them. "I've known this one a long time," she said, tipping her head towards Ricky. "I suggest you make him foot the cleaning bill."

Ricky nodded ruefully. "That seems only fair," he agreed. "Here." He pulled a silver penny from his purse and handed it to her.

"I'll get your change."

"Don't bother," he said. Then he whispered in a loud, mock-conspiratorial voice, "I'm hoping I'll be invited back."

The hostess chuckled and pocketed the coin. "By the way, I sent Aren for an officer like you asked. There should be one here at about eleven-thirty."

Jimothy's eyes widened and he stared a challenge at Ricky. The lanfis looked contrite. "Yeah," he said. "I was going to tell you about that."

"Oops," said Maeve. "That's my cue." She quickly vanished into the back.

Silence filled the space between the two men as Jimothy waited for Ricky to explain.

"Yeah," he said again. "You need to tell the officers what happened. Just give them the facts of the attack, that's all."

"Why?"

"Why not?" Ricky countered.

"It won't get us anywhere bringing in the officers. If it really was a political statement—which we are both convinced it was—then they're not going to be able to help."

"That's true, but it needs to be in the public record if—" He hesitated.

"If what?" Jimothy prompted.

"If it happens again." Ricky spoke quickly. "They told you to leave town, but you haven't and you're not going to, right?"

"Right."

"So it behooves you to have the attack on their books. One attack can be written off as random, a second will force the officers to investigate."

"But I don't want them to investigate, and I can't believe you do, either!" Jimothy leaned in, backing up his point with his presence. "An official investigation will put whoever did this on alert, make them go to ground."

"Yeah, it will, but that's the point." Unintimidated, Ricky leaned forward too. "If they don't try to get to you again, we can keep doing everything on the quiet, which is fine because this is a political matter that I hope we can snuff out before it gets public. On the other hand, if—Blessed Martha forbid—they attack you again, the officers will get involved, forcing whoever's behind this to withdraw for a while. Either way, it's good for us in the end."

"Except for that getting attacked again thing," snarked Jimothy. "Reporting the first attack won't prevent a second."

Ricky looked stricken. "I know. I wish I knew how to keep you safe."

The simple statement, full of concern and caring, completely deflated Jimothy's growing irritation. He leaned back in his chair, his shoulders slumping. "I'll be fine."

Ricky gave him a mirthless smile. "Promise?"

The clocks chimed ten as Jimothy answered, "I can't promise that, but I promise I'll be careful. I can take care of myself, you know." Ricky raised a dark and doubting eyebrow. "Most of the time," amended Jimothy, "I can take care of myself. I don't travel with a personal guard, you know. I've been on my own for a while now and I'm still here."

"All right, all right." Ricky put up his hands in defeat, then let them fall to his lap. "I need to go. I'm going to catch major crap from Mother when I get home." He rose and Jimothy stood, too. "I'll come back tonight."

"Even if you have to sneak out like a teenaged truant?" Jimothy teased.

"It'll take more than that mildly humiliating analogy to stop me." They left the bar room and headed to the back door. Ricky leaned into him and they kissed good-bye. "I'll see you tonight."

Jimothy watched him until he'd passed through the gate at the far end of the garden. Someone came to stand beside him and he turned to see Japheth looking rueful.

"He's something, huh?" the host said.

"He is."

"You and I are lucky."

"Why's that?"

"If Ricky had any interest in women, you and I would both be sleeping alone."

Jimothy cocked his head curiously. "You mean Maeve?"

Japheth nodded. "She loves me. I know she does. But she's loved him longer and she loved him first."

Spoken in that way, Jimothy realized it was true. The signs were all there if one knew to look for them. "You're right, Japheth. We're very lucky."

Chapter Six

His interview with the officer was thankfully brief. They sat in Japheth's little office under the stairs where they could be assured of privacy. Jimothy restricted himself to the facts of the attack, telling the stern-faced woman the same thing he'd told Sister Martha Joan: three men, nothing stolen, no idea why they selected him. She made note of it all with a charcoal stick in the small parchment booklet she carried. She tucked a lock of sun-streaked brown hair behind one ear, nodding as she wrote.

"Where were you when you were jumped?"

"I wish I knew. I was lost. Oh!" exclaimed Jimothy suddenly.

"What is it?"

"You've made me remember something I've totally failed to accomplish," he answered sourly. "I have two letters I still haven't been able to deliver. I was looking for the city clerk's office when I was attacked."

"Hm." The woman nodded again, making another note. "Where did you start your search?"

"A produce shop between here and The Heathers. Scarlet Apple was the name over the door."

"I know it. Why were you there?"

"I went in to ask for directions. It was on my way from The Heathers back here and I figured it was as good a place to ask as any. I bought some fruit, too," he added, doubting it was relevant.

"And was it these directions that got you lost?"

"I'm afraid so. This is my first time in Couvin. I find the layout...confusing."

The woman snorted derisively. "That's one way of putting it." She looked at him and her pale blue eyes sparkled with dry humor. "I call it a particularly nasty urban kluge." Jimothy snorted a surprised laugh and the officer looked amused. "Is there anything else you can tell me?"

"That's it."

"All right." She closed her notebook and tucked it into an inner pocket of her dark brown jacket. "I'm afraid there's nothing we can do at present, Minstrel Redwing," she said, her tone both regretful and professional. "If you'd come to us right away..." She left the sentence hanging, her meaning implicit.

Jimothy wasn't about to tell her that if he'd had his way he wouldn't be talking to her now. "I understand, and I appreciate you coming to see me even after the fact."

She harrumph, apparently mollified. "I'll put this on the books as soon as I'm back at the station. If anything like this happens again, I strongly advise you to send for an officer immediately."

"I will, of course."

The woman rose. Jimothy stood with her and ushered her out to the tavern's front door. He shut it behind her and leaned heavily against it.

"Was it that bad?"

He jumped and spun around. The woman from room eight

was there, seated in the corner booth, as brightly garbed as ever although she'd chosen to do without a hat this time. *How did I not see her sitting there?* She could easily have come from upstairs while he was in Japheth's office talking to the officer, but how could he have missed seeing her sitting *right there*? He frowned internally, angry with himself for being sloppy and unobservant. It was the kind of thing that could and would get him into trouble in the wrong circumstances.

"Not so bad as all that," he replied, putting on a casual expression.

"That's good. I never much like dealing with the officers, myself. Although I suppose they're just doing their jobs."

"Thankless jobs much of the time, I expect."

"Mm," she agreed with a slight nod. "I suppose that's true."

He gave a short nod and a tight, meaningless smile in return. "Excuse me." He turned to leave.

"Are you going out today?" she called after him.

He paused and turned back to her. "I haven't decided."

"Be careful if you do," she advised. "I enjoy your music. I wouldn't want to pass another evening in this drab and awful city without it."

"Thank you." Jimothy quickly left the bar and went upstairs. "That was odd," he muttered to the empty room. He leaned his back against the locked door and wondered again what, if anything, the Coral Woman had to do with what was going on. He wondered too if he and Ricky had made the right choice not telling Maeve or Japheth about last night's possible break-in. *Could she really have broken in?* It was a disturbing idea at best, thinking his next-door neighbor was spying on him. *There are two other guests now,* he reminded himself. Two guests who had arrived yesterday. And he still didn't have any proof a break-in had actually occurred—only a feeling in his gut. Suddenly Ricky's "healthy paranoia" seemed like just plain paranoia. Feeling foolish, he shook his head. It made no sense.

No, he silently corrected itself. It all made sense somehow, if he could just figure out what pieces went in which puzzle and then put those pieces together correctly. He heaved another weary sigh and crossed the room to look out the window. The Coral Woman's words came back to him: drab and awful city. *Drab?* That truly made no sense. This was the most painted city he'd ever visited; it was one of the first things he'd noticed. Compared to her flamboyant garb, the city might seem drab, but what other reference could she possibly be using? It was another piece of the puzzle that he couldn't place.

"Blast," he swore softly. There was nothing for it for the time being. Rather than pace the room thinking too hard to actually accomplish anything, he decided he would be better off doing something constructive. As often as not he found the answers he sought by not thinking about the problem. "I have got to get those last two letters delivered."

With a firm course of action in mind, he collected the letters from the chest, tucked them into his purse and added Maeve's map and enough coin to buy lunch. Another glance out the window revealed lowering skies to the east. The rain would hit the city by mid-afternoon, if he judged the distance rightly. He pulled his cloak on and went back downstairs. He passed the Coral Woman on the first floor landing.

"So you're going out after all," she said breezily.

"A Minstrel's work is never done." His reply was deliberately vague.

"Watch yourself. There's a storm brewing."

"Thank you." He pondered the potential multiple meanings of her statement as she continued up and he continued down. *Weird. Just weird.*

He reached the bar room and found Maeve preparing to open for the lunchtime crowd.

"How did it go with the officer?" she asked.

"As well as could be expected, I'd say." He sat down at the bar.

"I'm sorry. I thought you knew Ricky had sent for them." She paused in stocking cleaned earthenware mugs from a tray to the shelves under the bar. "Clearly I was mistaken."

Jimothy looked wry. "Knowing any sooner wouldn't have changed the results." He shook his head, forcing away the last of his lingering irritation with the lanfis. "I need your expertise once again."

"What can I do for you?"

"I need another map. I made the mistake of trying to follow someone's spoken directions last time and the results...well, you saw the results."

"What do you need to find?"

"The city clerk's office. I'll be damned if I'm not going to unload these last two letters today."

She smiled and teased, "Are they weighing you down that much?"

"Only my conscience," he answered.

Maeve chuckled. "Do you have the map I drew for you?"

"Yes." He removed it from his purse and unfolded it onto the bar.

"Hang on." She popped into the back and returned a moment later with quill and ink. She turned the map to her and began adding to the small work of art.

"Maeve, where did you learn to draw and paint so beautifully?" Jimothy asked, watching the city appear like magic on the page under her skilled hand.

"It's a knack," she answered evasively.

"Ah." He gave a knowing nod. "Like Ricky's knack for going unnoticed?" he asked.

Maeve looked up at him from under dark eyelashes. "I should have known that sort of thing wouldn't bother a Wand'ring Minstrel."

"You can't do my job if you hold many prejudices or taboos."

"Do you have any 'knacks' of your own?" she asked, turning her eyes back to her work.

"None of the sort you mean."

"Neither does Japheth, although his skills at business and money management are bordering on *cheel* if you ask me. He insists not, though. Here you go." She blew on the parchment to dry the ink and then turned it to face Jimothy. "Here we are." She pointed with a finger slightly stained with ink. "You know how to get to The Heathers. Start as you would to get there, but here—" she indicated an intersection shortly before the statue of the first lanpere, "—turn left. Follow this street to here, then turn right and take the second left."

"I think that's where I went wrong before," said Jimothy thoughtfully. "I'm not positive, but I'm pretty sure I turned left there, and then left again...somewhere along here." He indicated a section of the map at the top edge of what she'd just drawn.

"Really?" She frowned.

He looked more carefully. "I think so, yes. Why? What's wrong?"

"That's just not usually a dangerous part of the city. There are neighborhoods that are more respectable, but there are others that are worse."

"Huh. If I'd had any doubt before, that just adds to the list of confirming evidence."

Their eyes met across the bar.

"They were after you specifically, weren't they?"

"Yes."

"Why? You've never been here before. You can't possibly have made any enemies in the few days since you got here, could you?" She shook her head, answered her own question. "No."

"I don't think it's anything like that."

"Then what do you think it is?" The hostess leaned forward, resting her forearms on the bar and shifting her weight from one foot to the other. Jimothy guessed it was as much to ease her back as it was out of impatience or curiosity.

"When I figure that out for sure, I'll let you know." He folded the map and put it in his pocket. "Thanks for the map and directions, Maeve. I really appreciate it."

"Just don't come back beat up this time," she said with forced lightness, but there was real concern in her eyes. "You scared my customers last time."

He gave her a small smile of apology and encouragement. "I'll do my best."

She walked to the door with him and unlocked it for the start of the business day. "I mean it," she added quietly before he could slip away. "Be careful and come back safe. I do not want to have to pick up the broken bits of Ricky's heart if anything dire happens to you."

He answered her softly, "So it's that obvious, is it?"

"I've known him a long time, Minstrel. He's never..." She paused and Jimothy got the impression that she was weighing her words, deciding precisely what she wanted to say and how she wanted to say it. "You're special to him. Don't waste that."

Jimothy took her ink-stained hand in his, looked deep into green eyes that were bright with unspoken emotion. "I won't. I promise."

She sniffed once. "Good. See that you don't."

✧

Ricky sat opposite the lanmere, who eyed him across her polished maplewood desk. He'd always had mixed feelings about this room—her Office of State. The whorls in the wood of the desk had fascinated him as a child, but as he'd grown up it was the work that covered the desk that fascinated him most. This office was a place of knowledge and power; information was gathered and disseminated here. It was also the place where he'd been brought to answer for his ill-chosen actions as a child—and today.

Fallon's face was a mix of disappointment and anger—a mood that was enhanced by the heavy, dark clouds that he could see through the window behind her. A shock of lightning flickered over the landscape and thunder rumbled in the distance several seconds later. The rain that had slacked off earlier began to fall in earnest once again, adding still more to the grim atmosphere in the room. Ricky felt like the "teenaged truant" Jimothy had compared him with so lightly, and he fought not to squirm under his mother's intense gaze. It didn't help that he was seated on a straight-backed wooden chair that even with its leather padding was arguably the least comfortable seat in the house.

"Did you think I wouldn't find out?" Fallon asked at last, her stern tone unwavering.

"No, ma'am." Short, succinct answers were best in this situation; he knew it from childhood. Yes, ma'am and No, ma'am until she decided it was time to allow him his defense. Assuming she wasn't so angry that she wouldn't hear it. He hoped she wasn't that angry. The last time she had been, he'd been ten—and unable to sit down comfortably for three days after that particular interview.

"Do you have any idea of the position in which you've put not only yourself, but your Wand'ring Minstrel?"

"Yes, ma'am." Ricky's stomach twisted in worry at her words.

"Patrick."

He swallowed his fear for Jimothy and looked at her, forcing his expression to remain carefully neutral. "Yes, ma'am?"

She sighed and Ricky could hear the frustration and weariness in it. "You're not making this easy for me—not that you ever have." The corner of her expressive mouth curved up in a mirthless quirk of a smile and Ricky responded with a contrite half-shrug of acknowledgement. Fallon shook her head. She leaned forward and laced her fingers together, resting her hands on the desk. "You're my heir, Patrick. You've been taught all your life what politics are at their core. I thought that by now you knew how to play them. Was I wrong?"

He sat up straighter. "No, ma'am."

She continued to look at him, openly appraising the picture he presented. Again Ricky had to fight not to fidget. He kept his gaze steady and his body still, although his heart pounded in his ears. He could hear the clock on the nearest bookshelf, its soft tick-tick a counterpoint to his heartbeat and amplified by the tense silence. Finally, the lanmere's expression softened and Ricky relaxed the tiniest fraction. Fallon was far from smiling, however, as she sat back and rested her interlaced hands in her lap.

"Do you have anything to say?"

Ricky considered well before answering. She knew everything that had happened—how Jimothy had become lost and the circumstances of the attack. The daily officers' report that her personal secretary received and forwarded to her had seen to that. He'd known that was a possibility, but he'd risked it anyway. It was too important to him that the attack be in the officers' records. She must also know why Ricky had gone to him, must understand how imperative it had been that he see Jimothy right away and make certain he was all right.

When he replied, it was silently. He wouldn't lie to his mother aloud, and he *couldn't* lie to her this way. *I had to go. He's too important to me to risk losing him.*

Fallon nodded slowly in understanding. *I suspected as much. I could see it in your eyes when you looked at him. I'm sorry I asked you not to see one another.*

His eyes widened in surprise at her apology, and she was quick to forestall his next thought.

Don't think that means I'm pleased with what you've done. I made a request in good faith and you ignored it.

I didn't ignore— he began in protest. She held up a hand to stop him.

Ignored, disobeyed. Use whatever word makes you feel better about it. Semantics aren't the point. She leaned forward again and her expression grew stern. *As lanmere, I could have ordered you away from him. Instead, as your mother I trusted you to do what I asked. If the dons have operatives in the city—and it seems clear by recent events that they do—then the risk to both you and Jimothy is great, together or apart. But greater, I think, apart.*

"What?" Her words startled him out of silence.

She favored him with a wry smile. "I hope I'm not so

arrogant that I can't admit when I've made an error in judgment." Her smile vanished as quickly as it had appeared. "It's clear that I can't stop you by asking, nor can I condemn you for your actions up to now. Had it been your father who was hurt, I—" She stopped short and a sad expression flickered across her face. Ricky nodded, his heart heavy in memory. Fallon regained her composure and went on. "I will not order you to act against your conscience or your heart. So it seems my choice is to treat you like an adult and trust you not to behave foolishly."

Their eyes locked across the desk, and Ricky spoke firmly. "I may be rash sometimes, but you didn't raise any fools."

"I'm glad to hear it."

Ricky left Fallon's office feeling as if he'd dodged an arrow. He made his way from the office to the residential wing of the house feeling much lighter of heart than he could have dared to hope. He'd felt only dread going into the meeting with his mother. Now he smiled to himself. She understood why he'd done what he'd done, understood why he'd had to do it. That mattered more to him than he'd thought it would.

Lightning flickered again and thunder crashed shortly after. He paused and sidetracked to look out the window at the end of the corridor. While his mood was lighter, the weather had grown heavier over the short course of his meeting with Fallon. He smiled out at the driving rain, content in the knowledge that his Wand'ring Minstrel had a roof over his head and a warm fire tonight. He headed back along the hall towards his rooms. A glance at the grandfather clock on the way told him it was nearly half-past ten. How long would it take him to change clothes and walk down to the Cat and Turtle? *In this weather...*It would take longer than if it were dry; the streets were messy and could be slippery and treacherous on nights like this. He considered and decided it was worth it to spend the night in the arms of his lover.

He hurried back to his room and quickly changed out of his embroidered velvet tunic and good breeches, trading the obviously royal clothing for more homely garb. As he laced up his old, road-worn boots, there was a knock on the bedroom door. "Come in," he called, hoping it wasn't his mother. Despite her concession mere minutes ago, his decision to go into town was impulsive and less than wise. But as he'd assured her, he was no fool. He knew how to be careful. Still, he wasn't entirely confident he would have her blessing if she caught him tonight.

To his surprise, it was Coran who entered at his call. Ricky wasn't pleased, but he was a little relieved. His brother took in his working-class garments and leapt to the right conclusion as easily as Fallon would have. He gave Ricky a disapproving look. The difference between Fallon and Coran was that Ricky didn't care what his brother thought of him. "What is it?" he asked, his tone impatient. He finished tying his laces and stood up—a clear indication that he didn't expect Coran to stay.

"A messenger came for you," Coran replied evenly. "He was in quite a rush. Seemed very concerned that this get to you, so I said I'd bring it up myself." He held out a small, folded piece of parchment. "It wasn't sealed," he added as if he expected Ricky to accuse him of opening it.

Suspicious and uncertain, Ricky frowned and took the missive wordlessly. Coran was right to suspect a challenge; Ricky would have given him one had he not spoken first. He opened the note and read it, his heart racing at the few brief lines. The handwriting was familiar even without the signature.

Ricky~

Jimothy's been attacked.

He's hurt but living.

Will you come?

Please hurry.

~Maeve

His fear must have shown on his face, because Coran's expression grew anxious. "Is it bad news?"

Ricky hardly heard him. He stuffed the note in his breeches pocket as he rushed to grab his wool cloak. He hurried to the door, and Coran followed him into the hallway and downstairs.

"Is there anything I can do?"

The lanfis stopped for a moment at the door to outside, taken aback by the tone of concern his brother's voice. "There isn't, but thank you. I have to go."

"I hope your Wand'ring Minstrel is all right!" Coran called after him as he dove out into the dark and the rain.

So do I.

✧

It was nearly five-thirty by the time Jimothy delivered the last letter in his charge. The promised rain had come shortly after he'd finished a hurried lunch, and his cloak was now near the saturation point. Lightning flashed off to his right. He counted to ten before thunder rumbled distantly. *All right. I have plenty of time to make it back before—*

Lightning flashed again, closer this time. He only made it to five before thunder cracked loudly.

Crap. He took a moment to check his map once more, silently cursing the increasing precipitation as he tried to shield it under his heavy, damp cloak. Satisfied that he knew where he was going, he tucked the precious map away once more and hurried down the street to his left, feet splashing with every step. It was still about two hours until sundown, but the heavy clouds made it dark as evening. He rushed along like everyone else forced out in the inclement weather, hood up and head down, trying to watch both his feet and the people around him at the same time. Evening shoppers clutched purchases under long cloaks. Workers heading home pulled up the collars of their coats and pulled down the brims of their caps. No one was inclined to stop and chat.

Much to his relief, he made it back to the Cat and Turtle without incident. Customers already filled half of the tables in the bar room. The fire in the hearth was fully ablaze, beating back the damp air. He smiled a greeting at Nita who was serving dinner to a small group of folks in one corner. She nodded hello back at him. Maeve called him over to the bar.

"Everything go all right?" she asked with deliberate casualness.

"Fine, thanks," he answered, understanding her completely. "Last of the letters are safely in their owners' hands and I didn't run into any old friends."

"Good. Go dry off and come have some dinner. We won't be busy tonight, but I still want you playing for those who come in."

"I'll be right back."

Once upstairs, he took a moment to visually appraise his room before removing his cloak and draping it over the chair to dry out. It looked like no one had been in or out since he'd left that morning. The usual amenities were dealt with before he'd gone out, and he had no impression of any other activity in his absence. *That's a relief.*

He toweled his hair as dry as he could and ran his fingers through it so it would finish in a reasonably tidy way. He took off his tunic and put his map away. The sleeves of his shirt were damp, but they would dry quickly enough now that his cloak no longer covered them. He wished he had another pair of boots, but that was a luxury he couldn't afford. He pulled on his spare tunic. "Good enough for now." He locked his door, pocketed the key and headed back downstairs.

"That's better." Maeve smiled at him as he sat down at the bar. "You're looking much more respectable now despite the two days of beard hiding that battered jaw of yours," she teased. "You look ruggedly handsome now rather than scruffy, like you did the day you arrived."

"Thanks," he replied wryly.

"Would you like soup and bread or mutton pie?"

"I think this sort of weather calls for soup, don't you?"

"I do. Ale?"

"Definitely!"

She laughed at the vehemence in his voice. "All right then." She waved Nita over with one hand as she took a pint mug from under the bar with the other. "Nita, bread and soup for Jimothy, please."

"Right." The girl disappeared in the direction of the kitchen.

"Which one do you want?" Maeve asked, gesturing to the taps.

Jimothy had quickly grown familiar with the small selection and chose the amber. "The Rabbit's Foot, please."

Nita returned with a bowl of steaming soup and a wedge of dark bread at the same time Maeve finished pulling the pint of slightly bitter, hoppy ale. They set down food and drink in front of him, and Nita pulled a spoon from her apron pocket. "Such service," he joked.

"It's all in the timing," quipped the hostess and the waitress at once. They looked at each other and burst out laughing.

Jimothy ate the rich, hot potato and leek soup, enjoying the warmth of it as it filled his belly. A few more people trickled into the bar, dripping water with every step. The Coral Woman appeared just as he was finishing his pint. They nodded pleasantly to each other and she crossed to the bar.

"You're back in one piece tonight, I see," she said, barely glancing at him. "Wine, please," she added to the waiting hostess.

"I am."

"I'm very glad to know it. Will you sing tonight?"

"I'm planning to. Did you have a request?"

"Something rustic," she said. "I'm feeling inexplicably pastoral today. I'd like to hear something old-fashioned and countrified." It sounded almost like an insult the way she said it, but Jimothy nodded blithely at the request.

"I'm sure I have something that will fill that bill."

"Oh good. I'm certain you won't disappoint me." To his astonishment, she looked into his eyes and smiled warmly at him before taking her goblet and going to sit at her usual table.

Maeve shot Jimothy a tight-lipped look. "I'll be glad when that one checks out," she said under her breath.

Despite the Coral Woman's unexpectedly friendly manner, he too would feel happier when she left. Her attitude in general bothered him, although she'd always been pleasant enough towards him. *And then there's my conspiracy theory...* Even he couldn't quite take his suspicions seriously. There just wasn't enough support. "Why? Has she caused trouble?" he asked, equally subdued.

"No, but I don't like her. She rubs me the wrong way."

"Can you narrow that down?" He kept his opinions to himself, wondering if Maeve's would parallel them.

"She's pretentious," answered Maeve shortly. "You'd think

she was foreign nobility from the way she behaves, but her accent is all Korpi, eh? She's no better than any of us, but you'd never think so from her attitude."

"Korpi?" echoed Jimothy, his curiosity piqued.

"Yeah. Can't you hear it?"

"I heard it, but I couldn't identify it."

"University educated, no doubt," Maeve added disdainfully.

"Ricky was university educated," Jimothy pointed out.

"Yes, but he had the sense to get out after a year or so."

"Have you always been so anti-uni?"

"No. Only since Ricky told me why he left. I had to drag it out of him, let me tell you. After that I knew it was no place for decent people."

A new thought presented itself and voiced it. "What about his brother, Coran? Did he go to the university?"

"Oh yeah." She rolled expressive green eyes. "He was there, all right. Full three years, too. I think he'd rather have stayed there than come home."

"Why didn't he?"

"What?"

"He's not the heir. Why didn't he stay in Korpi after graduating? He did graduate, didn't he?"

"He was there for three years," shrugged Maeve. "I would assume he did."

"Well, I've heard of plenty of younger noble siblings becoming professors and the like. I wonder why he didn't choose that path."

Maeve shrugged again. "I don't know. I never thought about it. I always figured the lanmere made him come home, but now that you bring it up, I can't think why. I suppose she'd want him here for something." She seemed genuinely at a loss for why anyone would want Coran Rosslyn around.

"Maybe she's training him in politics so he can be an ambassador," suggested Jimothy.

The hostess considered it, her expression thoughtful. "I suppose so. Her husband, the late Lanfar Eamon, was the Foreign Minister. Without him, I suppose Coran would be the next logical choice—but only because it's traditionally held by an immediate family member. If it were up to me, I'd break that tradition. It's not like we've needed him to do the job since his father passed away."

"You really dislike Coran a lot. Why?"

"He's arrogant. At least..." For the first time since the subject came up, her demeanor softened. But only slightly. "I find him arrogant. I've been to The Heathers a fair few times even since leaving my parents' dairy farm, and he's always been at the lanmere's heel, never far from the center of power, so to speak. It strikes me as sycophantic."

Having only met Coran once, Jimothy couldn't confirm her view of the young man, but neither could he dismiss it. "Isn't it possible there's a more honorable motivation to his actions?"

"I guess it's possible," the hostess begrudged. "But I don't think so."

"What happened to Lanfar Eamon?" Jimothy asked, deliberately changing the subject.

"You don't know? He died several years ago." Maeve's eyes grew sad. "The top Healers from the Sisters of Martha couldn't save him. His heart was weak. Something in it didn't work right and never had. No one else knew until then—except maybe the lanmere. I mean, he must have told her, eh? He was a good man. I can't imagine he'd have kept something like that from her."

"How do you know all this? It all seems a bit personal to have come out in the sort of royal statements I'm familiar with."

"And have you found the Rosslyns to be the sort of royals you're familiar with?" countered Maeve.

Jimothy could only agree. "Good point. So they simply...told the truth?" She nodded. "How honest."

Maeve chuckled. "You seem to find that unusual."

"Unusual and refreshing, as a matter of fact."

"You know, Jimothy, you're making me very glad that I've never traveled further from here than the coast."

"Does he ever come in here?" Jimothy asked unexpectedly, surprising himself as much as he did Maeve.

"He, who?"

"Coran Rosslyn."

"Coran Rosslyn?" Maeve echoed incredulously. "Here? Not bloody likely."

"So you wouldn't necessarily recognize him?"

"I'd recognize him."

"You're sure?"

She relented. "Well, not necessarily. The last time I saw him face-to-face was at least four years ago. Still," she went on firmly, "he's not one to mingle with the working classes." Her gaze grew keen. "What are you driving at, Minstrel?"

"Have you noticed any new customers lately? For example, someone who's come in fairly often this week? Dark hair, workman's clothes? He stands here at the bar."

She frowned in thought. "Maybe. That's not a lot to go on, though. You just described a lot of people."

"I've seen him," piped up the old man at the far end of the bar. Jimothy almost fell off his seat in surprise. The fellow was such a fixture there that he'd become part of the décor to Jimothy's eyes, and he'd never heard him speak before now.

"What's that, Noah?" Maeve said.

"Fellow the lad's talking about," the old man said. "I've seen him, eh?"

"What have you seen?" Jimothy asked.

"Same as you have. Orders a drink. Stands there." He waved a gnarled hand in Jimothy's direction. "Doesn't talk, not even when you ask him nicely to pass the sunflower seeds." He looked pointedly at Maeve, who pursed her lips a little but placed a small bowl of sunflower seeds on the bar in front of him. He smiled and cracked one open with stained teeth.

"What else have you seen?"

"That's it. He drinks. He pays. He leaves."

"I know who you mean, now," said Maeve. "Dour fellow with dark eyes and a five-o'clock shadow. The brooding type, which is a shame," she added thoughtfully, "because otherwise he'd be quite handsome. What about him?"

"You don't recognize him? He's not at all familiar to you?" He was thinking of his own initial mistake, thinking the man was Ricky in disguise.

She frowned in thought. "Now that you mention it, he did seem a little familiar at first, but I couldn't tell you why." Her voice lowered as her eyes widened. "You don't think he's—"

Jimothy stopped her before she could go any further. "I don't know. Just...think about it when he comes in tonight."

"When?" the hostess echoed. "You're that sure he'll be here?"

"Pretty sure, yeah. When he is, keep an eye on your brightly colored guest in the corner, too."

"What? Why?"

"Just pay attention and tell me what you see, if anything." He was reasonably certain of a few things, but the last thing he wanted to do was make accusations against anyone without solid evidence. It would be particularly unwise of him to say anything that might bring Coran Rosslyn under suspicion when all he had to go on was an unpleasant gut feeling. "What about the two new guests?" he asked.

"What about them? They're gone."

"Gone?"

"Checked out this morning. They were only staying a night."

"Oh." *I should be glad, I suppose. I can probably throw that puzzle piece away.* Instead, he tucked it into a mental pocket in case he needed it later.

The town clocks began to chime in the distance. The Coral Woman piped up across the bar room. "Master Minstrel, when will you be entertaining us? I hope it will be soon." She put on a pout that he figured was meant to be coy or even cute, but was so obviously contrived that Jimothy found it a bit creepy. He wondered if her show was for him or for the room and decided it was both.

"I'm on my way to collect my things now," he called back affably, and rose from his bar stool. "I'll be right back. Remember what I said," he said softly to Maeve.

"How could I not?" she replied.

He popped upstairs and returned promptly with his guitar and his mug. In the short time he was gone, the man he'd been waiting for had appeared at the bar. He looked exactly as he had each time Jimothy had seen him, and like all of those previous times he was angled a little away from the fireplace. Jimothy and Maeve exchanged a brief, significant glance. Then she finished pulling a pint and set it before the fellow.

Jimothy sat at his post and quickly tuned his guitar. Choosing a dramatic classical piece, he began to play, keeping half an eye on the man at the bar as he did. All he could see was his back and a quarter profile of his shadowed face. The man didn't move beyond taking a long swallow of his ale, so Jimothy shifted his gaze casually over the small crowd towards the Coral Woman. She seemed lost in her own world, eyes focused on nothing, hand loosely draped around her wine goblet. *Just like last time.* When he reached the end of the first piece, he modulated into another seamlessly. Usually he chose not to do this because it gave the crowd no pause in which to drop tips into his mug, but he wanted to see if the tempo of the music had any effect. There was no change in the woman's expression. The man at the bar took another drink of ale.

Huh. I wonder... He was glad he'd picked a short, up-tempo piece. He reached the end swiftly and let the last chord ring a moment before stilling the strings. There was a smattering of applause and he thanked the crowd politely, but he kept his attention split between the curious pair. The woman snapped out of her reverie almost immediately. He glanced swiftly at the man. He couldn't be sure from that angle, but he got the impression from the fellow's stiff stance that he was... *What?* wondered Jimothy. *Startled? Annoyed?*

Continuing his experiment, he chose a romantic ballad—something pastoral and countrified, as requested—and began to play and sing. The man's shoulders relaxed marginally and the woman's eyes unfocused once more.

All right, he thought as he sang. *What have I proved?* The answer, unfortunately, was *Nothing.* But it had confirmed some of his suspicions. There was definitely a connection between the music and the woman's strange behavior. But was there a connection between her and the man at the bar? It was impossible to know for certain. Then, mid-refrain, Jimothy saw the woman come back to her surroundings once more. The man finished his drink and slapped a few coins on the bar. This time when he turned to go, he turned towards the hearth and Jimothy caught a glimpse of his face under his cap. Only his rigorous training kept him from missing a beat or a word as he recognized the man at last. As he'd feared, it was Coran Rosslyn. He surreptitiously watched him go, as did the Coral Woman.

That's it. There was definitely a connection there, but what was it exactly? If Coran could mindspeak like Ricky and his mother could—and Jimothy knew the chances were good, but not definite—could he be communicating with the woman from Korpi? But if so, how would she be communicating with the dons at the university? He fell back on his early supposition that their representative here would have to be acting autonomously. It was the only thing that made sense and it was all too much to ponder when he had work to do. He would ask Maeve later what she'd observed and talk to Ricky about it that night. *Assuming he comes tonight.* He was risking a lot, going against the lanmere's orders. They both were.

He forced himself to let that line of thinking drop. *Perform now,* he told himself. *Puzzle it out later.*

Later turned out to be past midnight. Although the bar was technically open for another half an hour, everyone had departed. Even old Noah turned up his collar and headed out into the wet before closing time. Nita swept the floor for the second time while Maeve polished the bar for at least the third. Jimothy still sat by the hearth, plucking out random snippets of melody, hoping for inspiration for the song he was writing. And Vashti sat at one of the empty tables knitting woolen booties for her impending niece or nephew.

"We should lock up," Maeve commented to the room in general. Then she called out deliberately towards the back, "We should lock up!"

Japheth came through the curtain shaking his head. "You never know. A late-customer might come in."

The hostess looked towards the windows, sheeting with rain, and looked back at her husband. She pursed her lips, put her hands on her hips and raised an eyebrow. One didn't need to be a mindspeaker to hear the words in her pose. Lightning and thunder punctuated her point as effectively as if she'd called it down.

"All right, all right," he relented. He crossed the empty bar room, pulling the ring of keys from where it hung on his belt. Before he quite reached the door, it opened suddenly and a soaking wet body fell through it.

Chapter Seven

Vashti tossed aside her knitting and pulled her knife; Nita let out a tiny shriek of surprise; Maeve jumped; Jimothy stood quickly; and Japheth exclaimed, "What the—?" Then the bedraggled form raised its head. "Holy shit!" exclaimed the host, reaching down to the fallen man. "Maeve! Send for the Sisters!" Maeve rushed to the back, shouting for a runner. As Vashti moved to the open door, Jimothy put aside his guitar and went to help him.

"Who is it? Do you know him?" The words were barely out of his mouth when Jimothy recognized the battered man. "Ricky! Sweet gods!" He knelt down, getting one of Ricky's arms over his shoulder as Japheth got under his opposite elbow.

At that moment, Aren sprinted past them all like a winged blur and out the open door into the driving rain. Vashti followed him outside.

"Nita, close the damn door!" the host barked, snapping the girl from her stunned daze. She rushed to shut the door as the men got Ricky to a chair near the hearth. Japheth tossed her the keys, which she caught with surprise. "Shutters!" She nodded and began covering and locking down the front windows.

Jimothy knelt in front of Ricky. He put his hands on either side of his lover's pale, wet, battered face. He held the other man's head up carefully. "Ricky? Ricky! Do you hear me? Open your eyes. Say something, please!"

One icy blue eye opened reluctantly and seemed to half-focus on Jimothy's face. The other was swollen shut, ringed with a dark purple bruise. Ricky smiled a little around a split and bleeding lip. "Heya."

"Hey, yourself," said Jimothy, almost laughing with relief. "You look terrible."

"You seen yourself lately?" countered Ricky a little breathlessly. His eye focused more and he frowned. "You need a shave."

Jimothy laughed at that, but it was tinged with hysteria.

Ricky searched his face with an intensity that Jimothy found disconcerting. "But you're all right."

"I'm fine, but—what happened to you? Are you hurt anywhere else?" He looked the other man over a little frantically, but could make out nothing through the wet layers of cloak and tunic.

Maeve returned at that moment with a bucket of hot water and towels. "Who is he?" she asked as she approached, and then froze mid-step, splashing water on her feet. "Ricky!" She rushed the rest of the way to them. "Is he all right? What happened?" she demanded as she reached them.

"We're trying to find out!" snapped Japheth, panic making his temper short.

The door opened again and Vashti stepped inside, shaking her head and dripping water onto the already wet floor. "You can't see three feet in front of you out there. We won't find anyone tonight. I caught Aren before he got too far, told him to tell the Sisters to send a Healer."

"Will they?" asked Jimothy.

"When they know who we have here, they will," Vashti said with authority.

Maeve set down her burdens and moved behind Ricky to take his cloak. She maneuvered the heavy fabric off of him with difficulty. Ricky hissed at the jarring movement. "Sorry! Sorry!" she exclaimed. She handed the cloak over to Nita who took it automatically and, left with nothing else to do, hung it on a peg by the hearth. Then she just stood there, at a loss.

"I'll go for the officers," Vashti offered, reaching for the door again.

"No!" Ricky turned towards her sharply and then clutched at his side. "Ow! Lazarus' bollocks! No officers." His words were firm in spite of the pain.

The night keeper looked angry, but didn't argue with the lanfis. "Come on, Nita." She took the waitress by the elbow. "We'll check the back," she said, getting them both out of the way.

All of Jimothy's attention was on Ricky. "What happened?" he asked again.

"I met up with some friends of yours." One of his arms was wrapped tightly around his torso and for the first time the others noticed blood seeping from between his fingers. "They were armed with more than fists this time, though."

"Gods, gods!" Jimothy exclaimed under his breath. He grabbed one of the towels Maeve had brought. "Let me see." He gently pried Ricky's hand away from his side. A clean slice had torn through his tunic and shirt and blood saturated the dark fabric, spreading out from the cut like the petals of a dying rose. He pressed the towel against the wound and swiftly it soaked up the crimson. "It's not too long. I-I can't tell how deep it is, though."

"Shit," breathed Japheth unhelpfully, and Maeve smacked

his arm.

"Go watch for Aren and the Sister!" she ordered, pointing to the door.

Again as Japheth reached it, it flew open. This time a blue-clad Sister entered with Aren on her heels. She assessed the situation with a glance. Dropping her wool cloak on a convenient chair, she set her blood-red satchel on the table nearest Ricky and knelt beside Jimothy. "Let me see," she said with authority.

"It's a knife-wound. I'm not sure how deep. There's so much blood." He was babbling and he knew it but found it hard to stop.

Ricky held up a bloody hand, thumb and middle finger spread as far as they could go. "About that deep, I'm guessing," he said through clenched teeth. He was shivering now, cold with the combination of blood loss and the rain that had soaked him.

"All right. I'll take care of him now. Move aside."

Jimothy's instincts told him to stay, but the woman's quiet command was impossible to ignore. He rose and moved a step away. The Sister worked with precision and knowledge, removing the towel and probing the wound with expert fingers. Several times Ricky hissed in pain or choked back a wordless exclamation, and each time Jimothy wanted to go to him but something held him rooted to the spot. The Sister took a small bottle from her bag and looked at Maeve. "A mug of drinking water, a knife, bandages, and blankets."

The hostess fetched a mug of water and a large knife, returning impossibly quickly. Japheth went for bandages and blankets and was back only seconds later with an armful. The Sister used a tiny dropper to add a dark liquid to the mug. Then she held it to Ricky's mouth. "Drink." He did as told, swallowing in shuddering gulps until she pulled the mug away.

The Sister's eyes landed on Jimothy. "Help me." Suddenly Jimothy could move. He closed the distance between them in a single stride. "Help me get him onto the blankets."

Japheth and Nita laid out the blankets near the fire. Ricky's good eye fluttered shut and the Sister snapped her fingers barely an inch from his nose. He started and the eye snapped open again. "Stay with me," she ordered, and again there was something in her voice that demanded to be obeyed. He nodded vaguely.

The Sister was stronger than Jimothy would have given her credit for. The two of them moved the injured man the short distance to the makeshift bed. Maeve was a step behind with the red satchel. She set it on the floor beside them. Once he was safely settled on his back, the Sister demanded the knife from Maeve and used it to cut open Ricky's tunic and shirt. She opened the soaked garments like the cover of a book, revealing moon-white skin washed with red.

"What can I do?" asked Jimothy, fighting rising panic.

"Make him look at you. Keep him awake and focused on you."

Jimothy nodded and knelt beside Ricky, taking his hand. He spoke in a soft but commanding voice. "Hey there. Hey, Ricky. Look at me."

The wounded man rolled his head to one side, turning a glassy blue eye on him. "Heya," he said with a frown. "I can't feel my feet."

Jimothy shot the Sister a terrified and angry glare. She shook her head at him. "That's the medicine. It will move up his body and I'll be able to stitch him up without him screaming. I can Heal some of the damage, but this comes at a bad time. My strength is low."

Jimothy swallowed hard and nodded once. He turned back to Ricky and patted the fading man on the undamaged side of his face. "Hey, hey. Stay awake. Why does he have to be awake?!" he hissed back at the Sister.

"Excessive blood loss; unwakeable sleep; death," she answered shortly. "Even at my best I cannot Heal that. Keep him awake." She spoke each word clearly, precisely, and forcefully. Jimothy didn't need the press of her *cheel* abilities to do as he was told.

His eyes met Ricky's fading gaze and he held it. "You still with me?" he asked intently.

"Uh-huh." A drugged, slightly goofy half-smile tugged at his lips. "Always."

Jimothy gave another half-hysterical chuckle. "That's right."

"Can't feel..." He trailed off drowsily. Jimothy squeezed his hand tightly.

"Can you feel that? I'm holding your hand. Can you feel it?"

"Ow." Ricky frowned. "Hurts."

Jimothy looked at the Sister again and immediately regretted it. The pile of bloody towels was bad enough. The blood-soaked needle and thread were an image he'd never needed to see, especially not when they were weaving in and out of the flesh of his lover. He promptly looked back at Ricky's face. It was pale even in the warm, orange glow if the fire. His dark hair clung to one cheek damply while the side by the fire dried slowly in the heat.

"Hurts," he complained again, his tone reproachful. He wiggled his fingers and Jimothy realized he meant his hand. He loosened his grip.

"Sorry. I didn't mean to hurt you." He pressed an apologetic kiss on the lanfis's cold knuckles. "Tell me what happened. Can you do that?" he asked, figuring to accomplish two goals at the same time.

Ricky's words were ragged and a little disordered, but he told his tale. "I was coming here—maybe half way here. Three guys...jumped me. They didn't say anything, but they were waiting for me. I could hear it in their heads. I was afraid and that made me careless. My own fault they noticed me."

"Afraid?" echoed Jimothy. "Afraid of what?"

Ricky seemed not to hear the question. He blinked so slowly that Jimothy feared he'd lost consciousness. Then his eye opened again and this time there was an edge of clarity in it. There was anger and sorrow there, too. "They didn't know who I was, only that I was their target. But I know who they are. I know who they work for." Jimothy had the feeling he knew what he would say and spoke before the words could leave Ricky's mouth.

"I know. He was here this evening." Ricky looked surprised and Jimothy went on quickly. "What were you doing out in this weather, anyway?" His worry made him angry with Ricky's impetuous actions. He hoped it didn't show in his voice.

"I got word you'd been attacked again. A note—I didn't stop to think." Ricky's good eye closed. "Shit. It was a setup. I should have realized it."

Before Jimothy could ask him to explain, the Sister spoke. "That's it. I've Healed what I can and physicked the rest. The wound is clean and stitched. It was deep, but it missed anything vital. You're lucky it wasn't an inch higher or you'd be drowning in your own blood right now." Jimothy took what small comfort he could in her blunt pronouncement. "I need fresh water so I can finish cleaning him up. Hot and cold."

Japheth took the bucket of bloody water and hurried to the

back. Maeve followed him and when they returned he carried two buckets of fresh water and she held a large woven basket. While Maeve collected the soiled towels in her basket, the Sister added herbs to the hot water and bathed Ricky's stitched side and his damaged face. When he was clean, Jimothy helped her get the lanfis's wet shirts out from under him. He added them to Maeve's growing laundry pile.

He held Ricky steady while the Sister placed a soft pad against the stitched wound and then wrapped a clean bandage around him. It was a careful process, but the Sister was sure-handed and made quick work of it. As Jimothy lowered Ricky back onto a fresh towel provided by Maeve, the Sister dipped a small cloth into the cold water and wrung it out. She pressed it gently against Ricky's bruised eye and looked at Jimothy, explaining and instructing. "The chill will help reduce the swelling. Change this when it gets warm." Jimothy nodded, placing his hand on the cloth where hers had been. The Sister's knees audibly cracked as she rose from the floor. She stretched her back, a pained look on her face. For the first time he realized this wasn't the young Sister, Martha Joan, who had treated him the other day, but a much older woman. "It's up to him to do the healing now."

"But when your medicine wears off..." Jimothy began, looking to her.

"I'll leave something for the pain that will follow," she assured him. She continued speaking as she tapped a brown powder into a paper cone. "Keep him warm and dry. Get the rest of those wet clothes off him for starters, and you'll want clean, dry blankets. Then keep him as still as you can."

"We can't leave him here," protested Japheth. Maeve glared at him, but he stood his ground. "Well we can't. We can't open for business with an injured man on the hearth!"

It was such a true yet absurd observation that they all burst out laughing—all but the Sister. Their relief was short-lived. "He can stay there until morning," Maeve declared, and Japheth didn't argue. She pushed the basket of water- and blood-soaked linens into her husband's arms. "I'll get more blankets and some pillows for you both," she added to Jimothy.

He thanked her, appreciating her understanding without him having to tell her that he would not leave the other man that night. The hostess went to fetch the stuff, and Japheth was close on her heels.

"That's fine," the Sister affirmed. "If he actually makes it through the night, you'll be able to move him to better quarters by morning."

Her brusqueness was too much for Jimothy. His emotions were raw and his temper flared at the woman. "Do you know who he is?" he demanded, his voice tight.

She met his glare evenly. "I do, Master Minstrel. I assure you the other Sisters are praying to Blessed Martha for his recovery at this moment, and I will join them as soon as I return to the hospital." She packed up her bag, leaving the paper cone—twisted shut at the top—on the table. "That will keep him pain-free," she said, indicating it, "but it will also keep him a bit loopy."

"Hm," chuckled Ricky. "Loopy. Loopy-loopy." He giggled.

"Like that. A teaspoon in his tea will do well. Keep him talking until you're sure he's warm through or until the medicine I gave him wears off. Then give him a dose of this and let him sleep. If you need anything, send your boy for me. I'm Sister Martha Miriam."

Jimothy looked around. He'd lost track of Aren in the hubbub. He spotted the boy curled up on the hard bench of the nearest booth, fast asleep.

Japheth returned and saw the Sister to the door. He locked it securely behind her. Maeve and Nita returned with fresh blankets and Vashti was close behind them.

Nita began putting out the candles on the tables and the lanterns that hung from the heavy ceiling beams. Japheth picked up Aren and carried the sleeping boy to the back while Vashti collected her knitting. "I'll be awake if you need anything," she said in a voice that managed to be strong and soft at the same time.

Jimothy took her empty hand and gave it a squeeze in gratitude. She patted his shoulder as she passed him. The others disappeared to the back, but Jimothy caught Maeve before she could vanish with the rest.

"Maeve, will you help me get the rest of his wet clothes off, please?"

She gave him an unreadable look, and then nodded. "Of course."

Jimothy removed the damp cloth from Ricky's eye and grimaced at the sight beneath. It would be days before that eye would open and focus clearly. He wanted to be the first thing Ricky saw when it did. Moving carefully so as not to jar their charge unduly, the pair managed to get him out of his boots, stockings, and breeches. Naked but for the bandage at his midriff, he shivered despite the warm fire beside him.

"Just another minute, sweetie," soothed Maeve. With careful maneuvering, they replaced the blanket beneath him—wet with water and blood—with a clean, soft one. Jimothy tucked a second blanket around him as Maeve put a fresh pillow under his head. Ricky grinned stupidly up at her.

"I'm in love, Maeve," he said in the loud whisper of a drunken man.

"Shh. I know, sweetie." She smiled and smoothed his hair

with a gentle stroke of her hand. She turned to Jimothy. “I’ll fetch you a pot of tea for his medicine.”

As Maeve went for the tea, Jimothy took off his own boots and tunic. He rinsed the cloth in cool water and replaced it over Ricky’s eye. Then he settled in beside him, taking hold of his hand once more.

Maeve returned and placed a teaspoon, a mug, and a clay teapot wrapped in a towel on the nearest table, next to the paper packet of medicine. “Call if you need anything,” Maeve said softly. “Vashti isn’t the only one who’ll be up tonight.”

“Thank you,” Jimothy said.

“Thanks, Maeve,” singsonged the drugged lanfis.

The hostess rolled her eyes, but the expression was warm and indulgent. “I can’t imagine what you two are going to talk about while he warms up.”

“I’m sure we’ll find something,” Jimothy replied with dry humor.

“Better you than me, Minstrel.” She disappeared behind the curtain and left the men alone at last, lying next to each other by the fire.

“You know,” said Jimothy, trying to keep his voice light, “there are far easier ways to create a romantic setting.”

“Huh?”

“You and me snuggled up together in front of a cozy fire. You could have just asked.”

Ricky snorted a laugh, and then giggled again. “I snorted. Did you hear that? That was funny!”

Despite the severity of the situation, Jimothy couldn’t help but laugh a little. It was all beyond absurd. He was laying on a bar room floor with his lover, who just happened to be the lanfis of Kanbec, who just happened to have been stabbed by someone who just happened to be working for his brother. "By all the small gods of fortune," he muttered.

"The who?" queried Ricky and then yawned. "Ow."

"No one," said Jimothy, checking to make sure Ricky hadn't reopened the split on his lip. Fortunately he hadn't.

"No, tell me."

"Promise to stay awake? I don't tell stories to people who don't listen."

It took a moment for Ricky to get his hand out from under the blankets, but when he did he held it up in a pledge. "Promise." Then he let it fall gently onto the cloth on his eye, keeping it in place.

"All right." Jimothy relaxed a little, falling into his storyteller persona with little difficulty despite the odd situation. He had to consciously remind himself to speak softly; he was so used to telling stories to a large crowd rather than an audience of one. *One sleepy, wounded, beautiful man,* he thought warmly. He took a cleansing breath and began.

"Long years ago, so long ago that no men or women walked upon the land, so long ago that all the land was a single island floating in a single sea, the world was peopled by spirits."

"Whose spirits?" interrupted Ricky.

Normally Jimothy would have scolded him for it, but in the circumstances he could abide the occasional interruption. It meant the injured man was conscious. "What do you mean?"

"People have spirits. When people die, their spirits move into other people—babies waiting to be born. Spirits don't exist on their own."

"Don't they?"

"No."

"Do they always move from one body to the next right

away?"

"No. The right new person isn't always ready for a spirit," answered Ricky in a tone of one explaining the most obvious of things to someone who was being deliberately slow.

"Then the spirits have to wait sometimes."

"Yeah. Of course."

"Where do they wait?"

"Huh? Uhh...Oh."

"May I go on?"

"Um, yeah."

"The spirits were many in number and each was different, just as humans are. No two were exactly the same, but many had things in common."

"Like humans."

"Exactly."

Ricky smiled sleepily, proud to have made the connection. Jimothy went on.

"Over time the spirits began to recognize the similarities amongst themselves and as a result began to gather in groups of likeness. Spirits of Love found one another as did spirits of Fear and Spirits of Fortune. The Spirits of Fortune found that within them there was another division—those of good fortune and of bad. Many people know them as one, as Luck." He paused to make sure Ricky hadn't fallen asleep and found the lanfis staring back at him with open admiration. He felt his cheeks flush and pretended to himself it was the warmth of the fire. "Each spirit of good fortune had an equal and opposite in bad fortune. This is how balance is kept in all the spirit realms." The city and hospital clocks struck two, their sonorous harmony muffled by distance and the continual downpour.

"Take the good with the bad," put in Ricky. "We can't

appreciate the joys without the hardships."

"Without rain and sun together, the beauty of the rainbow is forever hidden," agreed Jimothy. He thought there was more color in his lover's cheeks, wondered if it was an illusion of the firelight. But there was growing clarity in his good eye, as well. Encouraged, he went on with his story. "The spirits of each side of fortune banded their energies together. These are the two Greater Gods of Fortune. But each individual spirit maintains its own identity within the whole. They are the small or the lesser gods of fortune. They bring us dumb luck and lucky chance and—"

"And the misfortune of being in the wrong place at the wrong time," Ricky said bitterly.

"The drugs are wearing off, aren't they?"

"Yeah. I can almost feel my feet." He grimaced. "I can definitely feel the stitched-up hole in my side."

"Are you ready for some of the medicine Sister Martha Miriam left?" Jimothy started to sit up, but Ricky stopped him with a word.

"No. I mean, not yet. We need to talk about what happened before I get doped up again." He tried to sit up and failed, cursing, "Lazarus's bollocks!" He face went ashen with pain.

"Don't move!" ordered Jimothy. "You can talk lying down."

"There are other things I prefer to do when I'm lying down," Ricky groused.

Jimothy's heart warmed at this small but sure sign of recovery. Heartened, he teased, "Now I know you're on the mend. I was worried when you were in such bad shape that you couldn't manage a single sexual innuendo."

"You bring out the best in me." Ricky smiled and Jimothy was glad to see his color returning to a more normal, if still awfully pale, shade.

"I'm sure others would see it differently."

"They'd be dead wrong."

"The attack—" Jimothy began. He didn't want to draw out the conversation any longer than necessary. He wanted to give Ricky the medicine that would make his pain go away. "You said you knew who sent those men."

"And you said you knew, too. How do you know?"

"I saw him tonight, early on in the dinner hour. I've seen him other nights, I just couldn't identify him before."

Ricky's voice was heavy. "Coran."

"Yes," confirmed Jimothy. "I'm sorry."

"Why?"

"Because he's your brother. Because...I don't know. Because maybe none of this would have happened if I hadn't..." How could he explain to Ricky the sense of responsibility he felt? He could barely put it into words for himself.

"Coran's been moody and bitter ever since Father died. Mother tries not to see it, but it's there. I never thought he was..." Ricky trailed off. "The note he brought me tonight... What he said... I should have known."

"What note?"

"The one from Maeve. The one she sent when you were attacked. When the messenger didn't find me at The Heathers, he gave it to Coran. The little prick told me so himself." His venomous tone was mirrored in his good eye. "He just left out that it was several days ago." He let out a weary sigh, then sucked in a pained breath.

"You need more medicine." Jimothy was halfway out from under the covers before he'd finished speaking. Ricky forestalled him with a hand on his thigh.

"Hang on. I'm still thinking."

Jimothy waited, barely containing his impatience. The lanfis needed medicine and sleep, not more worry about a treacherous younger brother. He wondered if this was what it felt like for Ricky when Jimothy was hurt but kept refusing his medication. He resolved to be a better patient should the occasion arise again—which he knew it inevitably would in one form or another.

After a few tense and silent moments, Ricky shook his head against the pillow. "I don't know. This would have happened with or without you, though. I'm sure of that. You brought that letter from Korpi. That was written at least a fortnight ago, right?" He went on without waiting for an answer. "This was coming on its own. I just don't know how it got this far this fast. There's something we're missing." Ricky yawned and closed his eye. "I give up. I can't think anymore tonight."

"I'll get your medicine." Jimothy rose and moved to the table. He carefully measured the brown powder into a mug and filled it half way with hot tea. He returned to the makeshift bed and set down the mug on the floor beside it. "Let me help you." Ricky didn't fight as Jimothy gently levered him up into a half-reclined position against his own body. "Here." He reclaimed the mug, blew on the tea to cool it a bit, and then held it to Ricky's mouth. The lanfis used a hand to steady it as he drank. When the mug was empty, Jimothy set it aside and helped him to lie down again.

As Jimothy climbed back under the blankets, Ricky said in a slightly pouty voice, "You're not naked."

"No," confirmed Jimothy. "I'm not."

"I'm naked. Why aren't you naked?"

Jimothy gave a small, tired laugh. "One of us needs to keep his pants on tonight because you are not up to the alternative."

"I would argue, but you're right," Ricky said, disappointed. He yawned.

"Sleep now," advised Jimothy in a soft voice.

"Sing me a song." He was half-asleep already, the trauma of the night's adventure taking its toll on his battered body.

Jimothy brushed a lock of dark hair back from Ricky's forehead, continued to run his fingers through tousled locks. In a soft, tender voice he began to sing. It was nothing he had learned from his years of study, but rather a simple lullaby from his childhood.

"Sleep tight, my sweet one, I'll keep you near.

Sleep tight, my dear one, you've nothing to fear.

I'll hold you close all through the dark night.

Morning will rise and bring us new light.

Sleep tight, my darling, for I love you so.

Sleep tight, my loved one, I'll never let go."

He continued to hum softly even after Ricky's breathing deepened in sleep. He heard the clocks chime half past three before he finally drifted off to sleep, his lover cradled in his arms.

✧

Dawn had barely reached the city when Jimothy woke to Maeve's gentle but insistent shaking of his shoulder. He felt as if he'd barely slept five minutes, but when the distant clocks struck six times he knew it was more. *But not much.* He focused bleary eyes on the hostess.

"I'm sorry, Jimothy, but you have to get up. We have to get Ricky somewhere safer and more discreet than this," she said in a hushed voice.

"Why do I smell bread?"

"Baker is here. Has been since four." She answered his non-sequitur without hesitation before returning to her point. "There is another guest in the tavern, and who knows what time she'll decide to get up today? And there's always the chance that an officer will have heard about the attack and come here to investigate."

"Why—?" But then his tired brain put it together. "Of course." He sat up, carefully disentangling himself from his sleeping lover. He wasn't quite ready to wake him yet. Jimothy had woken to painful injuries a few times in his life and he didn't wish that unpleasantness on anyone—particularly Ricky. Reality, though, had other plans.

"You wake Ricky," said Maeve. "I've already sent Nita to your room with a warming pan for the bed and fuel for the brazier. Everything should be ready by the time you get there." She rose heavily to her feet. "I brought a robe to put around him for the trip." She nodded to the flannelled wool robe on a nearby chair and Jimothy realized that at some point while they'd slept someone—undoubtedly Maeve; she'd said she would be awake—had tidied up and taken Ricky's wet things along with Jimothy's discarded tunic and boots. "Your things and his are already upstairs," she said, following his gaze and his thinking. "I tried to mend his shirt and tunic, but they were beyond my skills to repair. I..." She shook her head.

He saw the dark circles under her tired eyes and said, "I'm sure he'll understand. Is it still raining out?" he asked, deliberately changing the subject. He couldn't hear the downpour as he had earlier, but that didn't mean it had stopped.

"Yeah, it is."

"All right. Maeve, I don't know how to thank you for everything."

"You don't have to, Jimothy." She looked at Ricky and there was unspoken emotion in her face. "I'll always be here for him when he needs me. Oh!" She reached into her apron and pulled out a crumpled piece of parchment. "I found this in his pocket. Jimothy, I—"

"It's the note you sent the other day," he cut her off, taking it from her.

"How did you know?" Her expression went from haunted to stunned in a blink.

Jimothy shook his head. "It doesn't matter."

"I should have told the messenger to report back, but when Ricky arrived that night I just assumed..." She trailed off, looking stricken.

Jimothy took her hands in his and looked deep into her eyes that were bright with unshed tears. He spoke with calm certainty. "This wasn't your doing, Maeve. I swear it."

She nodded and sniffed, apparently mollified. "Thank you, Jimothy." She turned and passed through the curtain into the back.

Jimothy shoved the note into his pocket and sat for a moment, marveling at the departed hostess. Then he shook himself out of his reverie and turned his attention to Ricky. The color was back in his cheeks and he seemed relaxed in his sleep. It was a shame to wake him, but there was no help for it.

He nudged the sleeping man, careful not to jar him but needing him to wake. "Hey," he said softly. "Wake up." He nudged him a little harder, hating that he had to do it. "You have to wake up, sweetheart. Come on."

Ricky mumbled something unintelligible, but to Jimothy's

sharp ears it sounded a good deal like "Blow me."

Jimothy smiled knowingly. "I will—later. First though you have to wake up and come upstairs with me."

Ricky's good eye opened a fraction. "You'd better not be toying with me, Minstrel-mine. I don't appreciate people waking me up, getting my hopes up, and then failing to follow through."

"I'm a big believer in follow-through," Jimothy assured him. "Now come on. That woman from room eight could be down here any moment, for all we know, and since I'm pretty bloody sure she's working with your brother—" He didn't have to finish the thought.

"Yeah, yeah. I get it." He pushed off the blankets enough to get an arm out from under them.

"Do you need my help?" Jimothy expected a protest and was pleasantly surprised to be proved wrong.

"Yes, please."

Jimothy rose to his knees, shoving blankets aside so as not trip either of them. He got Ricky's arm around his shoulders and gently helped him to stand. Then he turned and used both hands to hold him steady while Ricky got his feet under him. "Maeve brought you a robe." He reached out a hand and snagged it from the chair.

"She's always thinking, is Maeve," Ricky said as he slipped his arms into the robe Jimothy held for him. He wrapped it gingerly around his waist, careful of his bandages, and loosely tied the sash.

Maeve returned then to check on their progress. "Oh good!" she exclaimed, although her voice remained low. She looked to Jimothy. "Can you get him upstairs on your own or do I need to get Japheth?"

"We'll manage," Ricky answered for him. At Jimothy's

questioning look, he added, "I can make it that far. There's a railing to hold onto so I don't fall forwards. You just have to keep me from falling backwards."

"I can do that," confirmed Jimothy, who had already determined that he would carry the man up if he had to. *Although the logistics of that on the narrow stairs...*the more practical and less chivalrous part of him began. He beat the thought down.

"Good," repeated Maeve. "Then I can clean up down here."

"I'll come back and help," Jimothy offered.

"No, you won't," she contradicted. "You'll get him up to bed and you'll stay there. I'll send Nita up with your breakfasts later. Now go!"

Ricky put a hand on Jimothy's arm for support and Jimothy willingly took the extra weight. The trek upstairs was slow and tortuous, but they made it into Jimothy's room without incident. He helped the lanfis to use the chamber pot, and then got him onto the bed. Ricky shivered a little at the cool linens but they quickly warmed to his own heat. He pulled the robe about him as Jimothy settled the blankets over him.

Jimothy sat heavily on the single chair, an unexpected smile on his face.

"What are you looking so amused about?"

"I bet you wish now that you'd told me to get a room on the first floor."

It was a ridiculous, silly point and they both laughed—and Ricky promptly grimaced at the pain it caused. "Don't make me laugh, damn it." But there was no heat in his words.

"We left your medicine downstairs," Jimothy said in sudden realization. He rose quickly. "I'll be right back. Will you be all right for a minute or two?"

Ricky rolled his one working eye sardonically. "Where am I going to go to get into trouble?"

Jimothy nodded once. "Good point." He hurried out and was surprised to meet Maeve only a step past the first floor landing. She carried the paper packet of medicine in a clean mug in one of her hands and a fresh pot of tea in the other. He smiled. "Thank you."

"You're welcome." He turned to rush back up the stairs when she stopped him with a word. "Jimothy."

He turned back to her and knew his face showed more impatience than she deserved. He schooled it into kindness. "Yes?" She hesitated and it was the first time he could remember seeing her so uncertain. His expression became concerned. "Maeve? What is it?"

"You won't be pleased, and Ricky will likely be furious."

His concern grew and confusion joined it. "What's going on?" he asked more firmly.

"I sent word…" She trailed off.

"Sent word to whom? The officers?" She shook her head. His impatience was back and this time he felt it was warranted. "Then who?"

"The lanmere." She braced herself for his explosion, but he simply shook his head and sighed.

"When?"

"Just before I woke you. She's his mother," she went on, her tone defensive. "She needs to know."

"I can't blame you. Ricky won't either, though you're right that he won't be happy about it."

She nodded sadly. "I had to."

"I understand. Ricky will understand." He smiled, the expression a mix of encouragement and light humor. "He'll probably be asleep again when she comes, so you won't have to hear him complain for a while yet. She is coming, I presume?" he added.

"I can't imagine not, considering. Can you?"

"No." He shook his head. "I can't. All right. I'll tell him, just so he's prepared."

"Would you?" The relief on her face was almost comical.

"I will, but you're still taking the fall if he wants to know who sent the message to her."

"That's fair. Thank you, Jimothy."

"You're welcome."

They turned to go their separate ways, but Maeve stopped abruptly and called after him again, "Jimothy?"

He looked back down the stairs at her. "Yes?"

She stood straight and strong, her head held high. Her green eyes were bright again with guilt and he thought he saw a tinge of anger there too. "I told the messenger to deliver it into the lanmere's hands and no one else's under any circumstances."

Jimothy nodded once in understanding. "That was wise."

"I don't make the same mistake twice." She turned and disappeared down the narrow stairway, and Jimothy headed quickly back up and into his room.

Ricky roused a little at his return. "Heya. You were gone longer than I expected."

"Me too." Jimothy mixed up a dose of medication as he talked. "I ran into Maeve on the stairs, bringing this up. She had an interesting bit of news."

"What news?" asked Ricky tiredly. He once again accepted Jimothy's help in taking the medicine. It wasn't until the mug was out of the way and he'd tucked the lanfis into the bed once more that Jimothy answered.

"She sent word to your mother about what's happened." Like the hostess had before him, he braced himself for an outburst. As before, none came.

"Well...bollocks," cursed Ricky half-heartedly. "You know, she probably already has an idea what happened. Or at least that something has happened."

"What? How?"

"How do you think? She's a mindspeaker. Way more powerful than me or Coran. She'll likely have heard me when I was attacked, although I wasn't exactly sending out any coherent cries for help. And it was late. She may have been asleep and thought it was a dream."

Jimothy sat on the bed beside him, brushed a lock of dark hair from Ricky's face. "Is that how you knew when I was attacked?"

"Yeah. Maeve said she sent a note, but I never got it. No." He paused, frowning a little in his attempt to concentrate. "I got it, but I got it tonight. From Coran."

"The 'setup'."

"Yeah."

Jimothy nodded thoughtfully as several puzzle pieces clicked abruptly into place. "Can your brother mindspeak, too?"

"Yeah." Ricky gave a small chuckle—evidence that the medication was kicking in. "Duh! It runs in the family, eh? Actually," he added grudgingly, "he's better at it than me. Prick." Then he laughed again for no reason.

And without flinching, Jimothy noticed. He was pleased at this confirmation that Ricky wasn't in any pain. Then he forced his mind back on topic, determined to get what information he could before the lanfis was completely loopy. "How far can he mindspeak? Or your mother? I mean, she must have been at The Heathers last night, right? And you say she would have known from that far away that you were hurt?"

"Oh yeah." His vowels were growing longer as the drug spread through his system. "Sure. She could probably find me from that far even without the extra trauma. Trauma...trauma," he repeated, rolling the word around his mouth experimentally. "That's a funny word. Trauma."

"Yeah, it is," agreed Jimothy patiently. "And it—trauma—heightens her ability to reach you?"

"Yeah. Heightened emotions, eh?"

"How far, though?" This was the important part and he leaned forward knowing he had only a few more moments in which to catch Ricky before he'd gone completely silly from the meds. "Could she mindspeak someone as far away as, say, Korpi?"

"Korpi?" Ricky snorted. "Hardly. Why not try the moon while you're at it?"

"What about Coran? Could he mindspeak that far?"

"Coran?" One pale blue eye focused on him with effort. "Am I the one on drugs or is it you? No way could he talk to someone that far. No one can, not even with someone on the other end meeting you half way, eh?" He snorted again and then giggled and Jimothy knew it was all the sense he'd get out of him for a while.

"Get some more sleep," he said gently. "I'll be around when you wake up."

"All right. Gimme a kiss first."

Jimothy smiled indulgently and kissed the lanfis on one cheek. "Don't pout," he said, seeing the expression growing on the other man's face. "You look bad enough with the split lip and the eye swollen shut. Adding a pout would make you look ridiculous." His teasing tone belied the harsh words.

"Why do you have to keep being right?" Ricky pouted anyway and Jimothy gave a small chuckle in response.

"One of us has to be."

"Bastard," muttered Ricky without malice.

"Go to sleep."

The lanfis was nearly there already; in three breaths he was fast asleep. Jimothy indulged himself for a few minutes just watching him sleep. Ricky's face relaxed as the pain at least temporarily faded away and Jimothy smiled. Even battered and bruised, the younger man was stunningly handsome. Then his thoughts turned sad and angry. *How could his own brother do this to him?* Moody and bitter, Ricky had called Coran. It was a combination that could easily add up to jealous. *And jealousy has caused a great deal of pain all over the world, if the stories are anything to go by.*

He could too easily imagine an epic poem about a jealous younger sibling, covetous of the crown, who would go to any lengths to get what he wanted. Actually, if he thought about it, he could recite three epic poems along those lines—and four ballads. *Crap.* Put into that historical perspective it seemed all too likely that Coran was indeed after his brother's position as heir. Working with the university dons meant a built-in support network once he became lanpere. *Hiring thugs to attack me and then Ricky...* He shook his head grimly. Jimothy was sure that last night's attack was meant to kill the lanfis and he was equally certain he would be next if he stuck around. *I have a distinct feeling I'm expendable. Huh. I wonder if those guys realize that once they do their job their lives won't be worth a copper for the lot.* It was reasonable to assume that a man treacherous enough to hire someone to kill his own brother would have no qualms about then removing the witnesses of that betrayal—particularly if he could do it under the guise of avenging his brother's murder. "By the Gods of Fear," Jimothy swore under his breath. "It makes too much sense." Then he hit a brick wall. *But what about the Coral Woman?* How did she fit into it all? And how was Coran contacting the dons—assuming he was. He had to be. "Blast it!"

He paced the room, covering it in three long strides before turning and retracing his steps. He wished Ricky were awake. He needed to talk to the other man, needed him as a sounding board for all these terrible ideas churning in his mind.

There was a knock on the door, interrupting his frenetic thoughts. He stopped pacing in an instant. Expecting to see Nita or Maeve with a tray of food, he opened it—and found himself face to face with an extremely worried Lanmere Fallon Rosslyn.

"Where's my son?" she demanded, concern making her tone sharp. She was dressed well but simply, like a well-to-do merchant more than a royal ruler, but her bearing was all nobility.

"Asleep, your highness," answered Jimothy quickly, keeping his voice soft and hoping she would follow his lead. He stepped aside and she swept into the room. As she sat lightly on the edge of the bed, all vestige of her royal persona vanished and was replaced by the anxious mother.

Just as Jimothy had done last night, she brushed a lock of hair from Ricky's cheek. Jimothy felt like an intruder as he watched the intimate and tender act, wondered if he should slip silently out of the room and leave them alone. Then she turned and looked at him over one shoulder. He saw unshed tears in her dark eyes, and behind that a resolve and anger as hard and sharp as any diamond. "Do you know who did this?"

Jimothy nodded stiffly. *Greater Gods of Fortune, please don't make me be the one to tell her.* "He said it was three men, probably the same three who jumped me the other day," he said, stalling the inevitable.

She looked as though she was about to reply when she stopped as if she were listening to something. She turned again to Ricky, one hand still stroking his hair, and Jimothy realized that perhaps she was listening—to him. *Can they do that? Mindspeak one another even through sleep?* It certainly looked that way.

The silence in the room grew dark and heavy. The feeling was so foreboding that it almost eclipsed the dull morning light trickling weakly through the small, east-facing window. He saw the lanmere's shoulders and back stiffen. *He must have told her about Coran,* he surmised. He made a mental note to thank his lover later for sparing him from that decidedly unwelcome task.

The moments ticked past and Jimothy grew more uneasy with every passing minute. Again he felt like he should leave the room, let them talk in private. *Which is completely ridiculous,* he reminded himself, *since I can't actually listen as it is.*

"Minstrel Redwing," the lanmere said suddenly, startling him from his thoughts. "How much more can you tell me?"

Jimothy related the conclusions he'd reached only a short time before her arrival. "I think he must be in contact with someone at the university, but I can't think how."

Her expression grew contemplative. "You say the Coral Woman, as you call her, grows distracted and unfocused—was that the word you used?"

"Yes, your highness."

"Unfocused when you're playing and Coran is in the bar?"

"That's right, your highness."

She fixed dark eyes on him and said, “Let’s dispense with the title for the time being. It will only slow communication.”

Jimothy nodded once. “All right.”

“Good.” She fell silent again, introspective. When she spoke it was slowly, even uncertainly. “It’s possible that she’s a conduit.”

The term meant nothing to Jimothy in the current circumstances. “I don’t understand.”

“I don’t expect you to, although...” she paused and looked him up and down, “...if anyone did I would expect it to be a Wand’ring Minstrel. The Sect’s archives are legendary.”

“Legends aren’t always true and without a reason to research something...” Jimothy shrugged. “Please tell me what you mean.”

“Human conduits. There hasn’t been one in recent history to my knowledge, but there’s an ancient reference in our family archives. A person—an aide to Lanmere Kere Rosslyn—who could act as a sort of go-between for two mindspeakers. According to the records, the range he allowed her to cover was as great as five hundred leagues.”

“That’s...hard to believe.” He crossed his arms over his chest and leaned a shoulder against the wall.

“I agree, but it is a possibility. And Korpi is less than that distance from Couvin. You said the woman made a particular complaint about the night you didn’t perform, and there was that moment you observed between songs last night. I think that’s important.”

“You think...what? Is the music the trigger that makes the conduit open?”

“Something like that, yes.”

“In that case it seems to me that it was counterproductive

to incapacitate me for that one night." His tone was bitter and more than a little ironic.

"I doubt that hired thugs would think of that, even if they were aware of the possible connection." The lanmere's voice held an equally sardonic note. "Or perhaps they were simply overly enthusiastic in their job."

"True enough. But still, why have them tell me to leave town when he needed me here? Unless the thugs were improvising." Jimothy shook his head, dismissed his own argument. "I don't think they were smart enough for that."

"It may have been a test to see what you would do when threatened. There are a number of possibilities," said the lanmere. "None of which matter now."

She was right. Better to focus on the immediate problem: the conduit and how it worked. It was disturbing to think that he could have been used as a part of this conspiracy without his knowledge. It made him that much more determined to get to the truth and see justice done. "All right. How do we prove this connection, then? Or even test it?"

"How often have you seen Coran in the bar since you arrived?"

"Every night but my first—although I can't speak for the night I was attacked."

"Then we can likely count on him to be here tonight, especially after this." She looked at her injured and sleeping son. Suddenly the lanmere looked tired and older than her years. "I am sorry. My son Coran has much to answer for, including the pain you suffered."

There was nothing for him to say, so he simply shrugged again. "I don't hold you responsible any more than I held Ricky responsible when he apologized."

"You're more generous than some," Fallon said

enigmatically.

"I'm practical." To his surprise, his comment elicited a small chuckle from her.

"Are you?"

"I like to think so."

"Then see what your practical mind makes of this. I will join the crowd in the bar tonight. Don't worry," she assured him before he could protest. "I have a little of Ricky's ability to hide in plain sight."

"So he inherited that from you, too?" he asked.

"He did, but his talent at camouflage surpasses my own. In any case, I can keep myself well hidden when necessary."

"But what do you plan to do?"

"Why, I plan to spy on my son."

✧

The scene in the bar room that evening was like any other since Jimothy's arrival. Among the people seated throughout the room, three of them—prosperous merchants by the look of them—sat enjoying a meal at a table near the hearth. The woman among them had an unobstructed view of the bar, while the men who sat to either side of her could each survey either side of the room with a glance. The woman was Lanmere Fallon and the two men with her were members of her personal guard. Jimothy wondered if they, too, could make themselves unobtrusive the way she could, and then decided they probably did it through simple training and disguise rather than *cheel* ability. It only made sense that it would be part of their job.

Old Noah sat on his barstool nursing his pint. Two seats down from him, Vashti lounged in a casual fashion. Despite her relaxed appearance, Jimothy knew she was ready to handle any trouble at a moment's notice. He wished he could have warned her of the evening's plan, but all he was allowed to tell her was that a guard had been sent by the lanmere to watch over Ricky. *With luck, this won't come to a fight.* He wished it more than he believed it.

The Coral Woman occupied her usual booth with her usual goblet of wine. She smiled at him and raised the goblet in a small salute when she saw Jimothy glance her way. He nodded in reply, his smile as smooth and inscrutable as her own.

No one but the royal trio, Jimothy, and Maeve were aware of the plan. The lanmere was determined to keep the entire affair quiet, and that meant having as few people involved as possible. "Scandal I can manage," she'd said. "This goes well beyond scandal. And the longer we can keep the dons from finding out that we're onto them, the better our chances of bringing them down. We need to do this quietly."

She had also pointed out quite logically that the fewer people who knew of the plan, the less the possibility that a stray thought could give them all away. The likelihood of such a slip being overheard was slim, but Jimothy had eventually agreed. *Better safe than sorry,* he thought. The only other people in on their scheme were Ricky and the member of the lanmere's retinue who currently guarded him. At present they were upstairs in Jimothy's room. Ricky had been ordered by the lanmere to stay where he was. To emphasize her point, she'd commanded the guard standing watch over him to keep him there even if he had to tie him up to do it. Ricky's nonplussed expression at that had almost made Jimothy laugh before he clamped down on his mirth. The situation was serious and, besides, it was never wise to anger one's lover.

"Sister Martha Ruth said to stay in bed," Jimothy had reminded him firmly. The Healer Martha Miriam had been unable to attend the lanfis that morning, but her substitute—a portly woman who bustled about, clucked her tongue, and resembled nothing so much as big blue hen—had been very firm in her orders of continued bed rest. None of Ricky's protests had convinced her otherwise. Lanmere Fallon's command had added weight to the Sister's order, and so Ricky was stuck.

Now the group of counter-conspirators was in place. The only person missing from the scene was Coran.

He arrived shortly after the clocks struck half-past eight. He looked the same as he had each of the previous nights he'd come to the Cat and Turtle. Jimothy allowed his gaze to roam the crowd freely, as he did on every other night, not wishing to draw attention to the lanmere's party by either staring at them or deliberately avoiding them. He continued to play while Coran ordered his drink and Maeve pulled the pint, her manner as friendly and businesslike as ever. She set it before him and he nodded in thanks.

Jimothy's eyes flickered to the Coral Woman. He saw no change in her yet; she was as sharp-eyed as ever. He finished the piece and nodded gratefully at the smattering of applause. A couple rose and dropped coins in his mug before departing. He chose another instrumental piece, a lament that was simple but evocative, long, and one he could damned near play in his sleep. To his satisfaction he saw the Coral Woman's eyes glaze over when he was barely a phrase into the piece.

His gaze slid surreptitiously to the lanmere. There was no outward sign of what was going on in her mind, but she'd told Jimothy of her intentions. She was listening in on whatever message Coran relayed.

"Aren't you concerned he'll notice you?" he had asked her over a pot of tea that afternoon.

Fallon Rosslyn had smiled indulgently at him and shaken her head. “I am very good at what I do, Master Minstrel, and Coran’s abilities are limited. Trust me.”

Her manner was such that he did trust her. He only wished he could be in on what she was hearing. As it was he could only guess. Fallon’s expression never changed, never gave him a clue. Jimothy could only perform, wait and imagine, and each thing he imagined was worse than the one that preceded it. Not wanting to chance discovery, he allowed his gaze to shift throughout the crowd once more.

He was nearing the end of his song and wondered whether or not he should segue into a new one right away. He glanced again at the Coral Woman, saw her eyes refocus, and quickly glanced away before she could catch him looking at her. *That answers that.*

He held the last chord of the piece for several seconds before stilling the humming strings with his hand. Again he thanked his audience for their kind applause. “It’s time for me to take a short break,” he announced pleasantly. “I’ll be back in about fifteen minutes.”

Another smattering of applause met his words. He smiled and nodded again. Then he set aside his guitar and poured the coins from his mug into his hand. He made only a cursory examination of them before transferring them to his purse. Then he crossed to the bar and ordered an ale from Maeve.

“Good night?” she asked amiably as she pulled his pint.

“Not bad. It’s early yet.”

As he and the hostess chatted quietly, one of the lanmere’s guards waved Nita over. He paid the bill for their meal and waited while the girl went to fetch his change. While they waited, the other guard rose and went out through the curtain to the back. None of the other patrons even glanced up; it was the way to the privy after all, why shouldn't he go that way? But Jimothy knew better. It was quicker to send a man out back to guard the potential escape route than to send him around the block from the front of the tavern. Not knowing when the duplicitous lanbrou would leave, it was best to have a man ready at any moment. But if he stuck to form he would leave soon.

Coran paid his bill then and turned to go. A moment later, the first guard returned from the back, undoubtedly silently summoned by the lanmere. Fallon and her second guard rose. To any unknowing observer nothing was amiss.

Coran left the bar and the trio was a cautious but close distance behind him. If all went according to plan, they would apprehend him quietly and escort him to The Heathers until a circuit judge could be obtained to try him for his crimes.

A shout from outside alerted Jimothy that all was not going according to plan. Maeve looked up in concern. "That doesn't sound good," she said so only he could hear her.

"Probably just some drunk talking to his spirits," Jimothy replied nonchalantly, and met her stare.

She got the hint, nodded. "I'm sure you're right." At that moment, the guard who'd been left to watch Ricky rushed through the back curtain and out the front door. Maeve looked at Jimothy sternly. "So much for quick and quiet," she muttered.

The noise in the street began to attract the attention of some of the patrons. They looked up and tried to see out the windows. Fortunately the street was darker than the bar, making it impossible. Vashti sat up straighter, ready to react should the ruckus find its way into the bar. Jimothy sat up straighter, too. His first instinct was to go out and see what was going on. It was part of a Wand'ring Minstrel's training, after all, to observe and report. Instead, he stayed where he was and observed the Coral Woman.

At first glance she appeared calm, but years of practice had taught him what to look for. She was too calm, too unruffled, and she deliberately ignored the commotion outside. Her serene demeanor was worn calculatingly. She finished her wine and rose from the booth, leaving the goblet behind. Her actions were no different from any other night, but this time Jimothy knew it would be the last time. Her contact was compromised and there was no guarantee he wouldn't take her down with him. He had no doubt that she would be gone before morning. She headed out the back, presumably to pack her things and wait for her moment to disappear.

The racket outside subsided, and Jimothy concluded that Coran Rosslyn was now in custody. He took a chance. Concentrating on Lanmere Fallon, he thought, *Your highness?*

Her mental tone was surprised. *Minstrel?*

You have Coran?

Yes. The single word held sorrow and triumph in equal degrees.

The conduit is suspicious. I think she's going to try to skip out tonight.

Understood.

It was a dismissal. There was nothing more for him to do at that moment but keep up the pretence that this night was like any other. But he couldn't do that without one more reassurance.

He looked at Maeve over his ale. "Will you check on Ricky, please?" he asked. "Or no. Send Aren to check on him."

She nodded in understanding and was about to call for the runner when the third guard returned. He looked slightly winded but otherwise unharmed. He crossed the room towards the bar and nodded to Jimothy and Maeve as he passed them on his way back upstairs. Anyone not in the know would assume he was a guest from the way he moved unchallenged through the place.

"Do you still want me to send Aren?" Maeve asked softly.

"Please. Just send him up to make sure...I don't know. Just...to make sure."

"All right."

"Thanks." Jimothy sipped his drink, willing himself to calm down. It was foolish to be so paranoid. The Coral Woman had no reason to suspect that Ricky was alive and safely tucked in bed in room six with a plain-clothed royal guard beside him.

Aren appeared shortly and nodded his head at Maeve.

"Everything's fine, Jimothy. No need to worry," she assured him.

All the same, he couldn't stop it. For the rest of the seemingly interminable night while he entertained the crowd with songs and tales, he worried about what could happen upstairs. *There's a royal guard up there,* he told himself a thousand times. *He can handle one overdressed spy. And Ricky will call for help if he needs it. He's only two floors away. He can mindspeak over that short a distance. I'll hear him if he calls for help.* As many times as he reassured himself, he still held a kernel of doubt and was glad when the last customer finally left shortly before one.

The clocks chimed the hour and at that moment a man entered the tavern. Japheth met him only a step inside the door. "I'm sorry, but we're closed."

The man pushed back his cloak and the gathered company recognized the uniform immediately. He was a member of the lanmere's private guard.

"What is it?" Jimothy asked instantly.

But when the man spoke it was to Japheth and Maeve. "I've come to collect the guest in room eight." Japheth looked confused but Maeve nodded.

"Vashti, take the gentleman up to room eight. Give him whatever he needs," the hostess said. Vashti rose and led the guard out. Japheth looked as though he would protest; it wasn't good for business to have guests arrested even if there weren't any other patrons to witness it. Maeve went to him and took his hand. "I'll explain everything. I swear."

There were sounds of a scuffle on the stairs, but in a short time both guards—one liveried, one in common wear—appeared with the Coral Woman between them and Vashti only a step or two behind. The night keeper looked thoroughly puzzled by the whole situation. The guards flanked their charge as they marched her towards a horse and carriage that waited outside the still open front door. She shot Jimothy an enigmatic smile as they passed him. "I see your talents aren't just musical. Well played, Master Minstrel."

He tipped his head, acknowledging her double meaning.

The guards escorted her out the door and the tavern denizens all watched them load her securely into the carriage.

Japheth closed and locked the door without speaking. He turned to face the rest of the small group: Maeve, Vashti, Jimothy, Nita. He opened his mouth to speak and was promptly forestalled by Ricky's emergence from behind the back curtain. Like any mother would, Fallon had brought him proper nightclothes, and he wore them now under the flannel robe Maeve had loaned him. He leaned on the doorframe for support.

"I take it we were successful, eh?"

Jimothy moved quickly to his side and put a supportive arm around him. "You shouldn't be up."

"I'm not an invalid," argued the lanfis, but he accepted the taller man's help to reach one of the booths. He sat down heavily.

Jimothy sat across from him and Maeve crossed to behind the bar. "Do you need anything? You must be hungry. Nita, see what's left that's fit for family to eat." She shooed the girl towards the kitchen while she poured a short goblet of wine.

Ricky frowned thoughtfully, as if food hadn't occurred to him until she mentioned it. His stomach growled audibly before he could speak. "I guess I am hungry," he replied.

"The Sisters would say that's a good thing." Maeve smiled encouragingly and set the goblet before Ricky. She pulled over a chair to sit nearby.

Nita returned shortly with a bowl of stew and a slice of bread. "That's it. I hope it's all right."

"Thank you, Nita," Ricky said gratefully and tucked into the food.

There was a short silence.

"Will someone tell me what just happened?" demanded Japheth, obviously befuddled and a bit impatient.

Ricky swallowed a bite and answered. "You and yours have just helped avert murder and treason."

Another, longer silence fell over the gathered company.

Japheth sat heavily on the nearest chair, his expression dazed. "I think you need to start at the beginning."

Chapter Eight

"Are you sure you have to leave us so soon?" asked Maeve. She followed him out from the back into the bar room, one hand instinctively going to support her lower back. Her belly had expanded noticeably in the weeks that had passed since Jimothy's arrival, and he'd often seen her massaging her back when she thought no one was paying attention.

"So soon?" Jimothy echoed with a hint of mirth. He moved to stand behind her and used strong thumbs to ease the pain along the base of her spine. She sighed gratefully. "Technically, I should have left Couvin a fortnight ago if I still want to consider myself a *Wand'ring* Minstrel."

"Are you sure you won't at least stay for the Harvest Festival?" It was a discussion they'd had a dozen times already, always with the same result.

"You know I can't. And if I stay for that I might as well stay to celebrate Ricky's birthday. And if I do that I might as well hang around for Solstice since it'll be getting cold..."

"Would that be so bad?"

"No, of course not. It would be wonderful, but impossible," he added before she could protest further.

Maeve conceded the argument with a nod. "But you'll come back as soon as possible." Her tone brooked no argument. "You're not leaving for good."

"How could I leave for good? Ricky is here." The statement was simple and deep with honesty. Maeve nodded.

"You're lucky. The both of you."

A smile turned up the corner of Jimothy's mouth. "You just made me think of something Japheth said to me a few days after I arrived."

"What was that?" She cocked her head and looked over one shoulder at him, curious.

"Nothing." He shook his head and picked up his pack, slinging it over one shoulder where it bounced gently against the guitar case already hanging there. He glanced out the front windows of the Cat and Turtle. An early autumn drizzle had just begun to fall, dampening the streets and making the colorful stone buildings shine in the watery morning light. He slung his boiled wool cloak over his shoulders, leaned down and kissed the hostess's cheek. "Thank you, Maeve. For everything."

She flushed and waved him away, but her smile proved her obviously flattered. "Go on. I know you're spending your last day at The Heathers before you leave town, and with the nights outlasting the days now you'll need to leave early tomorrow morning. You'll want as much of today and tonight with Ricky as you can get, eh?" Then her keen green eyes caught his dark ones and her expression grew very still. "You will come back. I've told you before and I'm telling you again, I'll not be left to pick up the broken bits of Ricky's heart if you don't."

"Maeve, you have my word."

She nodded once, accepting that word. Then the moment passed and her tone was once more light. "Give my love to Ricky," she instructed. "Tell him to come visit us during the festival."

"I will. Tell the others I said good-bye."

"I will...when they wake up."

He chuckled at that and, pulling his hood up, stepped out into the rain just as the clocks struck half-past six.

The walk to The Heathers was familiar now that he'd taken it so many times, especially during Ricky's convalescence and the trial of Coran Rosslyn. He sighed sadly in remembrance.

It had been a quick matter for the officers to round up Coran's hired muscle once he'd named them. They were held on charges of assault and attempted murder. With no knowledge of the political conspiracy, they were tried separately by the local magistrates. That had been the easy part.

The lanbrou's trial was painful for all parties and made all the more so because Coran's actions hadn't been motivated by hatred of his brother, but rather by love for his mother and concern for his country. Years of watching the lanfis behave in ways Coran felt were reckless, selfish and sometimes even dangerous had driven him to join with the university's dons to bring Ricky down. He didn't even believe in their cause, but had taken it on in order to gain their support. It was a means to a sad, but in Coran's view necessary, end. Ricky's sudden demise was meant to spare Fallon the pain of watching him fall inexorably into ruin, for the lanbrou was utterly convinced that it would happen.

Jimothy had thought the lanmere's heart would break when the circuit judge passed sentence on her younger son. He could see it in her eyes despite all her outward composure. It could have been worse, but Coran had agreed to name his co-conspirators at the university, earning himself lifelong banishment from Kanbec rather than lifelong imprisonment. The guards that had escorted him to the coast and a boat bound for the Northern Continent had returned yesterday, their commission completed.

The Coral Woman—Portia Kylan, her named turned out to

be—hadn't been so lucky. She didn't carry the deference that Coran, as a member of the ruling family, did. Her offence wasn't grave enough to warrant execution, though, and there were mitigating circumstances. She had been hired to do a job and as it turned out possessed only limited knowledge of the dons' objectives. Her talent as a conduit was a passive one. She knew who communicated through her—and willingly identified the don with whom Coran regularly communicated—but she never knew what they said.

In the end she had been offered a deal designed by the lanmere and her primary security advisor. Rather than spending the next six years in prison, she would spend them working exclusively for Lanmere Fallon. It was essentially indentured servitude, but it was more desirable than imprisonment and she had accepted the agreement readily.

The judge's final decree was for both conspirators. The Coral Woman and Coran were under orders never to contact one another again. Should it be discovered that they had, both would be subject to life in separate, distant prisons without the option of petition.

Jimothy knew the lanmere and her advisors were discussing how to deal with the university's dons, but she'd not made him privy to their discussions. *It's just as well,* he said to himself as he reached the gates and nodded hello to the guards as he passed them. He was trained as a diplomat, but of all his duties that one was his least favorite. Let them have their secrets. There were some things he just didn't want to know. He was content to be the messenger and leave the intrigue to the professionals.

He reached the south door and rang the chime. Minutes later the ancient porter, Paul, opened the door and ushered him in. "Her highness left orders to send you up as soon as you got here," he said in his old, broken voice. "She's waiting in the conservatory."

"Thank you," Jimothy said. "I know the way."

Paul nodded and left him to make his own way upstairs. Jimothy waved hello to Sarah the cook as he passed the kitchen—the only room bustling at that early hour. But there were signs the rest of the house was waking. He thought he caught a snippet of a song played on the harpsichord and resisted the urge to stop into the music room and say hello to Linnie.

He took the most efficient route to the conservatory. Emerging from the servants' stair onto the hallway behind one of the many tapestries, he pushed it aside and turned down the long corridor. He was unsurprised to see the tall footman, Martin, approaching him from the far end.

"Good morning," Jimothy said pleasantly, and failed to elicit a smile or any sort of emotional reaction from the fellow. It was a challenge he'd given himself, and in all the hours he'd spent at The Heathers, he had yet to succeed. He laughed internally.

"Her highness will see you immediately."

"Thanks."

Martin turned one step before Jimothy reached him and led the rest of the way. He opened the conservatory door, announcing, "Wand'ring Minstrel Jimothy Redwing."

Jimothy heard the lanmere's response through the narrowly open door. "Thank you, Martin. That will be all."

Martin bowed respectfully, ushered Jimothy in, and closed the door behind him.

Fallon stood at the window, looking out over the small orchard where apple trees hung heavy with the last of their fruit. She was dressed as she had been the first time he'd been summoned to this room, in simple, well-tailored clothing of linen and lightweight wool. It was a contrast to the more formal garments she'd worn throughout the trial. Jimothy was glad to see the outward sign that things were returning to normal. She turned to him and smiled warmly, but the smile also held weariness.

"Come in, Jimothy. Please make yourself comfortable."

"Thank you, your highness."

Her smile turned rueful. "How many times will I have to tell you to call me Fallon when we're alone?"

"At least once more, I'm afraid," he answered with a smile of his own. He removed his damp cloak, hung it on the stand by the door, and then set his pack and guitar next to it. "You'll forgive me, I hope. It's just that in my profession it's dangerous to become too familiar with royalty." Fallon quirked a dark eyebrow, her meaning clear. To his eternal frustration, Jimothy blushed. *Why can she make me blush? My own mother can't make me blush!* "You know what I mean."

She relented and waved him over to the window. He joined her there. "I do know, and you're absolutely right. But here, Jimothy. Here it is different."

He nodded. They stood for several moments, silently watching the rain fall on the trees.

Eventually the lanmere broke the silence with business. "I have two letters for you to deliver."

"I expected that you would."

"The first is for Don Savion." Jimothy nodded again and Fallon went on. "There is much he and I can accomplish through our new conduit, but this—" She indicated the letter. "Some things must be written down. I need you to take it to him yourself. I know I can trust any member of your Sect," she went on before he could object. She turned her dark eyes on him. "I would feel better if I knew you were the one taking it."

"I understand." He smiled at her. "I've wanted to see Korpi and the university ever since Ricky told me how beautiful it is—visually, if not ideologically." The lanmere gave him a wry and understanding smile. "Where does the other letter need to go?"

"The other is for your Headmaster."

Jimothy made no effort to hide his surprise. "The Headmaster?"

"Yes." She offered no explanation and it was outside his purview to ask for one. Then Fallon turned from the window, drawing Jimothy's gaze with her own. "You are always welcome and, should you one day choose to settle, you will have a home here."

Jimothy's heart swelled and he was startled to find himself blinking back tears. "Thank you. I—" He stopped, shook his head, laughed at himself. "I don't know what to say."

Fallon smiled at the irony. "I hope that isn't a habit. A Wand'ring Minstrel should never be without words."

"No, he shouldn't, but there's something about your family that seems to have that effect on me."

They both chuckled, a comfortable, amiable sound, and Jimothy felt he truly could settle here. *If I'm allowed.* Another thought came on the heels of the first, unbidden and unwelcome. He pushed it aside.

"Is there anything else you need from me—Fallon?"

Her smile turned wide and bright. "Very good!" she praised him, clapping lightly. He gave a small joking bow, eliciting another laugh from the lanmere. "There's nothing else I need from you. Here." She crossed the long room to a cherrywood writing desk and took two heavy parchment envelopes from it. "They are addressed and sealed. Don't mix them up." She quirked him a grin so like Ricky's that he had to grin back. Jimothy took the letters and put them into the safety of the depths of his oilskin pack. "And this, of course." She handed him two silver pennies, instructing, "Keep the change."

"Thank you." The extra money was more than a tip; it was food for at least three days.

"I'm surprised that Patrick hasn't come bursting in here yet," Fallon went on. "I was certain word of your presence would have reached him well before now."

"It's early yet. Are you sure he's awake?"

"I don't know." She appeared to consider the matter very seriously. "But he did spend the night here and not with you, so I presume he got to sleep before dawn." Jimothy blushed again and Fallon laughed. "I'm sorry, Jimothy. It's mean of me to tease you."

"Actually, madam, I don't mind a bit." Her teasing made him feel more a part of her world and her family than all the welcomes she'd given him. It was honest and real, something you reserved for the people you cared about.

She nodded in silent understanding. "Go find Ricky. I know you'd rather spend your last day in Couvin with him than with me."

"My last day," echoed Jimothy, then he smiled wickedly, dared a bit of cheek. "And my last night."

Fallon laughed uproariously at his audacity. "Fair is fair," she said, nodding and laughing. "Off with you. Go continue to make my son happy."

Jimothy swept an absurdly low bow. "As you command, your highness." He picked up his things and left her laughing in the conservatory. It was a good sound, a good feeling.

He quickly followed the familiar path through the hallways

to Ricky's rooms. He knocked on the door and then opened it a crack to poke his head in. "Ricky?" he called softly, looking around. The vast four-post bed was unmade, covers heaped and rumpled behind half-drawn curtains. The fire in the small hearth glowed gently, testament to the increasingly chilly nights. He spotted the lanfis at the table, eating a breakfast of eggs, sausage and tea, and still dressed in nightclothes and robe.

Ricky rose swiftly, wiping mouth and fingers on a serviette, and grinning to light up the room. "Jimothy!"

"You're awake early," said Jimothy, kissing him hello. He set down his things in one of the large plush chairs and took a seat across the table from the lanfis. The last vestiges of his bruises still shadowed one eye, but his lip had healed well, and Jimothy knew from past examination that the knife wound was also healing nicely.

"I knew you were coming," Ricky said. "Do you need breakfast?"

"I wouldn't say no."

Ricky rang the bell and then sat again. "What shall we do today, for your last day in Couvin?"

Jimothy shrugged. "I don't care as long as I spend the day with you."

"Sweet talker." There was a knock at the door. "Come in," called the lanfis. A young woman entered the room and dipped a small curtsey.

"You rang, my lord?"

"I did. Jenja, would you please bring us another plate of food and a fresh pot of tea? And ask Quinn to prepare a hot bath."

"Yes, my lord."

"Thank you." He smiled at her and the serving woman dipped another curtsey and left, shutting the door. Ricky sipped his tea, looking coyly over the cup rim at Jimothy. "That is, if you want to have a bath."

Jimothy's expression mirrored the lanfis's. "I'd love one." His arousal had sparked at the very mention. A hot bath was a luxury at any time in Jimothy's world, and a hot bath with his lover was something extra special indeed.

They fell silent, eyeing each other tantalizingly. "We can't," Jimothy said softly. "Not yet."

Noise in the next room warned them of the presence of someone—presumably Quinn—drawing water into the large, claw-footed bathtub. It would take him several minutes even running the taps at full power. The hot water stove downstairs would have to be refilled twice before there was enough to fill the tub.

We have time, Ricky said silently.

There's still breakfast coming. We don't want to be interrupted.

Ricky nodded in reluctant agreement and at that moment a knock came again at the door. "Come in," he called. The door opened and Jenja entered carrying a tray laden with dishes and a fresh pot of tea. She set it on the table, unloading everything and reloading it with empty dishes. Her task complete, Ricky ushered her to the door. "Thank you, Jenja."

She smiled politely, the perfect balance of deference and friendliness. "You're welcome, my lord."

He shut the door and returned to the table. Jimothy tucked into his eggs as Ricky poured fresh tea for them both, adding a splash of milk to his own. He sipped and watched the other man eat.

Jimothy looked up at him. "Am I that interesting?"

Ricky shrugged one shoulder, hands cradling the delicate teacup. “You’re gorgeous and sexy and I’m thinking about all the other lovely things you can do with that delicious mouth.”

Jimothy laughed, almost choking on a bite of sausage. He washed it down with tea while Ricky chuckled lightly. “You’re wicked,” he said once he’d caught his breath, but his expression was mirthful.

“And you love it.”

“I do.”

There was a light tap on the door from the bathroom.

“Come in,” called Ricky.

The door opened to reveal a boy of about thirteen. “Your bath is ready, my lord.”

“Thank you, Quinn. You’re dismissed. Tell the staff we’re not to be disturbed unless we ring.”

“Yes, my lord.” He nodded and shut the door, and Jimothy presumed he disappeared back through whatever mysterious servants’ passage he’d used to get there. Ricky looked at Jimothy, blue eyes bright with anticipation. “Are you done?” he asked, nodding at the half-empty plate.

Jimothy’s lips turned up in the corners the tiniest bit. “Impatient much?” he teased.

“I don’t want the water to go cold.”

“Right.” He took a long swallow of tea and rose to his feet. He swept a bow. “After you, my lord,” he said, his tone lightly mocking.

“Oh no,” contradicted Ricky, sweeping an even lower bow. “After you.” He straightened up and his smile was lustful. “I love to watch your ass while you walk.”

Jimothy burst out laughing and dutifully led the way into the bathroom. A mosaic of blue and green tiles covered the floor and the walls to about waist height. The long exterior wall had a window above the tiles, eight small panes long and three high, filling the space to just below the ceiling. The opposite wall above the claw-footed tub boasted a painting of a sweeping landscape. The first time Jimothy saw it he'd guessed rightly that it was Maeve's handiwork. A table at one end of the bath held fresh towels, while one at the other held an array of soaps, lotions, back scrubbers and other accoutrements. A chair stood alone in a corner by the window. The two shorter walls, where they weren't broken by doors or covered with tiles, were painted a pale blue.

Ricky made certain both doors were locked before turning hungry eyes on Jimothy. "Bath time."

They undressed one another slowly, savoring what was likely to be their last time together for several months. Jimothy sat in the chair and Ricky started with his boots, removing them one by one and setting them neatly to one side. Then he stood, allowing the lanfis to unlace the neck of his tunic and pull it and his shirt off as one. Ricky set them aside, dropping them atop the boots, and ran his hands over Jimothy's lightly furred chest. Quick fingers rolled and pinched Jimothy's nipples to instant hardness and his cock began to harden with them. He moaned softly and Ricky caught his lips in a tender kiss that soon grew more passionate. He opened his mouth to Ricky's probing tongue, thrilled to the touch as the lanfis ran it over his teeth and then across the roof of his mouth. He could feel his erection pressing almost painfully against his breeches, demanding to be set free.

Ricky leaned into him, rubbing a cotton-clad thigh between Jimothy's legs, rolling his erection gently from side to side. Jimothy moaned louder into Ricky's mouth and felt him chuckle in response. Still, they didn't break the kiss. Ricky's roaming hand snaked down Jimothy's arm and he caught his hand, interlacing their fingers before guiding it between them and over Ricky's groin. Jimothy grasped his erection, hot through the thin fabric, and massaged it with strong, musician's fingers. It was Ricky's turn to moan with pleasure.

Minutes passed as they lovingly teased and toyed with one another. Ricky nipped at Jimothy's neck, growling enticingly into the taller man's ear. Jimothy responded by reaching up under Ricky's shirt to tug gently on the dark hairs around his nipples, drawing an excited growl from the depths of his gut. Small damp patches at the front of both men's pants betrayed the excitement contained inside.

Ricky inhaled deeply as Jimothy bent over to lick one hard nipple through the fabric of his light shirt. "That's...it," he gasped. He took a step back, reached for Jimothy's breeches, and had them down around his ankles in a flash. Jimothy sighed at the sudden release of his manhood from its cloth prison. He leaned a hand on Ricky's shoulders as the man helped him step from the garment before shoving it aside. Rather than rising, Ricky remained kneeling on the hard tiles, caressing Jimothy's penis with his hand and mouth. Jimothy let his head fall back and his eyes close, burying himself in the moment.

Slowly, Ricky kissed his way up Jimothy's belly, pausing a moment to suck and lick at nipples turned hard as marble. When he was on his feet, Jimothy met his roving mouth with his own, taking his turn exploring the lanfis's hot, wet mouth while Ricky shed his robe and undid the buttons of his shirt. He dropped it with the robe and Jimothy ran his hands lightly over Ricky's hairy chest, fingers careful of the partly healed stab wound.

They broke the kiss reluctantly and Ricky quickly slipped out of his pants. At last they were both naked and they moved together to the waiting tub. Ricky tested the water with one hand and smiled broadly at Jimothy. “Perfect,” he said, and Jimothy felt the pronouncement was for more than just the temperature of the water.

Carefully they stepped into the enormous tub and sat down. Ricky stirred the water with a hand, causing it to swirl in little eddies around them. They took turns washing one another from top to toe, scrubbing each other’s backs, and generally lapping up the hedonistic delights of a long bath with a lover. Twice Ricky carefully released the drain, sluicing some of the soapy water from the tub as the taps refilled it with fresh hot water.

Jimothy scooped water in his hands, using it to rinse the suds from Ricky’s hair, turned black as jet by the moisture. Satisfied it was thoroughly free of soap, he smiled and kissed the younger man on the head. He felt Ricky laugh and lean back against him, resting against his chest. He reached around him and took Ricky’s penis in one hand. It had grown soft and he massaged it back to tumescence.

“Mmm,” sighed Ricky. “That’s lovely.” He snuggled back between his lover’s legs, and Jimothy’s cock grew rapidly from half-hard to fully engorged. “Lovely,” he repeated.

“Very,” Jimothy echoed the sentiment.

Ricky turned in the water so he was facing the other man, half-floating atop him, their erections bouncing against one another. He leaned in and kissed Jimothy, a sweet, tender, warm kiss. “I have a request,” he whispered in Jimothy’s ear, and then licked it playfully. “Something I’ve never asked of you before.”

Jimothy had some idea what it would be, but waited to hear it from his lover’s mouth. “Name it.”

“I’ve never been inside you.” There was a pause and Ricky’s tone was hesitant as if he were almost afraid of the answer.

"May I?"

It wasn't something Jimothy usually allowed, wasn't something he had trusted most of his past partners to do. But he'd known for weeks, since the night after he'd been attacked, that if Ricky ever asked him he would say yes. Jimothy smiled and kissed him and nodded. "Anything you want."

Ricky's eyes lit up. "I—Thank you." He looked around as if momentarily at a loss, as if he hadn't expected the positive response. Jimothy found it entirely too endearing.

"Do you want to do it here or somewhere else?"

"I don't—" He looked around again and Jimothy could see him come to a decision. "No. The bedroom." Suddenly he grew shy and wouldn't meet his lover's eyes. "I've never...been on top before. I'm not really sure I could manage it in the bath." He laughed self-deprecatingly and Jimothy thought his heart would burst with affection.

He captured Ricky's face in his hands, kissed him soundly, made him meet his eye. "I'll help you."

Ricky smiled and nodded, a look of relief and gratitude on his expressive face.

They stepped out of the bath onto the cold tiles and dried themselves off quickly. Then they returned to Ricky's bedroom where the trays of food had vanished as if by magic and the bedclothes had been tidied.

Ricky looked at the bed and laughed out loud. "That was a waste of time." He quickly checked that the door was locked. Jimothy smiled to himself at the precaution. Ricky caught him smiling. "What?"

"You're perfectly happy to suck me off in the flower garden, but you're careful to lock the doors in the house."

"You think it's strange?"

"I think it's charming."

"Good." Ricky grinned and pulled back the richly colored blankets. Then his resolve faltered. "How do you want to do this?" he asked uncertainly.

"Well," began Jimothy, choosing his words carefully. "I know you like to see me when I come, but I would be more comfortable if you came in from behind."

"All right." Ricky nodded.

Taking the initiative, Jimothy moved to stand close to him, wrapped his arms around him, and whispered in his ear. "You have that liniment, right?"

Ricky's eyes lit up again and he nodded. It took only moment to fetch it from the bottom drawer of a massive dresser. He tossed the cap aside and dipped his fingers into the pungent stuff. Both men inhaled deeply. "Love it," the lanfis said with a smile.

"Me too." Jimothy took a dollop and warmed it with his fingers. Then he grasped Ricky's erection and rubbed the slippery stuff over it. Ricky leaned his head forward, letting it fall on Jimothy's shoulder at the same time he reached around behind Jimothy and carefully slid a slicked finger into the tight ring of Jimothy's anus. Jimothy tensed very briefly and then relaxed into the touch, the movement of Ricky's finger inside him, the hot and cold sensation of the salve. "Another," he whispered, and Ricky obeyed, sliding a second finger in, gently stretching and prepping. "Mmm, yeah. One more." Ricky shot him an uncertain look and Jimothy nodded encouragingly. He knew how big Ricky was, knew a little more prep was in order. Besides, it just felt so good. "I trust you," he murmured. Ricky smiled, reassured, and did as he instructed, very carefully adding a third slippery finger. "That's it. Good." Their eyes met, flashing like lightning. "Time to come inside."

They released each other and Jimothy climbed onto the big bed, kneeling on all fours, facing the foot and the room rather than the wall. Ricky climbed up behind him and Jimothy spread his legs enough for Ricky to get between them. He felt Ricky's erection press against his crack, rubbing a little from side to side. "It's all right," he assured him. "I'm ready if you are."

"I'm ready," Ricky said with conviction. He placed a hand on Jimothy's hip and used the other to guide himself in.

It had been years since Jimothy had allowed anyone inside him, so long that he'd almost managed to forget the incredible feeling of fullness it gave. And Ricky was better hung than anyone he'd been with before. The sensation was intense and pre-ejaculate dripped from his cock onto the bed sheets. Ricky pulled out and slid himself back in again cautiously. A gasp escaped Jimothy and the lanfis paused, holding very still.

"Are you all right?" he asked with concern.

"I'm...fantastic," Jimothy assured him breathlessly. "It's...I've never had someone like you inside. You're so big." He could hear the grin in Ricky's voice when he replied.

"Thank you."

Jimothy gasped a chuckle, and Ricky withdrew completely and entered him again. "By all the Greater Gods!" he exclaimed. "That's so good!" Ricky did it again, and then reached his free hand around to grab Jimothy's hard cock. He stroked it, moving ever so slightly in and out of Jimothy's ass. Words escaped him. He made inarticulate noises of delight, savoring every sensation without and within. "Ricky, I—" He couldn't complete the thought.

Ricky leaned forward, laying his belly and chest along Jimothy's back and kissing him between his shoulder blades. "Tell me what you want me to do," he murmured, and Jimothy felt more than heard the words.

His mind flashed back to their first time together, in the waycabin a day's ride out from the city, and echoed Ricky's words from that propitious meeting. "Fuck me hard."

Ricky laughed gleefully, recognizing his own command that had been a staple in their couplings over their time together. He increased his stroke with hand and cock, jerking and pounding in an increasingly passionate rhythm.

"Yeah," gasped Jimothy, moving with him, his ass tilted at just the right angle to allow Ricky the best access. "That's it. Nearly...there." Another thrust and he felt Ricky release inside him, felt the pulse of his pleasure against inner walls of his ass. It sent him over the edge and he shouted out as he came, semen shooting from his cock, leaving a trail along the bed three or more feet long—a testament to some of the best sex he'd had in his life with the best partner he'd ever been blessed with. He gasped and laughed, giddy with joy and pleasure. He rested his head on the pooled blankets between his forearms, carefully avoiding the wet streak.

Ricky slid out of him, his cock soft and spent, and Jimothy took several moments to catch his breath before falling heavily and happily onto his side. Ricky lay down opposite him, arm bent, and leaned his head on his balled fist. He trailed a finger along the broken line of ejaculate, licked the light residue from its tip. "I'll take that as a huge compliment."

"And you?" Jimothy asked with a tired smile. "I hope you enjoyed that as much as I did."

"Mm-hmm." Ricky nodded. "That was..."

"Mind-blowing?" quipped Jimothy.

"Mind-blowing," his lover agreed with a grin.

They spent the rest of the day together, alternately making love and strolling around the estate grounds. The rain stopped shortly before noon and the autumn sun broke through the clouds to warm the air comfortably. No one bothered them or interrupted their solitude. They ate when they were hungry, not keeping to any set schedule. They spent that night in Ricky's big bed, but it might have been no more than a small cot for all the distance they put between them, sleeping naked and sated, arms and legs twined around one another.

They rose early the next morning, just as dawn streaked the eastern skyline. Jimothy bathed, shaved and dressed quickly before they sat down together for breakfast.

"I promised myself I wouldn't ask you," Ricky said over a plate of griddlecakes drenched in honey.

"Wouldn't ask me what?"

"How long it would be before you came back."

Jimothy was thoughtful. "I don't know for certain. I'm sorry."

Ricky shook his head, dismissing the apology. "Don't be sorry. I know you don't know the answer. My mother's sending you leagues away to Korpi, and then half a world away to that Sect of yours." There was a hint of bitterness in his tone that he didn't quite manage to hide. Jimothy wondered if he'd really meant to.

"I have to go. You know that. I thought—I hoped you understood that."

"I do," Ricky hastened to assure him. "I do. But that doesn't mean I have to like it, eh?" His usual grin was tinged with sadness. Then he seemed to deliberately cheer himself up. "But you are coming back."

"I am," affirmed Jimothy. He looked at Ricky intently. There was something the lanfis wasn't saying. Something Jimothy suspected he wouldn't let himself say. "What is it?"

"Nothing."

"Don't lie. Not today."

Ricky looked chagrined. "I was wondering something, but I don't think it's fair of me to ask it."

Half a hundred possible questions leapt to Jimothy's mind, but he couldn't guess what his lover wanted to ask him. "Go ahead. Whatever it is, we'll both be happier if you ask it."

Ricky nodded, but his demeanor was still hesitant. "I was wondering," he began and paused. "I was wondering if, when you come back, you might come back for good."

It wasn't one of the fifty and more questions that had occurred to Jimothy, but neither did it take him entirely by surprise. His answer, however, surprised them both. "I will," he said, and added a qualifying, "if I can."

Ricky smiled brightly at first, and then the light in his eyes darkened slightly. He nodded. "I understand."

"I'm not sure you do completely."

"You have obligations. I know all about obligations, eh?" Jimothy nodded, conceding the obvious point. "You travel all over, and someone who didn't know better might think you were as free as a bird. I know that's not the case. You have people to answer to—the Headmaster of the Sect for one. But." He paused a moment and Jimothy could see him thinking, see him fighting to make himself say what he had to say. "But, if you had it to choose, do you think there is any possibility that you could choose me?" His eyes were open, hopeful, a little frightened, but he didn't flinch or look away as he waited for Jimothy's answer.

Jimothy reached a hand across the table, placed it gently over his lover's. Ricky raised his hand and with their palms together, they interlaced their fingers. "I promise you that I will come back. I promise you that when I'm ready to stop Wand'ring, I will stop here." He paused, took a breath, and went on. "But can you promise that you will be here waiting for me when that time comes? You have obligations—not the least of which will one day be running this country and...and providing it with an heir. I can't give you that."

"You don't have to give me that." Ricky's tone was firm, decisive. "I've already made that arrangement." Jimothy's eyes widened in shock, and Ricky actually laughed. "I'm not saying I'm going to be a father any time soon!"

Jimothy relaxed, laughing too at the absurdity of the situation. "Then what do you mean?" he asked, growing serious once more.

"I mean I love you. I want you. Yes, I have to provide an heir and unfortunately the laws require that it be one of my blood and not one I've adopted. I'll change that if I can when I'm lanpere but that won't be soon enough for this. But I have made arrangements." The last was said deliberately, finally.

Jimothy wanted to ask more, but kept silent. He had an idea of what Ricky meant. It made no difference at that point whether he was right in his guess or not.

Then Ricky went on. "But when the time comes, I need—I would very much like for you to be there."

It was obvious that the decision was in Jimothy's hands. He wasn't sure at that moment what he would decide. He didn't know yet if he could watch the man he loved make love to another person—even knowing it was for the sake of an heir. "I will try."

Ricky nodded in understanding. "I know it's not really fair of me to ask, but it would be just as unfair, I think, not to include you. I love you."

"I love you, Ricky." Jimothy smiled at the lanfis, his heart full. Indeed it seemed to fill more every time he said those words.

Ricky grinned back at him, eyes alight. "I have something for you."

"You what?" He was taken aback by the sudden change of tone and topic.

"Call it a going-away present." Ricky rose and went quickly to the big dresser. He opened a drawer and fished way into the back, pulling out a small, brightly wrapped package. The paper rustled in his hands as he returned to the table. He placed the soft bundle in front of Jimothy and waited expectantly.

Jimothy reached out and picked it up, his expression curious.

"Open it," said Ricky eagerly. He looked like a kid on Winter Solstice morning, waiting to see the gift he'd given opened, to see the reaction of its recipient.

Jimothy untied the string and opened the colored paper. Inside was a pair of gloves made of beautifully tanned and buttery soft hide. The stitching was exquisite and the backs boasted some of the finest embroidery he'd ever seen. He looked at it closely. It was musical script, stitched into the skin. He read it, hummed a little, and then smiled. "The Love Song from Chendon's *Heart of the Rose*," he said, identifying the piece.

Ricky applauded. "I knew you'd know it. Put them on."

Jimothy did and found both hands wrapped in soft, furry luxury. "Is this—?"

"The fur and hide of the rabbits I shot the first night we were together," he confirmed, nodding. "Well, one of them. I have a pair to match made from the other. They fit you well, don't they?" His expression was worried and hopeful.

"They're perfect."

"Oh good! The textilist was reluctant to make them without the proper measurements, but I swore to him that I knew your hands plenty well enough to get it right." Now he looked a little smug. "I'm looking forward to telling him I was right."

Jimothy laughed. "Thank you." He removed them and set them on the table. "I have something for you, too." He laughed again at Ricky's perplexed look. He rose and went to his pack, taking his gloves with him and packing them away safely before pulling out a folded sheet of parchment. "Call it an early birthday present," he said as he sat again and handed the paper to his lover.

"I—" Ricky hesitated. "Should I open it now or wait until my birthday?"

"That's up to you."

He considered for another moment, turning the page over in his hands, examining the small wax seal impressed with the form of a harp and a writing quill—the ancient sigil of the Sect of the Wand'ring Minstrels. "I'll wait."

"All right." Jimothy reached a hand across to his lover once again. They sat in silence for several moments and Jimothy wished that time would stop, but that was impossible. Eventually the estate clock chimed seven times. Ricky's face grew suddenly somber and he squeezed Jimothy's fingers a little tighter. Jimothy saw him fight not to say what he knew the lanfis wanted to say, and answered him anyway with a promise. "I'll come back." Ricky nodded, his blue eyes too bright with unshed tears. Then a tear did spill over and run down his cheek. Jimothy reached out and brushed it away with his thumb. He cupped the younger man's cheek in his hand, and Ricky leaned into the touch.

"Blessed Martha, but I'm going to miss you," Ricky said softly.

Jimothy felt a tear escape his eyes and nodded. "I'll miss you, too."

There was a knock on the door. The men released one another and wiped away their tears. "Come in," called Ricky, a tiny hitch in his voice. He cleared his throat and forced his expression into calm impassivity.

The door opened and Fallon stepped into the room. "Good morning, boys," she said in a gentle voice. "I've come to walk you to the stables and to say good-bye."

Ricky had offered Jimothy a horse for his travels, and after deliberating, he had finally agreed. Feeding and caring for it was an extra burden, but the alternative was spending twice as long on the road on foot through the cooling autumn and the cold of winter.

The men rose from the table. Jimothy gathered his things and the trio made their way silently to the stables. The hostler was prepared for their arrival. A stocky, somewhat shaggy black gelding by the name of Jacques was saddled and waiting. A bag of provisions was strapped behind the saddle and Jimothy secured his pack alongside it. He turned to face Fallon and Ricky.

"Your highness," he addressed the lanmere formally. "Thank you for everything. The hospitality of your realm is—" he couldn't help but shoot a glance at Ricky, "—unparalleled." To his delight, Fallon laughed.

"Now you're getting the way of it," she replied, and he was certain he'd pleased her with his brazen humor. "I have something for you." She reached within her cloak and pulled out two rolled sheaves of parchment. "These are current maps of Kanbec. One is for you. One is for the archives at the Sect. I understand from my son that the map you arrived with is shite." There was a mirthful and slightly wicked gleam in her eyes.

"Indeed, madam, it was utter shite." He took the maps and secured them safely in his pack. When he turned again to the lanmere, she surprised him by suddenly wrapping her arms around him in a warm embrace.

"You will be missed in your absence, Jimothy," she declared as she released him.

"I'll miss you, too, Fallon."

She gave him a kind, motherly smile and he smiled back. Then she stepped aside, taking the hostler with her in order to allow the men one more moment alone together.

Jimothy reached out and took Ricky's hands. The lanfis looked up and tears fell from his eyes. He smiled sheepishly. "I've become a bit of a sentimentalist," he joked. "Maybe you noticed?"

"Have you?" Jimothy feigned surprise. Then he smiled tenderly. "I never would have guessed it."

Ricky gave a short laugh. They fell silent, simply holding hands and looking into one another's eyes for several moments. The morning sun crept higher in the east and began to warm the damp sod of the stable yard. Ricky sniffed and shook himself into motion. "You should go. Days are getting shorter and you need to cover as much ground as you can before dark."

Jimothy finished the thought for him. "Because the sooner I get where I'm going, the sooner I can return."

Ricky stood up straight and looked at him sternly. "Exactly." He cracked a wide grin and then leaned in the short distance between them. They kissed long and tenderly, knowing it would be spring or later before they felt that shared warmth again.

Finally, Jimothy forced himself to break the kiss and step

back. Reluctantly they let go of one another's hands and Jimothy turned to take his horse's reins. He swung into the saddle and turned Jacques towards the gate, which the hostler held open for him. "Your highness." He swept a bow from horseback, and the lanmere acknowledged it with a nod. Then he looked at Ricky, thinking, *Watch for me in the spring. I'll be coming from the west.*

I will.

Jimothy clicked his tongue and nudged his horse forward. He passed through the gate and turned eastward into the rising sun. It was nearly a fortnight's ride to Korpi, and as Ricky had said, he wanted to cover as much ground as possible before dark. *At least this time I have a decent map.*

Ricky stood at the paddock fence and watched until Jimothy was only a dot on a far hill. Then he returned to the house and went up to his rooms. The parchment Jimothy had given him lay undisturbed on the table, although the detritus of their early breakfast had been cleared away and the bed made. He picked it up and turned it over in his hands several times, deliberating silently. *I've waited long enough,* he thought. Smiling, he slipped a finger under the seal and broke it open. Carrying it to the desk by the window, he sat and unfolded it. Jimothy's clean, precise handwriting covered the page in verse form. There was no musical notation, Ricky noticed. *A poem then.* He smiled to himself and began to read.

Summer morning breaks over the land

I look up and see you atop a chestnut mare

Your eyes are so blue that I wish I could dive in

Your smile is so broad that my heart warms at the sight

The sight of your mile-wide smile

Summer evening falls on a small cabin
I look up and see you sitting across from me
Your eyes are so open that I nearly fall in
Your smile is so wide that I'm sure I'll be devoured
Devoured by your mile-wide smile

Summer night is moonless and dark
There's no one in the world but you and me
Your eyes are alight with passion that makes my blood hot
Your smile is so sexy that I have to kiss you
Kiss your mile-wide smile

You are my morning, my evening, my night
You are my midday sun and afternoon rain
Your eyes see me with such love that I want to cry
Your smile warms me with such love that I want to cheer

You excite me and calm me
You thrill me and soothe me
You are clarity and confusion
You are serenity and tumult
You are tenderness and strength
You are the one who makes me whole
My man with the mile-wide smile

Ricky read it through again before carefully folding it once more and tucking it in the inner pocket of his tunic. He rose and stood staring out the window—the west-facing window—and wished for an early spring.

About the Author

Maia Strong is a native Pacific Northwesterner whose banes in life are intolerance, ignorance, and bad coffee. In high school she developed an affinity for writing about boys who love boys, but it was only when she discovered slash fanfiction that she realized there was a vast audience who enjoyed reading about them. Thus was a love affair born. When she's not writing about sexy boys, which frankly she's been doing a lot of recently, she works in local theatre, watches too much Food Network, and generally just hangs out with her husband and cat. She loves baseball, bellydancing, cooking, daffodils, grey skies, Shakespeare, travel, yoga, and a damned fine cup of coffee.

To learn more about Maia Strong, please visit www.maiastrong.com. You can also check out her blog at http://maiastrong.blogspot.com, or send Maia an email at maia@maiastrong.com.

LaVergne, TN USA
24 October 2010
202067LV00002B/1/P

9 781605 041766